LEGITIMATE BUSINESS

LEGITIMATE BUSINESS

A Valentin Vermeulen Thriller

———◆———

Michael Niemann

cp
coffeetownpress
Seattle, WA

coffeetownpress

Coffeetown Press
PO Box 70515
Seattle, WA 98127

For more information go to: www.coffeetownpress.com
www.michael-niemann.com

Cover design by Sabrina Sun

ISBN: 978-1-60381-587-1 (Trade Paper)
ISBN: 978-1-60381-588-8 (eBook)

Library of Congress Control Number: 2016956949

Printed in the United States of America

Acknowledgments

———— ◆ ————

No book is written by one person only. There is always a community that offers the author support, encouragement and honest feedback. My biggest thanks goes to my co-conspirators of the "Monday Mayhem" writing group, Carol Beers, Sharon Dean, Clive Rosengren, and Tim Wohlforth. They read and commented on two versions of this novel, keeping me from going down the wrong alleys and fixing my typos and commas. Robert Weppner read the entire first draft and his frank criticism pushed me to add complexity to the plot. Fred Grewe evaluated two different openings and nudged me toward the one now in the book. Melody Condon provided expert editing. Catherine Treadgold and Jennifer McCord at Coffeetown Press, my new publisher, gave me great feedback on the manuscript when I thought it was already done. The final version is much better because of it. All remaining shortcomings are, of course, solely my responsibility.

For background on the Darfur crisis, I'm particularly indebted to Mahmood Mandani's *Saviors and Survivors. Darfur, Politics, and the War on Terror* and Julie Flint and Alex de Waal's *Darfur. A Short History of a Long War*. Both offer a critical look behind the headlines and the sometimes facile responses to this terrible and protracted civil war.

Since writing the novel, the Doha peace process has unraveled. Violence, particularly attacks by the Sudanese government, but also intra-group fighting, has increased, leading to renewed refugee flows and displacement. UNAMID is still there, providing services in camps, but not able to contain the violence.

CHAPTER ONE

---◆---

Wednesday, March 10, 2010

THERE IS NO RUSH HOUR IN a refugee camp. No jobs to get to, no appointments to keep. Just waiting. Waiting to go home. The Zam Zam camp for internally displaced persons, some ten miles south of El Fasher in Darfur, Sudan, was no different. The closest Zam Zam got to a rush hour was when the food aid arrived.

Garreth Campbell drove his pickup into the camp at ten in the morning. It wasn't rush hour. The air was still a little cool from the previous night and people were milling about, waiting for something to happen. He drove carefully. No need to give anyone a reason to remember him.

The pickup was entirely unremarkable. A white Toyota Hilux, a workhorse truck used throughout Africa. White vehicles were a common sight. The United Nations, the African Union, and all kinds of aid organizations were everywhere in Zam Zam.

An armored personnel carrier waited in the distance. The acronym of the United Nations/African Union Mission in Darfur—UNAMID—was emblazoned on its side. Campbell knew it would be there. He turned left and followed a small detour past a group of tarp-covered stick and straw shelters. A makeshift fence made of dried branches stuck into the ground surrounded the compound.

The GPS unit in the cab recalculated the distance to his destination. It was a half a mile away. The female voice admitted that it had no local road information and expressed regret that it could not supply turn-by-turn navigation. The shacks and the paths between them didn't show up on the display, only a red dot indicating the coordinates he had entered.

He reached an unoccupied area the size of a soccer pitch. Thin layers of reddish sand and beige grit covered a rocky surface. Not the place where one could keep a shack standing. There were tufts of hard yellow grass here and there that would pose a challenge even to goats. At the center sat an outcropping, covered with green bushes, which looked like an alien craft on a lost planet.

Some aid organization had installed a water pump that tapped into a vein of water hidden somewhere below. Campbell parked next to it. A sign with English and Arabic script hung from the pump. The English text explained that the pump was out of order. Red plastic tape with the words 'Keep Out' was strung around the pump. The signage had done its job. No one was waiting to pump water.

He lifted a long bag from the truck. It contained an M24 rifle with a Leupold scope and a bipod. A sniper rifle, effective range a half mile. Accurate to a quarter inch over a 300-foot distance. He took the rifle from the bag and inserted the five-round magazine.

Behind the pump and hidden by the bushes was a ledge, a perfect rest for the bipod. He knelt, positioned the rifle, and levered a match-grade hollow-point round into the chamber.

Two minutes.

He focused the scope on a spot six hundred yards away, where two paths intersected. A bit of a stretch, but doable. He took a deep breath, held it for seven seconds, and exhaled slowly, taking eight seconds. Repeated three or four times, it slowed his heartbeat sufficiently.

Zam Zam took its time.

The sound of a large diesel engine starting came across the shacks. It had to be the armored personnel carrier. The engine died again.

He waited.

A crowd appeared near the intersection. Campbell expected about twenty people. There were more, maybe twenty-five, all men. The commotion had attracted some passersby. What else was there to do?

He watched. And waited.

The men surrounded two women in colorful camouflage uniforms wearing blue berets. One was shorter and had her hair tucked under the beret. The tall one had clasped her long black hair at her neck. Campbell heard snippets of sound and saw hands gesticulating. The two women stood back to back, pointing their pistols at the crowd. A very defensible position, given their circumstances. They knew what they were doing.

Campbell scanned the faces through the Leupold scope. The distance made them unreal, like faces on a TV with the sound turned off. He wondered if drone operators had a similar feeling before they pushed the button that blew up some terrorist's truck.

The defensive posture of the two women worked. The crowd around them backed off. Some men on the outside turned to leave.

He stopped waiting.

The scope came to rest on the forehead of the old man, just under his dirty *kofia*, who stood closest to the two women. Campbell pulled the trigger. The bullet made a crack when it left the barrel. A fraction of a second later, it hit the old man in the head and killed him instantly. He levered the next round into the chamber, moved the barrel a fraction of an inch, and pulled the trigger again. The second bullet raced toward the tall policewoman. She'd turned just a bit, and the bullet hit her neck rather than her head.

The moment of absolute surprise ended with the second bang. Pandemonium broke out. Some in the crowd dove to the ground, others ran in panic, while the rest stood frozen with fear.

He chambered another round and aimed for the head of one of the young men who stood still. The guy went down. Three hits in four seconds. He stopped shooting.

His heartbeat sped up. It always did, afterwards. He'd never been able to figure out that sensation. Was it the release of tension? Or was it something deeper, darker? He used his breathing technique again.

The distant diesel engine started again. It was time to leave. He pulled the magazine from the rifle, folded the bipod, and slid the rifle back into its bag. Two of the ejected casings glimmered in the sun. He pocketed them. The third casing had bounced off a rock to somewhere. No big deal. He walked back to the pickup. The door was still open. He shoved the bag into the cab. The tape and the sign at the water pump were no longer necessary. He threw them into the cab and drove off. From the corner of his eye, he caught sight of a girl. For a moment their eyes connected. Nobody else took notice of the pickup.

* * *

CONSTABLE PRIYA CHOUDHURY WAS ON PATROL with her partner Ritu Roy. They were members of an all-female police unit from Bangladesh, one of the many contingents from around the world that made up the United Nations/ African Union Mission in Darfur. When she heard the first shot, she thought some idiot was playing around with his old hunting rifle. There were plenty of idiots in Zam Zam. The cloud of pink mist rising from the head of the old man in front of her told her she was wrong.

The old man had been the leader of the crowd hectoring them, talking the crowd into a frenzy. They'd appeared out of nowhere. Usually, a gaggle of children followed her and Ritu on their patrols. Female UN police officers were a reliable source of treats. This time, grown-ups had taken the kids' place, the old man out front, shouting. Their UN-appointed translator had run away the moment the crowd formed. Amina, the whip-smart twelve-year-old girl who helped translate, wanted to stay, but Ritu sent her away. So Priya had no idea what all the fuss was about.

The old man was just skin and bones. He'd dropped to the ground and almost disappeared under the pile formed by his ratty *jalabiya*. For a split second she thought Ritu had shot him. A silly thought. Ritu had never killed anyone, and the man, although loud, had never threatened them. It was the younger men in the crowd that had Choudhury worried. They were likely to become physical. That's why she and Ritu had pulled out their pistols and radioed for backup.

They always patrolled in pairs. Their backup—Nepali police in an armored personnel carrier—loitered in the distance in case there was trouble. The Nepalis hadn't come. She'd heard the engine start and die again. That happened far too often. The running joke in her unit was that the APCs were just for show. Half the time they began their patrols late because the damn things didn't start.

The crack of the second shot turned the stunned silence into a crazy free-for-all. People running, diving to the ground. Choudhury scanned the surroundings, trying to locate the shooter.

"Did you see where the shot came from?" she shouted over the din.

Ritu didn't reply. She wasn't standing against Choudhury's back anymore. Choudhury turned and saw her friend lying on the ground. Blood formed a dusty puddle around Ritu's head. She dropped to the ground and crawled to her friend.

"Where are you hit?"

The answer was no more than a gurgle. She saw why. A ragged hole in Ritu's neck spurted blood that fed the puddle.

The third shot barely registered with Choudhury. From the corner of her eye, she saw a young guy fall to the ground. She couldn't worry about him. Her hands were already pulling the first aid kit from her pack. She pressed a bandage against Ritu's wound. It turned red immediately. She took another one, pressed it against the wet one. It turned red too. She kept pressing against the soaked bandages.

"Ritu, stay with me. You hear me. Help is coming."

Ritu's eyes were full of fear.

Choudhury pushed the call button on her radio.

"Police down! Police down! I need immediate medical evacuation. Repeat, I need immediate medical evacuation."

When the medics finally arrived, Ritu's blood had stopped flowing. There was none left.

CHAPTER TWO

———◆———

Twenty-eight hundred miles northwest of Zam Zam, Valentin Vermeulen sat in a sleek *Café-Konditorei* in Düsseldorf, Germany. Even a casual observer would have noticed that he'd bet on the wrong side of the thermometer. His jacket, shirt, and trousers were meant for a much warmer climate than Düsseldorf, where freezing wind blew ripples across the gray Rhine. Add to that his deep tan, something the northern European latitude couldn't have produced at this time of year, and the observer might have thought that he hailed from a warmer place—southern Spain, Greece, or possibly Central America.

A closer look revealed a different provenance. He had grizzled blond hair, an errant forelock of which hung down on his broad forehead and stubbornly resisted the flick of his fingers. His eyes were the washed-out blue of hazy summer skies over the North Sea. His features were on the coarse side—a large nose and a generous mouth—reflecting his Flemish heritage. Just over six feet tall, he was neither bulky nor lanky, occupying the middle ground of forty-something men who keep in shape without overdoing it.

Vermeulen hadn't acquired his tan through the usual shortcuts employed by northern Europeans—tanning spas or the lotions that create a telltale splotchy orange hue. He'd earned his tan the hard way, sunburn and all, in the performance of his duties as investigator for the United Nations Office of Internal Oversight Services. The OIOS had been created to ferret out fraud throughout the world-wide net of United Nations operations. Which meant Vermeulen visited UN missions in places very much warmer than Düsseldorf in March.

The two-week holiday he had managed to extract from his bosses in

New York was almost over. He'd reserved the last three days to visit with his daughter Gaby, whom he hadn't seen in eight years.

"Let's meet at the *Medienhafen*," she'd said on the phone. "My office is in one of the Gehry buildings close to the TV tower. The stainless steel one in the middle. I'll get off at five."

The café was a steel and birch plywood affair. Modern, but not comfortable. Vermeulen sat at a table near the door. If Gaby got off early, he could see her crossing the plaza. Two elderly women occupied a table toward the rear, talking continuously in low voices. There was a large glass case displaying complicated cakes with more layers than the plywood of his table. The pastries looked dainty and fragile. Behind the case stood a blonde waitress, maybe twenty-five, her eyes glued to her phone, her fingers tapping the screen.

A flat-screen TV hung on the wall across from his table. It was tuned to a news channel with the sound turned off. He didn't pay attention to it until he saw a white vehicle with the letters 'UNAMID' painted on its door. He signaled the waitress.

"Can you turn the sound up on the TV?"

She nodded, went to the bar, and fiddled with a remote. When the sound came on, the face of a dark-skinned woman wearing sleek titanium glasses and an unruly tangle of thin braids filled the screen.

"The latest attack on the peacekeepers has frayed the nerves of all members of the UN mission here. This is Tessa Bishonga reporting from El Fasher, Darfur."

The two elderly women at the other table looked at him, frowning at the sudden disturbance.

The news anchor came back on. The next story was something about a Russian tycoon. It was none of Vermeulen's concern.

"Thanks. You can turn it down again," he said. The waitress shrugged and hit the mute button.

Vermeulen's interest was more than cursory. He was scheduled to audit the UNAMID mission in two days.

* * *

AT FIVE MINUTES TO FIVE, VERMEULEN stood outside the Gehry buildings. He'd heard of Frank Gehry but had never seen one of his designs. These were crazy. Not 'out of your mind' crazy. More like 'I didn't expect that' crazy. Impossibly undulating curves of stainless steel, brick and white panels, slanting walls, and windows sticking out at strange angles. The longer he looked at it, the more he liked it. There were enough buildings with ninety-degree corners in the world.

A gust blew across the river, and he folded up the collar of his jacket.

Somewhere a church bell tolled five times. The office exodus began right on time.

He recognized her the moment she came through the door, even though she looked quite different from what he remembered. Her pale blue eyes shone. Her hair was long again, parted on the left and tied into a ponytail that couldn't contain the willful lock she tried to brush from her forehead. He didn't remember her freckles, but he recognized her lips—not full, not thin, and not needing any lipstick.

His hand rose to his forehead to brush back a few strands of hair. The gesture brought a smile to her face. She stopped in front of him and grabbed his arms, examining him as if to make sure he was genuine. Tears appeared in her eyes, rolled down the smile lines on her cheeks. His eyes grew moist, too. It had been such a long time.

He pulled her close and they hugged for what seemed like hours.

She pushed him back to arm's length.

"You look older, Dad," she said, smiling through her tears.

"I'm glad I can't say the same about you. You look beautiful. So different than …." He stopped, wanting to kick himself for even thinking about the past—the messy divorce from his wife back in 2002, Gaby running away because of it, his desperate need to get the hell out of Antwerp and Belgium because it was too small for the two of them, and the unexpected job opening at the United Nations in New York City.

"You've done well for yourself, no?" he said.

"I think so. I'm happy with my work and I'm good at it. Just got promoted to this new job." The new job being head of the Africa section of a large Belgian logistics firm. The promotion had brought her from Antwerp to Düsseldorf.

"Sorry for calling you old," she said. "I didn't mean to be rude, I just remembered your face less—"

"Less drawn? Less gaunt?" he suggested.

She nodded.

"The result of a restless life," he said. "Assignments all over the world, no decent food, not enough sleep except on airplanes. I can't always take care of myself the way I should."

She didn't dwell on his appearance. "It's nice you came to visit during your time off. It must be a relief not having to jet off to those faraway places. What's that department you work for?"

"Office of Internal Oversight Services. We investigate fraud."

"I didn't think you had to travel so much?"

"That's because I got into trouble at the OIOS," he said.

"How'd you manage that?"

"A year after I started, we began the investigation of the Iraq oil-for-food program. I thought I found some evidence that the son of the Secretary-General at the time was getting paid off by a contractor."

"And you didn't hesitate to shout that from the rooftops, right?"

He cringed. Gaby was right. Although he hadn't quite shouted it from the rooftops, he'd sent his assessment up the chain of authority. There was evidence—good evidence, in his opinion—and his job was to get to the bottom of that affair. His colleagues had tried to warn him, telling him that the UN hierarchy didn't appreciate airing dirty laundry, especially if it provided more ammunition to American UN skeptics. He'd ignored them.

"How did you guess?" he said.

"You were always so stubborn when you thought you were right. It drove Mom crazy."

The mention of his ex-wife touched a raw nerve. He looked out at the Rhine. Gaby noticed the shadow on his face.

"So, how did it turn out?" she said.

"I was wrong. Not about the evidence, but about how it all fit into the larger picture. The man was cleared and I was sent to the UN equivalent of Siberia."

"Now you're exaggerating."

His smile was rueful. "Only a little. Rather than working in a comfortable office in New York and staying at my wonderful apartment in Greenwich Village, I'm sent to peacekeeping missions in out-of-the-way places to investigate petty fraud. It might as well be Siberia."

"Why not come back to Antwerp if you don't like it? Maybe you could get your old job back."

His old job at the Crown Prosecutor's office in Antwerp. It seemed like a lifetime ago. He'd done well in law school and the prosecutor's financial crime division was looking for someone with his dogged drive to find culprits. He'd loved his job. Chasing swindlers and nailing crooked companies became his life. He spent more and more time away from home. In hindsight, the divorce seemed inevitable.

"It's complicated. You know that," he said.

She pushed the lock of hair out of her face.

"It's not complicated. Just talk to Mom."

He shook his head.

"She doesn't want to talk to me."

"Come on, Dad, take the first step. Don't be so stubborn."

"If I hadn't been stubborn eight years ago ...." He instantly wished he could take those words back, reverse time for two seconds, say the right thing. Gaby's face hardened. She looked away, out at the river.

Eight years ago. The nightmare every parent dreads. Gaby had disappeared.

His friend, the chief inspector of the judicial police, shrugged. "Give it a few days, Valentin. Most runaways come back." When that didn't happen, he'd searched for her on his own. The search shattered the illusion of his comfortable existence. He saw the other side of Antwerp. The down-and-out drunks. The underage prostitutes hovering in the shadows of *Oudemansstraat,* hoping to make enough for another hit. The endless procession of filthy squats. The hollow eyes and wasted faces.

When he found her, strung out on heroin in an abandoned building, she looked nothing like his daughter. A pale face, a buzz cut, and empty eyes. He'd endured the screaming fits and dragged her to rehab. She made it through. She'd also refused to speak to him again. Until a year ago.

Yes, he'd been stubborn. He wasn't sorry about that. But he didn't need to remind her.

"Sorry," he said. It was too late.

She kept looking at the river. When she turned around, her voice was defiant.

"Has it ever occurred to you that I might not have ended up in that place if you had been civil to Mom? If you had been home more often?"

Of course it had occurred to him, but Gaby saying it was a punch in the gut.

"It's cold out here," he said. "Let's go and sit somewhere and get some tea. Then have dinner later."

Her face betrayed her inner turmoil. It always had. She shook her head.

"Where are you staying?" she said.

"Some hotel in the *Altstadt.*" He fished in his pocket for one of the cards he'd taken to tell cab drivers where to bring him. "Metropol Hotel."

"I'll call you."

* * *

THE COLD WIND PROPELLED HIM ALONG the promenade toward the city's old town. A barge maneuvered through the bend in the Rhine, coming close to the bank. A small car sat on the rear deck, and a dog ran along the deck gangway barking. The skipper waved from the wheelhouse. Vermeulen didn't wave back. By the time he'd reached the old town, his mood was as dark as the evening sky.

He meandered through the narrow passages of the *Altstadt*, looking for a suitable pub. Being Flemish, he loved good beer. Of course, his favorite Belgian brews ranked the highest. But Düsseldorf's specialty, *Altbier,* came pretty close. A brewpub called *Schlüssel* drew him. Despite the cold weather, patrons stood at wooden counters outside to grab a quick glass. Although he craved a cigarette, he was too chilled to drink outside. Inside, the pub was filled with thick wooden tables and chairs. The walls were paneled in wood the color of the beer served there. The barkeeper filled glass after glass from a brass tap stuck into the bottom of a large wooden barrel. Aging waiters, their bellies held in place by blue aprons, packed their trays, four glasses at a time. One of them slapped a glass in front of Vermeulen and marked his coaster with a thick pencil. No need to ask. If you sat down, that's what you drank.

The beer was good but didn't fill the emptiness in him. The second followed quickly. After the third, he paid and left. The cold evening wind propelled him to the next brewpub, *Zum Uerige*, where he drank more beer. Even though the old town was packed with people, he felt like a shipwrecked sailor, stranded on a faraway island. He ate something somewhere but didn't remember what. He forgot the names of the pubs where he stopped to drink. His alcohol-addled brain threw out ideas on how to patch up things with Gaby. Send flowers. Send chocolates. Fortunately, he was still coherent enough to know that these were just as dumb as his behavior that afternoon. In any case, he didn't know where she lived.

Well after midnight, he found a taxi stand, fell into the first Mercedes, and showed the driver one of the cards. His hotel, it turned out, was right around the corner. He crawled back out of the cab, almost tripped on the cobblestone street, and stumbled to the hotel. It took the considerable help of the night porter to navigate the narrow stairs to his third-floor room, where he crashed onto bed without taking his coat off.

CHAPTER THREE

———◆———

Diary of Ritu Roy

THE FLIGHT WAS LONG AND BORING. Not much fun sitting in the belly of a transport aircraft. Our trucks were strapped down in the middle. We were sitting in hard seats along each side. It was very cold, too.

No matter, we made it to El Fasher, all one hundred forty of us. So far it's exactly as I imagined. Our tents—six women to a tent—stand on concrete pads. It doesn't make for a nice feel underfoot, but it's easy to keep clean. Maybe I can find a little mat or rug in town. The advance team did a good job setting things up. We each have a cot and a footlocker to keep our things in. It's a bit strange to have no privacy, but I'll get used to it.

The mess tent is large and the kitchen made a decent supper for us. I think I'll make good friends. But I'm glad Priya is here with me. I don't think I would have been brave enough to do this without her.

After supper, we had a little ceremony to mark the beginning of our mission. It was an amazing sight. One hundred forty policewomen, all dressed in our new uniforms, standing in formation. Our commander made a nice speech, and Commissioner Duah, the head of UN police at UNAMID, welcomed us. We're ready to do the work we came here to do.

Thursday, March 11, 2010

PRIYA CHOUDHURY WENT BACK TO THE scene. Her commander had assigned her to camp duty. Choudhury disagreed with that decision. The image of Ritu lying on her back, the blood pulsing from her neck wound, was etched into her mind. It appeared every time she closed her eyes. She had to do something, find who killed Ritu. It was clear to her that Ritu had been the target of the attack.

Three of her colleagues accompanied her. New security rules. A Nepali APC followed them. When they reached the spot, the APC stopped, but its engine kept idling. A lesson learned too late.

The place where Ritu was killed didn't look like a crime scene. There were none of the markers the crime scene technicians in Dhaka used. Just the dark spot where Ritu's blood had seeped into the ground. A few more days and the sun would bleach it to the same orange color as the rest of the sand. For now, those passing gave it a wide berth.

The last frames from the day before played in her mind again. The first bandage getting soaked. Pressing the second one against the first. It turning red as well. If only she could have stopped the blood. She tore her eyes away from the patch.

Choudhury stood in the place again, facing southeast, the shelters just a few yards away. Ritu had stood against her back, facing northwest. The bullet had torn through the left side of her neck, severing the external carotid artery. It couldn't have come from the shacks in front of Priya, because it would have had to pass through her head before hitting Ritu. It also couldn't have come from the opposite side. Reverse logic.

That left the westerly direction.

An outcropping in a bare area was the only suitable place. A slight elevation, bushes for cover. A perfect location for a sniper. She jogged over to the rocks. Tire tracks indicated that a car had parked next to the water pump. A bit of red plastic tape with the letters 'p Out' was stuck to a thorn. She took it with her fingertips and put it in a bag. Footprints led around the bushes. The wind had already smoothed whatever tread pattern the soles might have left.

Behind the twigs, she saw indentations in the sand. Someone had knelt there. She looked across the rock ledge. Her three colleagues were clearly visible. This was the spot where the gunman had set up.

She scanned the area. Nothing left behind. No fibers stuck to the thorns. No bit of paper, carelessly thrown away. The site was clean. She knelt down, looked under the leaves of the bushes. Nothing. A glint caught her eye when she rose again. It came from a crack in the rock. A casing had rolled into the crevice. She used a twig to coax the brass from the crack. A standard 7.62x51mm NATO casing. Not very common in Darfur. Most weapons in use here were the Chinese M-56 variant of the AK-47 using 7.62x39mm ammunition.

* * *

GARRETH CAMPBELL WATCHED THE WOMAN COP from behind a shack. He'd left his pickup a few rows back. The woman who lived there was happy to accommodate him. He'd given her a little money, which was more than anyone else had done for her.

The death of a peacekeeper wouldn't go by without an investigation. Campbell knew that. Shortly after the shooting, Bangladeshi and Nepali police had swarmed to the spot where the policewoman died. According to the woman in the shack, they'd searched the area, but hadn't found anything. More importantly, she told him that the outcropping hadn't been part of their search. That news had reassured him.

He was about to leave when he saw four of the Bangladeshi women cops arrive. He recognized the short, stocky one from the day before. She took her time examining the area, turning one way, then another. She knew where to look. That worried him. When she walked to the outcropping, he swore under his breath. He saw her check the tire tracks, pick up the stray piece of plastic tape. Then she disappeared behind the bushes. That wasn't good at all. She took longer than she should have. When she came back, she was holding a plastic bag. Whatever was in the bag glinted in the sunlight.

Damn, he thought. *She found the casing.*

Chapter Four

A PERSISTENT BUZZING WOKE VERMEULEN. IT SOUNDED like the horseflies from his father's farm, back when he was a kid. He waved a hand to shoo them away. The buzzing continued. Moving his hand directed his attention to a rhythmic pounding, as if someone was hitting a plaster wall with a sledgehammer. Each pounding was followed by a wave of pain. He swallowed. His throat was dry and his tongue a dead animal in his mouth. The buzzing stopped. The pounding continued.

He forced his eyes open and saw gray morning light through a gritty film. It dawned on him that the pounding was actually inside his head. Something sharp dug into his back. He tried to roll to the right, but he was stuck. His arm was pinned behind his back. He pushed himself up with his other elbow. His stomach heaved and he let himself fall back on the bed. The buzzing returned. This time, he located its source. The room phone. He forced himself up again and pushed the receiver against his ear.

"Yeah?" His voice was a rasp scraping against a piece of hard maple. He needed water more than anything.

"Dad?"

The memory of their quarrel the day before squeezed past the blows in his head. *Damn*. He was in no condition to talk, but he couldn't hang up either.

"Hang on a second," he said, then put the receiver down and dragged himself into the bathroom, where he drank greedily from the faucet. Another heave told him to stop, and he splashed some water onto his face before returning to the phone.

"I had toothpaste in my mouth," he said.

"I'm sorry for how I behaved yesterday," she said. "So many memories are still raw."

"No reason to be sorry, darling. I was the boneheaded one."

"Could we have breakfast? Maybe even spend the morning together? I took time off."

He would have danced a jig if his condition hadn't been so precarious.

"Sure," he said. "I'd love to. That's why I'm here."

"Great, I'm downstairs in the lobby. I'll come up."

"W-wait," he said. "Let me get dressed."

"I bet you didn't even get undressed after you got back from drinking last night."

"Who says I went drinking?"

"Come on, Dad. You should hear your voice. Remember, I have some experience."

A HALF-HOUR LATER, THEY SETTLED INTO A café and ordered coffee, croissants, butter, and jam. Vermeulen gulped the coffee, burning the roof of his mouth. The coffee, on top of the quick shower and the two aspirin he'd swallowed, restored him to a semblance of normality. Gaby kept looking at him with a crooked smile.

She told him about her job, and he marveled at her command of the complexities of global trade. His daughter, controlling the flow of millions of dollars of goods from around the world to Africa and back. Working for OIOS seemed a lot less exciting in comparison. She asked about the places he was sent, and he admitted that he rarely had time to really get to know the cities where his work took him.

"Isn't it dangerous? I mean, there are wars going on. Otherwise, the UN wouldn't be there, right?" she said.

He told her that his work was mostly inside and that he was usually far from the actual conflicts. He didn't tell her about the times when the crooks he investigated weren't as petty as he made them out to be, or that he'd had a few close calls. There was no need to worry her. It was their moment together.

"Where are you going next?" she said as they strolled along the Königsallee, Düsseldorf's premier shopping boulevard.

"To Sudan. An audit of UNAMID, the United Nations/African Union Mission in Darfur. And all the work that comes with that."

"Are you looking forward to it?"

"Yes and no. Sometimes I meet interesting people, but the work can be tedious."

They stopped and looked at the shoe display in a large window. They were stylish and of good quality but well beyond his budget.

"So, is there someone important in your life?" he said.

"Maybe," she said after a moment's hesitation. "His name is Uli. I met him a couple of months back. I like him. It's too early to say if it's serious."

"Does he work at your firm?"

She gave an impatient wave of her hand. "Goodness, no. I'd never date someone in my office. Too complicated. No, he's a lawyer with a small firm specializing in company law."

"Am I going to meet him?"

Gaby shook her head. Pushing a lock of hair from her forehead, she said, "No. I'm not even sure about him. Having him meet you would make the relationship more than it really is. Let's wait for your next visit and we'll see where we stand."

"Be careful with lawyers," he said.

She punched him in the side.

They'd just turned toward the Rhine again when his phone rang.

The voice at the other end was depressingly familiar.

"I still have a day left," Vermeulen said. "Don't ruin it."

"You would if you weren't in Germany," Suarez, his boss in the New York headquarters, said. "There's only one flight a week from Frankfurt to Kenya, and that leaves tomorrow. So suck it up. You'll get the day credited. Take it some other time. Your tickets will be at the airport. The briefing in Nairobi is on Sunday. You go to Sudan on Monday."

CHAPTER FIVE

———◆———

Diary of Ritu Roy

W**E'VE FINISHED OUR FIRST WEEK OF** patrols in Zam Zam camp. I patrol with Priya. For a moment I was worried when I was assigned to work with a different woman, but then the Commander reassigned me to go out with Priya. It's good to work with my best friend. Especially here.

Zam Zam is a sad place. Over fifty thousand refugees. But they are called IDPs, 'Internally displaced persons.' The commander explained that you become a refugee only if you cross a border into another country. If you run away from your home but stay inside your country, you're an IDP. Seems like a distinction only bureaucrats could make. It makes no difference to the people. They are just as miserable.

We focus on women and their needs. We listen to their complaints through our interpreter. We help them get medical attention. Sometimes we mediate arguments. The worst are battery and rape. Sometimes it feels like the civil war has destroyed whatever respect the men had for law and morality.

This week alone, we saw three women who had been beaten. Priya and I spoke with each of them. The stories are depressing and very similar. Their husbands beat them for the slightest reason. One of them snuck some food to her children. Her husband caught her. Doesn't he know that his kids need food more than he does?

The worst was the girl who'd been raped. Her eyes were just black holes. She didn't speak, just barely nodded or shook her head when we asked what happened. Did she know the rapist? She shook her head. But I'm sure she knows. She's afraid. There are so few of us. We can't protect her. At least we got her an appointment at the hospital.

Friday, March 12, 2010

PRIYA CHOUDHURY REPORTED TO COMMANDER MITRA, her commanding officer. She knew her to be a patient leader, concerned about the welfare of the women under her command. So it was logical that Commander Mitra would follow up and make sure Priya showed no signs of post-traumatic stress.

The meeting started out friendly enough. Yes, there were nightmares. No, she wasn't isolating herself. No, she wasn't lashing out at others. No, she didn't think someone was after her. Why did she go back to the spot where Ritu had been killed? To collect evidence. They had to find the killer. Wasn't that what police did?

Commander Mitra told her that she shouldn't investigate Ritu's death. Tried to explain that in random shootings like this, they'd never find the shooter.

"Two other people were killed at the same time, Constable. Don't forget that."

"I know. Maybe the killer had to warm up."

"Then why did he shoot the young man after Constable Roy? You told me the sequence of shots. First the old man, then Ritu, then the youth. No, Constable, it was a random attack. Ritu was caught in the wrong place. It could have been you."

"I wish it had been."

The commander shook her head. She put her hand on Priya's arm. "How can you say that?"

"Ritu was younger. She still had so much to live for."

"That's very valiant of you. But it doesn't change what happened. We'll never know the reason. This country is full of enmity, and we won't have figured out who hates whom by the time we go back home. All we can do is help the most vulnerable."

"What about the NATO casing?" she said. "That's a clue. Who's got a rifle that uses NATO ammo? A sniper rifle, to boot. Not the poor buggers in the camp. I checked the casing, it's got 'RG' stamp on the head. We could find out where it was made."

The commander threw up her hands. "That's not our mission, Constable. We don't have the crime lab facilities here that we have in Dhaka."

"We don't need a crime lab. We just have to look at the facts. The person fired three perfect hits over six hundred yards. That takes skill. I couldn't do it."

"It was a crowd of people. Anyone able to aim into the crowd would have hit someone."

"Two shots into the head and one into the neck doesn't sound like someone fired randomly into a crowd. Also, why did he stop after three shots?"

The commander didn't even stop to consider. "Maybe that was all the ammo he had. Let it go. That's an order. For the next week, you are not to go back to Zam Zam. Report to the support team. They'll have work for you. And check in with me every day at noon. Dismissed."

* * *

VERMEULEN SAT ON THE LEFTMOST AISLE seat of row 23 in a Boeing 737-300 en route from Frankfurt to Nairobi. He preferred the aisle seat because the UN wouldn't pay for business class and he had to put his legs somewhere.

It was an overnight flight, but he didn't intend to sleep. On his tray table lay a folder containing the necessary background information for his next assignment. Short histories of Sudan, the Darfur conflict, the relevant UN Security Council resolutions, the particulars for UNAMID, and a detailed listing of all participating units and their home countries. Enough to put him to sleep.

He caught the eye of a passing flight attendant and asked for another beer. The brand offered by the airline didn't even rank among his top twenty.

The historical summaries didn't include any earthshaking revelations. A businesslike summary of Omar al-Bashir's rise to the top Sudan's government after the coup in 1989, his consolidation of power, the second civil war with the southern provinces. Typical UN speak—just the dates, some facts, no innuendo or any pronouncement on the obvious fact that al-Bashir was a brutal dictator.

The summary of the conflict in Sudan's western province of Darfur contained several interesting bits. Vermeulen didn't know how complex the shifting alliances between the various groups in Darfur were. He'd relied on the Arab versus African image that dominated the media since the conflict burst onto the world stage in 2004. The report pointed out that those designations were far from accurate, often imposed by outsiders and altogether not useful in describing the different parties. Pro-government groups and rebels included people fitting both categories.

Since the renewed negotiations at the beginning of the year, there had been as much in-fighting on each side as conflict between the two sides. He also hadn't considered the environmental component of climate change and desertification that had disrupted the annual treks of the pastoralists and their camel herds.

Add to that the colonial hangover of unequal land distribution and

Vermeulen wondered why it had taken so long for the whole thing to blow up.

The cabin lights had long been dimmed and his seat neighbor at the window had pulled the blanket over his head to shut out the beam of his reading light. A few screens in the seat backs in front of him glimmered, but most of the passengers slept.

He tackled the particulars of the UNAMID mission. Nothing much new there. If anything, it showed the reluctance of the Security Council to get involved. He could just imagine the big powers on the Council telling each other that Darfur was an African problem. Let them fix it. That strategy hadn't worked at all. The first mission fielded by the African Union had nowhere near enough personnel to make a dent in the violence. So, after enough dithering, the Security Council approved UNAMID with a much more robust military presence drawn from member states in Africa and elsewhere.

The list of participating countries was long. About fifteen thousand military personnel and some forty-five hundred police officers. With an assortment of civilian employees, the total came to twenty-five thousand. A big operation by United Nations standards. Which meant a lot of matériel coming in and going out. Which meant a lot of opportunity for fraud. It was his job to uncover that.

CHAPTER SIX

———◆———

CAMPBELL PARKED HIS PICKUP UNDER THE canopy of a tall acacia tree near Lake Fasher. The water was brown with a layer of green scum covering the southern end. He glanced across the water and saw the fence of the soccer field. It was quiet. Too early and too hot for a game.

His mobile phone rested in his hand. He should have called yesterday. The instructions were clear. Report any new developments immediately. He sighed and pushed the speed dial button.

"Yes?" a voice said. It belonged to Dale Houser.

"There has been a new development," Campbell said.

"Yes?"

"One of the Bangladeshi cops came back and poked around yesterday. She found something. I think it was the missing casing."

"Does it pose a problem?" Houser said.

"No, it's a standard casing, nothing special."

"I don't like it."

Campbell noticed the Newcastle accent creeping into Houser's voice. It meant Houser was getting angry.

"Think about it, boss. Leaving the casing makes the whole thing look unprofessional. We don't want anyone to think it was a professional hit."

"Then you should have left all of them. What kind of casing was it?"

"NATO 7.62x51mm." Campbell hesitated. Then he added, "Match grade."

"You idiot. Anybody with half a brain will figure out that it wasn't some yokel taking potshots. All they need to do is check the head stamp."

"Why should they?"

"Why shouldn't they?"

Campbell was quiet.

"Is there anything else?" Houser said.

"After I fired the shots, everyone ran away. When I drove away, I saw a girl. I don't think she was watching me. But she might remember my face."

"Goddamn it," Houser said. "Can the girl connect you to the shooting?"

"I don't think so."

"That's not good enough. The cop you saw poking around might talk to her. She'll put the pieces together. Get rid of the girl and find out what happens in that Bangladeshi unit. They're all chicks, right? Get to know one. The moment someone asks more questions, I want to know."

* * *

DALE HOUSER LEANED BACK IN HIS chair. It creaked. Like everything else in his Port Sudan warehouse, the chair was old. He had no plans to refurbish the office. Port Sudan was not a place he visited often. Fortunately, he did enough business around the world that Sudan was low on the list of places where he had to spend time. Except the current project required his presence. The Sudanese liked doing business with a British company, and he had to make sure that everything went smoothly.

Garreth should have cleaned up after himself. The man was a great shooter, one of the best marksmen in the Third Battalion of the Royal Parachute Regiment. That's why Houser had hired him. But ex-military men often had difficulties transferring their skills to the civilian sphere.

He had seen Garreth pick off Argentinean soldiers during the Falklands War as if he were plinking bottles off a fence. The man could calm himself, even when the world around him was crazy with the clamor of battle. Back then, Garreth never had to worry about leaving casings behind. It was war. Killing was legal.

Lieutenant Houser's squad led the charge during the bloody battle for Mount Longdon, the strategic point overlooking Port Stanley, the main port on the Falklands. They'd killed plenty of Argentineans then. Most before they surrendered, others afterwards. They didn't have time for legal niceties, distinctions between combatants and noncombatants, and such. All Argentineans were enemies. And enemies were killed.

Back in Britain, Houser and his men got medals for it.

A decade later, all that changed. Some asshole from the battalion wrote a memoir, which happened to mention the shootings of POWs. The Ministry of Defense investigated. Then Scotland Yard. Houser left the service before they could kick him to the curb. So did Garreth.

It was the mid-nineties. Regular armies were shrinking after the end of the Cold War. Private military contractors were booming. Both found gainful employment with a South African company. They fought in Angola and Sierra Leone and trained special forces around the world.

By 2005, Houser had enough contacts and cash to start his own private military contracting business, Assured Sovereignty. He bid on contracts that larger competitors would skip because they weren't lucrative enough. His list of clients grew, even included the British and U.S. governments. He leased a few transport planes and became a one-stop-shop for delivering dodgy cargo to dangerous areas. Throughout it all, Garreth followed him like the loyal soldier he was. But he never did learn to clean up after his missions.

* * *

The Medea, a Panamax-sized container ship, docked at the north quay of Umm Qasr, Iraq's only deepwater port. Umm Qasr wasn't a large port by any stretch of the imagination; it was a small enclave in the desert next to Kuwait. Its fortunes had waxed and waned, depending on the needs of the country and the degree of enmity between Iraq and Iran, which affected use of the Shatt al-Arab waterway, Iraq's only other access to the Persian Gulf. Starting in March 2003, Umm Qasr blossomed as it became the gateway for the matériel needed by the United States and its 'Coalition of the Willing.' Since the end of hostilities, it had continued in that role, albeit for different customers.

Two large gantry cranes began the choreographed routine of unloading the containers. The crane operators had the printout of the unloading sequence, and they went to work accordingly. Their spreaders descended; the twistlocks clamped into the corner castings; the steel boxes rose thirty feet; the trolleys wheeled back to the quay; and the containers came down to the concrete front apron, where the spreaders released them. A camera scanned the barcodes on the containers and directed the reach stackers to grab them and deposit them at their respective destinations in the container yard.

A blue container with the inscription 'Excelsior' descended to the concrete. It was no different from the blue containers that preceded it. The radio on the belt of a port employee crackled. A voice said something in Arabic. The man blocked the camera, keeping it from scanning the code. A stacker operator hoisted the container and turned around. Instead of adding it to one of the three stacks where all the others had been deposited, he carried the box to the rear apron of the next berth.

With that, the box ceased to exist. 'Lost at sea' was the official explanation.

CHAPTER SEVEN

———◆———

Diary of Ritu Roy

Priya is so down-to-earth. She's my rock, really. When I talk to the women, I get so emotional. I cry with them, hug them. Priya does that, too. But she knows how to keep a little distance. She's practical that way, always thinking of what we can do right then and there. That's very helpful in a place with so few options. I wouldn't know what to do without her.

The dryness is getting to me. The temperatures are no different from home, but at home we have moisture in the air. Sure, it makes you sweat, but it also keeps your skin soft. Here, my hair is getting brittle and my skin dry. I use lotion, but supplies are scarce. The dust is the other thing that bothers me. It gets into everything. It clogs my sinuses. I drink more water than I ever have.

Monday, March 15, 2010

Early on Monday, the *Gloria*, a rusty small feeder sailing under the Liberian flag, docked at the south berth of Umm Qasr. She made regular runs along the Persian Gulf shores and into the Red Sea. Nobody rushed in to unload her. The ship just sat there, a little less than half loaded.

The crew got six hours of shore leave, which they took advantage of, only to find out that Umm Qasr's entertainment options were sparse even by conservative Gulf standards.

While the crew was gone, the port machinery next to the Gloria came to life. The cargo it took on was minimal. Just a blue container with the inscription 'Excelsior' that sat on the rear apron.

The reach stacker grabbed the steel box, deposited it under the gantry crane. The crane's spreader locked into the corner castings, lifted the container, and deposited it in the forward left bay on the *Gloria*.

The ship's bay plan did not reflect the additional cargo.

* * *

THE DE HAVILLAND BUFFALO FLEW LAZY circles south of the El Fasher airport. Vermeulen sat strapped into what amounted to little more than a garden chair bolted to the aluminum floor of the aircraft. He was as ready to get back to solid ground as he'd ever been. The flight from Nairobi had taken almost nine hours, counting the stopover in Juba, Sudan. Nine hours was bad enough in economy class, even with movies. In the Buffalo, it was pure misery. Noisy as hell, buffeted by turbulences, and no movies. About five miles out from El Fasher, the pilot informed him that the El Fasher tower told him to circle until another plane on approach had landed. The mission wasn't off to a good start.

The briefing at the UN complex in Nairobi had been a waste of time. OIOS had been doing audits of peacekeeping missions for a decade and a half. Vermeulen had done them for the better part of eight years. Bookkeeping hadn't changed during that time. Nobody had invented a new way to tally up numbers in columns. It was the same tedious job as before.

Arne Bengtsson, head of the Nairobi office of the OIOS, didn't really want to update him on accounting practices. Bengtsson considered himself Vermeulen's immediate superior, an opinion Vermeulen didn't share. Vermeulen considered the New York headquarters as his home base, not Nairobi. But that didn't stop Bengtsson from telling him to stay out of trouble. As if Vermeulen were looking for trouble. He wasn't. It's just that when he saw a problem, he tried to deal with it rather than duck, like so many of his colleagues did. Like the whole UN did, if you really thought about it. The organization depended on the support of its members. That often meant couching problems in diplomatic language. Vermeulen called it as he saw it. For Bengtsson, that meant trouble.

The Buffalo turned again. From his window, he saw the exhaust trails of a large white jet coming from the North.

"Another UN flight?" he asked the copilot.

The man shook his head.

"No, that's an Ilyushin 76 cargo jet. We don't have any of those under contract. It could be Azza Air or Assured Air Services. They both operate IL-76s."

"What are they bringing in?"

"I don't know. Probably supplies for the Sudanese Armed Forces."

The pilot turned the Buffalo again. Vermeulen peered through the opposite window. The jet lined up with the runway and glided to its touchdown. After the next turn he could see it taxi to the far side of the airport. There was crackling on the intercom. The pilot said something into his microphone, righted the plane, and aimed for the tarmac below.

They touched down with a mighty bump. The plane yawed left and right, but the pilot managed to keep it straight and braked. They taxied to the cargo area and stopped. The copilot opened the side door. Vermeulen grabbed his bag and stepped onto the tarmac. Darfur greeted him with a red sun at the horizon and a blast of hot wind. He knew right away his jacket, shirt, and trousers weren't meant for this climate either.

A white Nissan Patrol with UNAMID insignia came to a stop nearby. The driver, a tall man with a face as dark as espresso, approached him. The patch and flag on his uniform told Vermeulen that he was with the Kenyan contingent.

"Mr. Vermeulen?"

"Yes?"

"Welcome to the United Nations/African Union Mission in Darfur, sir." He saluted. "I'm Corporal Winston Wambui, Kenyan military police. I'm your driver and liaison. Let me bring you to your quarters."

"Where am I staying?"

"You are housed at the World Food Programme guest house. It's not far from the airport." He pointed into the distance.

On the way out, Wambui drove past four fighter jets painted in brown and green patterns.

"What are those?" Vermeulen said.

"Sukhoi-25 jet fighters of the Sudanese air force."

"What are they doing here?"

"Attacking rebel forces and villages."

"Isn't that illegal?"

"Yes."

At the far end of the tarmac stood the IL-76. It was bigger than any aircraft Vermeulen had seen. Surrounding the plane stood soldiers in desert fatigues. Unlike Wambui, they didn't wear blue helmets or berets. Khaki-colored vehicles were driving off a ramp from the rear gate of the plane.

"Sudanese reinforcements," Wambui said. "Also illegal."

"What's the UN doing about this?"

"There's not much the UN can do. They protest. But not too much. Otherwise, Sudan will rescind its permission for UNAMID's deployment, and that would be far worse."

* * *

The WFP guesthouse sat in a compound about two blocks away from the UNAMID headquarters, just across from the maternity hospital. His room was in an aluminum shed, but it was air-conditioned. There were no en-suite facilities. Hygienic needs were taken care of in an ablution shed that was fed by a large blue plastic tank sitting on a scaffold.

Vermeulen didn't mind. Better than sitting in a hotel. He could walk to HQ. He took his trousers and spare jacket from the suitcase and hung them on the rod provided. There was just one outlet, but he always carried a small power strip. He plugged in his phone, his iPod Touch, and the Bluetooth speaker he'd picked up at the Düsseldorf airport duty-free.

It took a few moments before the appropriate lights came on indicating that the speaker could be paired with the iPod. A few taps later, the Clash, his all-time favorite band, played their 1977 track, "Career Opportunities." The new speaker sounded better than he'd expected.

He stretched out on the bed, lit a Gitane Papier Maïs, and wondered which career opportunities had never knocked on his door. It wasn't that he didn't like his job with OIOS. It certainly allowed him to visit places he wouldn't have seen otherwise. It also let him go after crooks, something that gave him deep satisfaction. Still, he couldn't help wondering if there had been moments along the path where he could have made a different choice.

Like most of the draftees in 1983, he'd resented having to interrupt his life for what seemed a useless eighteen months in the Belgian army. After basic training, the unfathomable logic of military bureaucracy sent him to Army Intelligence, where he did well, rising to the rank of corporal. His commanding officer urged him to enlist and stay with the service. At the age of twenty, he'd found the prospect of spending the rest of his life in uniform preposterous. Looking back, he realized his life hadn't turned out so different. Sure, he wasn't wearing a uniform, but the strictures of bureaucracies certainly ended up shaping his life. First as a law student at Antwerp University, then as staff attorney at the Crown Prosecution Service in Antwerp.

When everything fell apart in 2003, he was able to leave Antwerp so readily because he'd grown tired of being a cog in a hierarchy. What irony that he should join the most intricate hierarchy there was, the United Nations. No wonder he got into trouble so quickly. But also it was the best thing that could have happened to him.

He hadn't been completely honest with Gaby. Yes, he disliked bouncing from one mission to the next on some OIOS errand. It was a hard life and it took its toll. But the real reason he didn't want to come back to Antwerp wasn't that his ex-wife lived there. Hell, the city was big enough; he could live there until he died without ever running into her. The real reason went deeper. He could no longer abide by the rules of the convoluted pecking orders by which people organized their lives and those of others.

So, considering everything, life wasn't so bad. He was his own man. He cleared his cases in his own way. No use worrying about what might have been.

CHAPTER EIGHT

———◆———

Diary of Ritu Roy

IF I SEE ONE MORE WOMAN beaten by her husband, I'm going to strangle that man. Who do they think they are? Greedy, lecherous bastards, the whole lot of them. The women are afraid to talk about the bruises on their faces. The children hide behind them. The husbands just sit there, goddamn prayer beads in their hands, giving me that "What are you gonna do about it?" look.

We take the women outside, ask them what happened. Ask if they want to file charges. They are horrified by the prospect and shoo us away. I feel the heft of the Glock 17 in my holster, and I just want to pull it out, storm into the hut, press it against the man's head, and tell him that I'll blow his head off if he ever touches her again.

This place weighs on me. The women are just part of it. My anger sits simmering just below the surface. I never felt this way back home. It's not the poverty here. There's plenty of that in Dhaka. Maybe it's the bleakness of it all, the hopelessness I see in the faces. It makes me wonder what I'm doing here. This isn't an adventure anymore. It never was, really. It just took me two months to notice. The same routine, day in and day out. No change. Just more people arriving. I can't bear hopelessness.

Priya worries about me. She told me so yesterday. I don't know what to tell her.

Tuesday, March 16, 2010

SCORES OF UN POLICE OFFICERS STOOD in neatly formed rows on the central square of the UNAMID compound. It made for an impressive sight. A fat man wearing a blue uniform faced them across a lectern. It was Police Commissioner Duah, commander of UN police units in Darfur. Vermeulen had seen his photo on the UNAMID website. Next to the commissioner stood an easel with a large picture of a woman wearing a blue beret.

Someone turned on the PA system and the speakers popped. A man approached the lectern and tapped on the microphone. The sound echoed across the assembled police. The man nodded to the commissioner.

"We come together here today," Duah began, "to remember one of our own who gave her life to promote peace in this war-torn country. Constable Ritu Roy came to Darfur because she wanted to help women find their voices. She left her country, her home to follow her vocation …."

The commissioner listed Roy's achievements. Vermeulen's attention wavered. He looked around. The Bangladeshi female police unit stood front and center. The camouflage pattern of their uniforms was unique. The color patches—light blue, dark blue, and purple against a khaki background—looked stylish but did little to help the wearer blend into the background, least of all the orange soil of Darfur.

Duah continued, "Focusing especially on the most vulnerable displaced persons, women, and children, Constable Roy put her training to good use with regard to the special problems women face …."

Other units, both male and female, were flanked the Bangladeshis. Vermeulen saw both men and women with tears in their eyes. Ritu Roy's death must have struck a deep chord among her colleagues. Were casualties so rare that they could elicit such emotional responses? Or was her death particularly tragic? Wambui might know.

"Constable Roy leaves behind her parents and two brothers, who live in Dhaka, Bangladesh. I have personally extended UNAMID's condolences to her family."

The commissioner then awarded Ritu Roy a medal posthumously. A trumpeter played a soulful tune. The police units stood at attention. After the last sounds of the trumpet died away, the units were dismissed. The square quickly turned into a sea of milling uniforms. Vermeulen let the crowd drift around him, catching bits of conversation in more languages than he could understand. The first item on his agenda was meeting the UNAMID commander, a brigadier general from Nigeria, to introduce himself and his task. After that the tedious work began.

Someone tugged at his jacket and he turned. Next to him stood a policewoman wearing the Bangladeshi designer camouflage.

"Wait a moment, then follow me past those sheds."

Before he could ask her anything, she turned and pushed through the crowd toward a row of aluminum sheds. Her cloak-and-dagger manner was odd. He looked around. The square was teeming with personnel. Nobody would've paid attention to them talking. The woman had disappeared in the crowd. He hurried to catch up.

The UNAMID headquarters reminded him of the 1950s public housing estates at the outskirts of Antwerp—the same bureaucratic grid, the same deadening uniformity, the same lifeless buildings. Except here, the edifices were single-story aluminum huts instead of concrete blocks. What made this compound even worse was the lack of any adornment. In Antwerp, even the poorest spruced up their housing, if only by hanging laundry on their balconies. Here, the only markings were the institutional lettering indicating block and unit number.

The concrete path turned right after a set of five sheds, revealing an identical path running between more identical sheds. Without a map, he'd be lost in this labyrinth. The path ended in a T-junction. Unsure whether to turn left or right, he hesitated. A hiss sounded from the right. He followed it. A few steps later, a pair of hands pulled him into the space between two sheds.

She was of medium height, and her uniform was clean and neatly pressed. Her black hair stuck out from under the blue beret and showed the first white strands. She had an oval face with olive skin, dark almond-shaped eyes, and a slender nose. Her mouth had the hard edges of someone who'd faced plenty of challenges in life. A smile might have softened them, but she looked angry and determined.

"Ritu was my friend," she said in a low voice. "We patrolled together a lot, and I was with her on the day she was killed."

"I'm sorry for your loss," he said, "but how do you know me? What's your name?"

She ignored his first question.

"I'm Priya Choudhury. Ritu and I worked together in Dhaka. We were the only women in our precinct, so we stuck together from the beginning. She wanted to volunteer for the UN and I came along. We were excited to be part of an all-female police unit."

Her eyes focused on an invisible horizon. The hardness around her mouth softened. Tears appeared in her eyes. She swallowed and wiped them away.

"I held her, I pressed the bandage against her wound. I couldn't keep her blood inside. I couldn't keep her alive until the medics came."

More tears rolled down her cheeks. He wanted to tell her that she'd done all she could, but thought better of it. She straightened and wiped her face. Her mouth grew hard again.

"I don't believe it was a random killing."

Vermeulen pricked up his ears. "What do you mean?"

"The official story is she was killed during a random attack. I don't believe that."

"Why not?"

She talked about their patrol in the New Arrivals section of the Zam Zam refugee camp, how they stopped to chat with women and to distribute advice and medicine, and how the usual band of kids following them suddenly became a gang of men.

"Up to that point, there was nothing unusual. The men sometimes get upset when we tell women to stand up for themselves. We usually defuse that by telling them how it will help their sons grow stronger and keep their family healthy. This time an old man got very upset and talked himself into a frenzy. Pretty soon everybody was shouting and accosting us. Then the shot rang out."

"Has anyone ever shot at you?"

"No, that's the point," she said, her face animated again. "They argue and yell, but they don't attack. Something else was going on that day."

"But you didn't see who shot her?"

"No, the shots came from an outcropping about six hundred yards away."

She wiped her eyes again. Vermeulen touched her shoulder. "What else do you remember from that day?" he said. "Was anything different?"

"Yes, I don't know how to explain it. It all seemed set up, artificial. The old man wasn't even related to anyone we had talked to. None of them were. Ritu had just told one man not to hit his wife. That man had a reason to be upset, but I didn't see him in the crowd."

"Do you know what kind of gun was used to kill her?"

"I found a casing at the outcropping: 7.62x51mm. NATO ammunition."

"That sounds odd to me. Don't they mostly use AK-47s here?"

"Yes, but there's all kinds of guns around, from hunting rifles to AK-47s. I think this was a special gun. The shooter killed three people. Two were head shots, and he hit Ritu in the neck. He did that from far away. Nobody can shoot that well unless they have a sniper rifle."

"So the shooter killed two more people?"

"Yes."

"Why do you think she was targeted?"

Choudhury hesitated a moment and peeked around the corner of the shed. "I think it's because she complained about the lousy armored personnel carriers of the Nepalis." His face must have shown his bewilderment, because Priya explained, "In Zam Zam, we patrol in pairs. The Nepalis in their APCs always serve as backup, usually staying back because those things are so intimidating. If that damn APC had started, she might still be alive today."

"You called for backup and it didn't come in time?"

"We heard the engine start and then die. It happens all the time. It made Ritu mad. She was very outspoken about anything that wasn't done properly. Her biggest complaint was the lousy equipment the Nepalis brought. All units are supposed to bring proper equipment. She even wrote to the head of mission about it."

"Let me get this straight," Vermeulen said. "Ritu Roy complained about the poor equipment and you believe she was killed in retaliation?"

Choudhury nodded. He pushed a damp lock of hair from his sweaty forehead. He wasn't sure what to make of her proposition. It did sound far-fetched. But she had a better sense of what could happen on the ground.

"What about the other two victims?"

"Maybe he shot them because he wanted to make it look like a random attack."

"Did she receive a response to her letter?"

"She never told me. She sent the memo a couple of weeks before she was killed. I know it sounds crazy. But why else would someone kill her?"

Because you are patrolling in a war zone where people get killed, because refugee camps also house criminals, because this place is full of rivalries that no outsider really understands. The rational part of his mind could have listed more reasons he couldn't tell Choudhury. She'd lost her best friend, she wanted answers, and she'd come to him.

"I'll look into it," he said. It was all he could promise.

* * *

THE UNAMID COMMANDER WAS OUT OF the office, so Vermeulen went to his temporary office, if you could call an aluminum shed an office. The inside was as depressingly institutional as the rest of the compound—a concrete floor, two steel desks, two chairs, and an air conditioning unit fitted into a hole in the wall. Even though a light indicated it was running, he didn't feel any cool air.

Wambui pushed a dolly with three boxes through the door. "Where do you want these?"

"Just put them in a corner," he said and put his jacket over one of the chairs.

He plugged in his laptop, entered the Wi-Fi password listed on the instruction sheet lying on one of the desks, and checked his email. There was just one message from Gaby, asking if he had arrived safely. He replied, telling her that he was fine and promising more details soon.

The onsite audit focused on two aspects of the mission: local procurement and direct deliveries. Local procurement covered everything a UN mission bought from local vendors. The longer a mission lasted, the more it tended to rely on local purchasing—as long as the local economy could sustain it—and the more cases of petty fraud occurred. After six years, UNAMID in its various forms had put down substantial roots.

Priya's suspicion had piqued Vermeulen's interest in direct shipments involving matériel sent to a unit from abroad. If the Nepali unit brought their APCs with them from Nepal, there was nothing he could do. But if they were delivered to the unit after they came to Darfur, there'd be a paper trail.

He lit a Gitane and wished he had a cup of coffee. There'd better be a decent coffee shop around. With all the memorial activity, he'd never gotten a proper orientation.

"You can't smoke in here!" a voice said from the door. "The UN has a strict non-smoking policy."

Vermeulen turned. The man standing in the door could have passed for one of Hollywood's B-list actors who regularly made appearances at refugee camps—crisp khaki pants, a safari shirt with way too many pockets on the chest and arms, a photographer's vest with even more pockets, and an Aussie bush hat. He had a longish face with a weak mouth and a small nose. No more than twenty-five, he looked like someone who spent most of his time indoors.

"And hello to you too. You must be Antonio Gianotti."

Bengtsson in Nairobi had told him he'd be working with an auditor new to field audits.

"Yes. Please put out the cigarette. I'm allergic to smoke."

Vermeulen had met Gianotti's type before—insecure but ambitious, sticklers for the rules. It made the prospect of tedious work even more unpleasant. Still, there was no need for a confrontation this early. He stepped outside, crushed the cigarette with his heel on the concrete path, and came back inside.

"Okay, no smoking. I'm Valentin Vermeulen."

Gianotti closed the door and shook his hand. Gianotti's felt like a wet dishrag.

"Wambui is just delivering the documents," Vermeulen said. "If you deal with local procurement, I'll get started on direct deliveries."

He didn't expect Gianotti to agree without objection—insecure but ambitious junior bureaucrats usually felt the need to mark their territory—but it was worth a try.

"We should first go through the audit template," Gianotti said.

Vermeulen sighed.

"It's just like any other audit."

"That doesn't matter. Every audit starts with the template."

Vermeulen looked at Gianotti in his ridiculous outfit and wondered why his life always got worse at the precise moment he'd decided it was bad enough. He sighed again.

"Listen," he said, trying for the paternal approach. "Doing an audit is not rocket science. The majority of it will be done elsewhere anyway. All we have to do is check the direct deliveries and local procurement. We split up the work, get done quickly, send in the report, and go home."

"That's not what the manual says."

Okay, this was getting tiresome. Either Gianotti was just plain stubborn or there was something else going on.

"Oh, for pity's sake. Forget the bloody manual. It's just a bunch of instructions that don't apply to us anyway."

"No. I've heard all about your cowboy methods, and I have no interest in causing trouble."

Which confirmed Vermeulen's suspicion that the Nairobi office must have had an orientation just about him. He stepped forward, his face inches from Gianotti's.

"What did they tell you?"

Gianotti shrank back. "Uh, nothing. I just don't want to upset my superiors. I plan to follow the rules."

"You do that. In the meantime, I'll start with direct deliveries."

Vermeulen sat down at his desk, lit another Gitane and exhaled the smoke noisily. He'd tell Bengtsson where to stick it when he got back there.

"I asked you not to smoke in here," Gianotti said. "It's against UN rules to smoke in offices."

Vermeulen considered ignoring that remark but decided against it.

"We are in a goddamn shed in Sudan, not an office. If you don't like my smoking, sit outside. Make sure to wear your hat."

* * *

VERMEULEN HAD JUST OPENED THE FIRST box of invoices when his phone rang.

"Goddamn it, Vermeulen!" It was Bengtsson. "What did you say to Gianotti?"

"To Gianotti? I just proposed a strategy for this audit. He took exception to my suggestions and left."

"I asked you not to stir things up, and on your first day, you pick a fight with your colleague. Is it too much to ask you to smoke your filthy cigarettes outside the office?"

"Mr. Bengtsson, last thing I knew, I report to headquarters in New York, not to you. But for your information, I smoke when I work. It helps me do my job well. It's not my fault the so-called office the UN sent me to is an aluminum shed with ill-fitting windows and poor ventilation."

"When you are working in Africa, you report to me. When are you going to get that into your thick skull? Show some consideration for Gianotti."

"I could ask the same of Gianotti. Who, by the way, shows up here as if he's going on a goddamn safari and then goes on to tell me how to do an audit. By the way, what did you tell him about me?"

"I just warned him about your habit of ignoring the rules."

"Maybe you should have told him to do his job."

He pushed the red button on his phone and pulled the first folder from the open box.

Fifteen minutes later, Gianotti appeared again and took his chair at the second desk. Vermeulen ignored him and continued examining the documents. Gianotti spent another quarter hour on busywork before he cleared his throat.

"I guess we could divide up the work as you suggested, Mr. Vermeulen."

That was a surprise. Given Bengtsson's tone on the phone, Vermeulen had expected Gianotti to come back with a chip on his shoulder.

"Okay. Let's do that. Local procurement records are in the last six boxes over in the corner. Let me know if you have any questions. If things don't check out, make a note for follow-up. I'll smoke outside from now on."

"Sounds good. And please, call me Tony."

"Okay. I'm Valentin. I'll be working on direct deliveries. Is there a place around here to get a cup of coffee?"

"Yes, there's a mess hall near the entrance."

Vermeulen nodded and called Wambui's name.

"Do you want anything?" he asked Gianotti.

"Are you going to send Wambui to get you coffee? He's not your servant."

Technically, that was true. But Gianotti didn't know the first thing about military life.

"I'm just helping him look busy. If there's one thing officers can't stand, it's seeing soldiers idle. Being our assistant is a plum job for Wambui. I'm just helping him keep it."

CHAPTER NINE

Diary of Ritu Roy

Amina. It's uncanny how this ray of sunshine comes into my life just when I feel as low as I ever have. She's twelve, kind of gangly, with hair black as mine. And she's chosen me. I can't find any other word for it. Kids follow us all the time. Once the novelty wears off, they leave. Not Amina. She's there when we start our patrol. She takes my hand and off we go. Her big smile when she sees me makes me forget my worries. She speaks a little English and helps me communicate in Zam Zam. Much better than that jackass of a translator the UN gave us.

She doesn't talk about herself. All I know is that she has a mother and a brother. Her father's dead. I don't know where she learned English or how her father died.

She's better than a newspaper when it comes to the latest gossip from her section of Zam Zam. Who's had an argument with whom. Which boys are getting into trouble. Whose husband is spending too much time at another shack. I'm glad to have her company.

* * *

Vermeulen had a choice. Check the invoices in chronological order and wait until he found something related to the APCs, or search for them. The latter option would be preferable if he knew such records existed. Since he didn't, he decided to just slog his way through the paperwork. That way, the work would get done while he followed the lead.

Most invoices were for food and other consumables. The food shipments were enormous. Vermeulen had seen before how much food got shipped to peacekeeping units. UNAMID was a very large operation, almost ten percent of El Fasher's population. Which meant that most of the food couldn't be sourced locally but had to be shipped in from abroad.

Uniforms, weapons, communications equipment, computers, even vehicles—anything that wore out or broke and needed to be replaced. The logistics were more complex than he could grasp. He thought of Gaby. She'd be perfect at managing the supply chain for a UN operation.

As long as each unit had signed for the deliveries and didn't register any discrepancies, he simply checked off the entry in the template. Some units consumed significantly more expensive food than comparable units from other countries. He flagged those for further attention.

The work was tedious. No surprise there. How could it not be? Columns of numbers, a CPA's dream. Except he wasn't a CPA. He was an investigator, sent to ferret out fraud. If it hadn't been for Priya's suspicions, he'd be deeply depressed by now. Gianotti didn't seem to have that problem. He dug through receipts with the fervor of someone hoping to find the prize inside the cereal box. Some people were born to do this work.

He finished the dregs of cold coffee and stepped outside for a cigarette. It could well be a wild goose chase. The armored personnel carriers in question had probably come with the Nepali unit when they deployed. The fact that they were in poor condition didn't mean anything. Used vehicles were all they could afford. Nepal wasn't a rich country. That's why they sent the unit in the first place. The UN payments helped balance national defense budgets. It also kept the men with guns busy, always preferable to having them plot mischief at home. He crushed the butt against the concrete step.

The next folder included an invoice from a British company with a strange name: Assured Sovereignty. Ten months ago, this firm delivered eight Pandur I armored personnel carriers to a Nepalese Formed Police Unit. He sat up straight.

"Hey Tony, how is a Formed Police Unit different from regular UN police?"

"They come as a group, a hundred and forty police plus support personnel. FPUs are used for crowd control and protecting other UN staff in civil war situations where there are many refugees."

"Do they have to bring their own equipment, too?"

"Yes, they're just like the military contingents."

"It says here that the Nepalese FPU got eight APCs delivered by some British outfit. Is that common?"

"Hmm, I don't think so. The UN is very strict these days. If a country sends a unit, it has to come with the proper equipment. Maybe they didn't have the right vehicles in Nepal and had to order them to equip this unit."

Vermeulen checked the roster and found that the unit was the only Nepali contingent deployed with UNAMID. Its task was to patrol Zam Zam. These had to be the APCs Priya had mentioned. He checked the document line by line. It was smudged in many places, hard to read, like so many faxes. One line made him stop. The vehicles were listed as new. He could imagine one lemon among the delivery, but eight? That seemed far-fetched.

He grabbed his jacket and left to speak to Choudhury again. On his way, he called Gaby. She didn't answer her phone. He left a message, asking her if she could find some background information about Assured Sovereignty. With her connections, she would find what he needed faster than he could using the official UN channels. The name was odd but fitting for someone selling weapons. Then he remembered the huge Ilyushin jet at the airport. What had his pilot said? It could be Assured Air Services. He called Gaby again and left another message, asking her if Assured Sovereignty and Assured Air Services were related.

* * *

THE BANGLADESHI ALL-FEMALE POLICE UNIT HAD its administrative office inside the main UNAMID compound, but the policewomen were quartered in a separate compound. The sun sat low on the horizon when Vermeulen asked the guard at the gate for directions to Choudhury's tent. The compound had the same maze-like layout as the UNAMID headquarters, with the difference that tents, rather than sheds, sat in groups of five along the concrete paths. A large parking area filled with neatly lined-up white SUVs covered the area to the right of the gate.

He soon lost his way. The aroma of food being cooked reminded him that the coffee and sandwich he'd had for a late lunch were wearing thin. The skinny yellow dog sniffing the corner of a tent probably had the same feeling.

He stopped a policewoman and asked for directions. The woman, tall, with short black hair under her blue beret and wearing the unique blue-and-tan uniform, eyed him with suspicion. The name patch on her uniform said "Khan."

"Who are you?"

"My name is Valentin Vermeulen, Officer Khan. I'm with the OIOS, and I'd like to talk to Priya Choudhury."

"Does she know you are coming?"

"I doubt it. We only met this morning."

Officer Khan remained suspicious. Two more policewomen joined her. Khan said something to them in Bengali. She turned back to Vermeulen. "How did you get in here?"

"I showed my credentials to the guards." He pulled out his UNAMID-issued ID. The woman studied it and nodded.

"You must excuse us," she said. "We're all upset since our colleague was killed."

"I understand. It must have been a shock."

"Yes, it was. Priya took it the hardest. She's very fragile right now. Can't it wait until tomorrow?"

"She approached me this morning with questions, and I think I have some answers for her."

"Maybe it'll be good for her," the second policewomen said. "She's been holed up in her tent and needs some contact."

They led Vermeulen to a tent a couple of rows farther, shouted something at the door. The flap folded back and Choudhury looked out. Her eyes looked red and dull.

He hesitated, not sure if she had shared her suspicions with the other women in her unit.

"I found something that might help," he said.

Choudhury raised her eyebrows. "Come." She pushed back the flap of the tent.

"You gonna be okay?" Khan said.

Choudhury nodded.

The living quarters were spartan. Six cots were evenly spaced on a square concrete pad, a footlocker at each end. A table and six chairs completed the furnishings. He noted a small vase with two sprigs of green at the center of the table and an open book on its corner. A framed, smaller version of Ritu Roy's photo was positioned on the bed in the far corner.

Choudhury pointed to the chair opposite the open book.

"I've just found an invoice for eight armored personnel carriers that were delivered to the Nepali unit at Zam Zam," Vermeulen said.

"So what?"

"The invoice states that the vehicles were new. Would you agree with that description?"

Choudhury looked up. Her eyes were no longer dull.

"No, they can't be new. They've been repainted … a rather sloppy job if you ask me."

"Most vehicles get repainted for UN missions. The manufacturers don't make them white."

"You have to believe me. These vehicles are used."

"Okay, I do. But the larger question is why someone would want to kill your friend over this. In my experience, fraud, even if it's big, rarely leads to murder. What else can you tell me about the attack?"

"I've told you all I know."

The weariness showed again in her face. The harsh light of the fluorescent tube overhead turned her complexion ashen.

"Wait." A small flash in her eyes. "The casing I found? It has a stamp on it. L45A3 RG 09. Maybe you can find out where it came from."

He wrote the code into his notebook.

"Can you think of anyone who saw what happened?"

"How about all the men who were there?"

Vermeulen decided to ignore the snippy response.

"I mean someone you know, someone I could talk to. How about your interpreter?"

"That jerk? He disappeared as soon as he smelled trouble."

"Anyone else who was with you and not part of the mob?"

"No. Nobody." She hesitated. "Well, there's Amina. The girl sort of adopted Ritu. She spoke a little English and translated for her."

"Where can I find her?"

"It doesn't matter." Choudhury shook her head. "Ritu sent her away before the mob got nasty."

"Kids don't always do what adults tell them. She might have hung around," he said.

She shrugged.

"I'm going to Zam Zam to check up on the APCs anyway. I might as well talk to Amina. Where can I find her?"

"She lives with her family in the New Arrivals section of Zam Zam. I don't know exactly where. It's not far from where Ritu was killed."

"I'll try to find her. Has your friend left anything that might help? Maybe she heard back from the head of mission and didn't tell you. Have you checked her belongings?"

Choudhury shook her head. "No, we just put her things in the footlocker. It'll be shipped to her family soon."

"Would you check it? Any additional information might help."

CHAPTER TEN

THE AREA BORDERING THE UN COMPOUND had attracted a number of fast food places that catered to the demands of foreigners. It wasn't the kind of food Vermeulen enjoyed. So, after speaking with Choudhury, he took a battered Chinese-made taxi—no comparison to the ones he had enjoyed in Düsseldorf—to the city center of El Fasher.

The streets were busy. People hurried along sidewalks, spilling into the street, causing cars to honk and swerve. The main street split around the mosque. Spotlights illuminated two minarets that stood on either side of a structure topped with two domes. He let himself drift, following the crowd past shops lit by hanging bulbs and displaying everything from groceries to hardware. He reached a large soccer field. No one was playing. A car repair place next door was just closing up. The wail of the muezzin interrupted the street noises. That explained at least part of the hurry in the streets. It was time for evening prayers. Out of nowhere, the line from "Rock the Casbah" about the muezzin on the radiator grille drifted into his mind. He grinned. Leave it to the Clash to have a suitable lyric for El Fasher. Four blocks later, Vermeulen found another mosque. The Grand Mosque, as the Arabic/English sign explained, occupied an entire city block and was a much larger building than the first he had passed.

There were no restaurants or bars on the main street. He circled southwest, following the wall that surrounded the soccer field. Across the street, two yellow dogs were fighting over a plastic bag. His stomach knew how they felt. The smaller dog yelped and ran away. It hadn't been a fair fight. The larger dog, flush with victory, looked at Vermeulen, daring him to come near the bag. He declined with a smile.

Once Vermeulen passed the soccer field, the road veered due south. There were few lights in that direction, not a promising sign. He should have asked the taxi driver. A beer would be good just about now. The muezzin's final call for evening prayers reminded him that Sudan was a Muslim country. There'd be no beer anywhere. He sighed.

He turned into a side street. A block farther, he was rewarded by the aroma of roasting meat. He passed through a dirt passage to the next street and found the Al-Waha Restaurant. It was busy, despite the evening prayers. A good sign. He stopped in the door and tried to decipher what looked like a menu painted on the wall. The numbers were obviously prices, but the rest was Arabic script.

A fat man dressed in a white tunic and wearing a white *kofia* that covered most of his gray hair hurried to him.

"Welcome, my friend," he said in strongly accented English. His wide smile showed teeth as dark as the night outside. "Very best meal here for you. Please, sit."

The man pulled out the chair at the last empty table, wiped it with a rag of dubious color, and gestured to Vermeulen.

"You want to eat, no?"

"Yes, I want to eat. What do you recommend?"

He sat down.

"Recommend? Oh, I give you *kharouf,*" he hesitated for a moment, searching for the word, "*sheep* cooked over fire. Very good."

"Good, I'll take that."

"You want drink?"

"Yes, what do you have?"

"Coffee, Coca Cola, tea, *karkadeh.*"

"What's that?" Vermeulen said, hoping that it contained alcohol.

"Is a red tea from—flower."

"Okay, red tea. Thank you." Roasted mutton with red tea. It would have to do.

"Thank you, my friend."

The other patrons checked him out. Obviously, European visitors were uncommon at Al-Waha. He didn't mind. He stuck out, and the locals made no secret of their interest in the tall white man. It was more honest than the furtive glances Westerners used.

A woman in a long dress and a scarf brought him a steaming glass of red tea. The aroma reminded him of something Gaby had liked as a kid. He took a careful sip. It was surprisingly good. The global no-smoking campaign hadn't reached El Fasher yet. There were ashtrays on every table. He pulled out his pack of Gitanes and lit a cigarette.

The restaurant was plain, its walls painted in a yellowish hue. A low wall near the rear divided the kitchen from the dining area. Two women were busy prepping food, and a man labored over a stove and an open fire. The fat man presided over the place from a director's chair near an ancient cash register.

The other customers, mostly men, wore everything from dark suits to *jalabiyas* with *kofias*. The few women all sat with men, likely their husbands, most of their bodies covered.

Vermeulen studied the faded posters on the wall. One depicted a large river—probably the Nile—and several others featured individual soccer players. The newest one showed an entire team in red jerseys and shorts. The fat man saw his glance, slipped from his chair, and pointed to the poster.

"Sudan national soccer team, Sokoor Al-Jediane ..." he hesitated again, searching for the translation.

"That means Desert Hawks," a female voice said from the entrance.

All faces turned to the newcomer. A woman with cinnamon skin stood in the doorway. She wore a blue jacket over a white blouse, baggy khaki pants, and a scarf that covered her hair. It was the news reporter Vermeulen had seen on TV in the café in Düsseldorf.

"Yes, Desert Hawks," the proprietor repeated. "Will win next African Cup of Nations."

He turned to the woman. "Welcome, Madame Bishonga." Then he fell into a rush of Arabic. They shook hands and she added her own greeting. Her arrival had stopped all conversation. People here knew her.

She came to his table. Vermeulen got up. Despite her clothing, he could tell she had a wiry build. Her walk had the spring of a gazelle. She was about a head shorter than he.

"You're a brave man, venturing into a restaurant without speaking the language," she said. "Most Europeans don't go far from their compound after dark."

"I had to eat something, so I took a taxi to town and strolled around until I found this place. Obviously the right choice. Otherwise, you wouldn't be here."

She had an unusual face, with dark eyes set close together, a wide nose, full lips, and pronounced cheekbones. Tiny braids peeked out under her scarf. She looked to be in her late thirties. Her eyes sparkled behind titanium-framed glasses. She brought a palpable energy into the room.

Vermeulen rose from his chair and stretched out his hand. "Valentin Vermeulen. Please join me."

They shook hands.

"Tessa Bishonga."

"I know. I saw you on the news in Düsseldorf, a week ago."

She smiled, hung her bag on the back of her chair, and sat down.

"What brings you to Darfur?" she said.

"I'm with OIOS, and we're doing an audit of UNAMID."

"And OIOS is …?"

"Office of Internal Oversight Services, kind of a watchdog outfit, reporting to the Secretary-General. Making sure that the Americans' money is spent properly."

Her eyebrows arched.

"Watchdog? Sounds interesting. Is there anything improper going on?"

"Oh, no. Just a routine audit. Tedious stuff."

"This your first time in Darfur?"

He nodded.

"How are you getting on without Arabic?"

"It's an obstacle, but not insurmountable. Most people are friendly and want to help. I couldn't read the menu, but the owner told me that roasted mutton was his specialty. I just ordered that."

The owner brought a glass of dark tea to Bishonga and looked at her expectantly.

"I'll have the mutton, too. Thanks, Samir."

Samir went back to his director's chair and barked something in Arabic to his cook. The foreigners' novelty having worn off, the other patrons went back to their meals and conversations.

"How come everybody here knows you?" Vermeulen said.

"I come here regularly, and they've seen my reports on Al Jazeera. I'm the biggest celebrity they'll ever see, so they treat me with respect. Samir is also a great resource. He knows what's going on around here."

"But you're not from Sudan, are you?"

"No, I'm Zambian. I haven't been there in a while."

"Tessa doesn't sound like a Zambian name."

"I grew up in Ndola, the heart of the Copperbelt, close to the Congolese border. My dad was a miner there. My mum was very Catholic and named me after Saint Teresa. I just shortened it."

"Saint Teresa," he said, and nodded. "The patron saint of lacemakers."

"Patron saint of what?"

"Lacemakers. I'm from Belgium, which is famous for its lace. I know all about Saint Teresa."

She looked at him over her glasses. "Don't be presumptuous. That isn't me."

"Not you as in protecting lacemakers, or not you as in being a saint?"

The server brought two plates filled with pieces of seared meat, rice, and stewed tomatoes, sparing her an answer. The aroma of earthy spices wafting from the plates was too much, and Vermeulen dug in. She followed suit. They ate in silence for a while.

"So, what's your real job here?" she said after a suitable pause. "I don't believe they sent someone from Belgium just to check the books."

He lowered his filled fork.

"I am here to conduct a long-overdue audit. That's all."

"You sound just like a UN statement. Calm and boring." An impish smile appeared on her face.

It was his turn to raise his eyebrows.

"What do you mean?"

"I'm a journalist, Valentin—can I call you Valentin?—and I know when I'm being stonewalled."

There was an edge to her voice, a challenge. An old journalist trick. Accuse someone of stonewalling and they get defensive. He'd seen it used when he worked at the Crown Prosecutor in Antwerp. It gives the impression you know more than you do to get interviewees to say more than they want.

"Can I call you Tessa?" She nodded. "No, I'm not stonewalling. That's why I'm here."

"So you weren't sent to investigate the death of that Bangladeshi policewoman?"

"No, I was not."

He shoved another forkful of rice and tomatoes into his mouth to hide his surprise at her question. Although he had promised Choudhury he'd look into her claims, he didn't know how much he could do. Only one thing was obvious: it wasn't going to be easy. Since the local hierarchy had already written off the death as random violence, anyone claiming something else would be a nuisance. The last thing he needed was a journalist drawing attention to what he hoped could be settled with a few quiet inquiries.

"You might find it difficult to believe, but OIOS conducts regular audits of all UN missions. Should we find something amiss, we'll investigate, of course. That's our mission."

"Is it really as boring as you make it sound?"

"Often it is, sometimes it isn't. Why did you ask about the policewoman?"

"When peacekeepers get killed, it's usually because something else is brewing. Maybe a new government offensive, or some rebels making a point. But my sources haven't indicated anything of that sort."

"So it was random violence," he said, doing a little fishing of his own.

"It's hard to tell. How much do you know about the Darfur crisis?"

"I suppose as much as anyone who follows the news," he said. "The Darfuris want independence, or at least autonomy. The government doesn't like that, so it uses militias to attack the rebels. The rebels retaliate by attacking the government and militias. The government and militias, in turn, burn villages. The result is a huge humanitarian crisis and a large UN-African Union peacekeeping mission. There's also an environmental component having to do with pastoralists and their conflict with farmers."

She nodded. "I'm glad you didn't fall for the Arab versus African thing. It's been the biggest bit of misinformation out there. It was the Brits who, always eager to categorize the people they conquered, divided the Darfuris into Arabs and Africans. The ethnic divisions in Darfur are far more complicated. You'll find Arabs and Africans, if you insist on using those terms, on both sides of the conflict."

"But the government militias—Arabs—have killed over three hundred thousand Darfuris."

Tessa glared at him.

"You're sounding just like a Darfur Alliance press release. It's not at all clear how many civilians have been killed by the militias, the *janjaweed*. Since the new round of peace talks in Doha began, most recent clashes haven't even been between the *janjaweed* and the rebels. They were among different factions of the rebel movement. The *janjaweed* are having the same problem. The whole Darfur Alliance campaign just gives Westerners an excuse to be anti-Arab."

It was his turn to glare at her. He pushed a lock from his forehead.

"Rubbish! You're sounding just like an apologist for General al-Bashir."

Vermeulen signaled for another tea.

"Don't you call me that." Tessa's eyes were blazing. "Of course, al-Bashir is a nasty dictator. It just doesn't help when outsiders pick sides without understanding the issues."

They glared at each other for a long moment before Vermeulen broke into a smile.

"We barely know each other and we're already fighting like an old couple," he said.

"As I said before, don't be presumptuous."

But he could see the smile playing at the corners of her mouth.

"Okay," he said, "tell me about the issues."

"Land and access to land," she said. "Darfur means 'homeland of the Fur.' Over the past two hundred years, various peoples here, Fur and others, were given their *dar*, or homeland. Most of the pastoralists didn't get any land. They are nomadic. In the summer they come south in search of grazing lands, and in the winter they move north again."

The woman set down a new glass of red tea. She looked at Tessa, who nodded.

"So, what do nomads grazing their camels have to do with genocide?" Vermeulen said.

"There you go again. Using that word doesn't help solve this conflict. This is where the environmental issues you mentioned come in. Drought and desertification have disrupted the annual circuits of the pastoralists. They stay longer in the fertile places. These issues used to be dealt with through negotiations. Now it's done with AK-47s. The influx of weapons from Chad only makes things worse."

"Chadian weapons?" He knew Chad bordered Sudan to the West. But the flow of weapons across the border was news to him.

"Yes, ever since Gaddafi's meddling in Chad in the 1980s, waves of Chadians have taken refuge in Darfur, bringing their guns with them. The Sudanese government supports some and expels others. Whatever Chadian government happens to be in power goes after their opponents. The border is really a sieve. The *janjaweed* operate on both sides. So do the JEM, and to some extent, the SLM."

"That's quite an alphabet soup."

Tessa nodded.

"JEM stands for Justice and Equality Movement. They want an independent Darfur. SLM stands for Sudan Liberation Movement. They are so splintered, it's hard to keep track of who wants what. There's also the UJM, the United Justice Movement—they are more hard line. But everybody wants al-Bashir gone."

"Does that violence spill over into refugee camps like Zam Zam?"

"Of course. Especially if one side thinks their enemies are hiding there, which they often are." Tessa pushed her glasses up her nose. "Refugee camps, especially big ones, are just like cities. In Zam Zam, you've got fifty thousand people living in a small area. It doesn't take much imagination to understand what happens there. What little police presence there is comes from the UN. Nothing more than the proverbial bandage."

Vermeulen had no idea that Zam Zam housed so many people, or that they were antagonistic to the UN. Somehow he'd thought that refugees, having gone through trauma, would be more cooperative.

"So the refugees don't like the UN?"

"Hell no. Why should they? They've lost everything. The UN isn't doing anything to get it back."

Samir took away their plates and asked something in Arabic. Tessa answered.

"Did you ask for the bill?" Vermeulen said.

"No. I ordered *bishbosa* and coffee." She anticipated his question and smiled. "Just wait, you'll like it."

"I went to the memorial for the policewoman, and it struck me how shocked everyone seemed by her death. Are such casualties rare?" he said.

She shrugged. "It depends on what you consider rare. Every casualty is one too many. UNAMID has more than the smaller operations. The troops are careful. They only go out in convoys and patrol with backup. Casualties usually occur during ambushes, and then there are three or four at a time. A single death is rare."

Samir came back with the coffees and two plates holding small pastries that smelled of lemon and coconut. Vermeulen stirred his coffee longer than necessary. Should he raise the topic of Roy's death with Tessa? The obvious reason against it was her being a journalist. He'd known too many to ever trust one again.

He took a sip of the coffee. It was good and had a thick layer of grounds at the bottom of the cup. The pastry had a light, tangy crust that melted in his mouth. Quite delicious.

On the other hand, Tessa could provide information and context. That would help him assess if Choudhury was off her rocker or had a good case.

"Good choice," he said. "Thanks for ordering for us. To go back to the violence, if a single peacekeeping casualty is uncommon, then the death of the policewoman would be a rare exception, wouldn't it?"

Tessa smiled.

"I knew it. You were stonewalling. You are here to investigate her death."

"You are wrong. That's not why I'm here. My itinerary was set way before I heard you report the news last Wednesday. I'm just curious."

"Why don't I believe you?" she said, still smiling.

He shrugged. "I haven't the faintest idea."

"Come on, Valentin." She pushed up her glasses.

"Okay," he said. "I do have an ulterior motive. I spoke to someone who claims the incident wasn't random mob violence, that the constable may have been targeted. I'm just wondering if there's anything to that claim. Have you heard anything at all?"

She sipped the tea, then shook her head.

"No. I've put out a few feelers about recent violence in the area, but I haven't heard anything about someone targeting a UN policewoman."

"What have you heard?"

"The government has ratcheted up its attacks against rebel positions, both with air and with ground forces. You've probably seen the reinforcements at the airport. They want to improve their negotiating position in Doha. What was the policewoman doing at Zam Zam?"

"She patrolled with her friend. I believe they were helping women."

Tessa shook her head. "That'd be enough to upset the men. First their cattle are stolen, then their houses burned, and to top it off, someone comes to tell their wives they have equal rights. Don't get me wrong—I support that." She took another bite from her *bishbosa*. "Still, I don't think they'd kill a cop over that."

Vermeulen thought back to what he'd heard from Choudhury.

"I don't know. According to her friend, the usual gang of kids following them suddenly changed into a mob of men. They were shouting and some became physical. The two policewomen drew their weapons and radioed for help. Then three shots were fired from a distant rock outcropping and the constable and two men died before help arrived. Her colleague thinks it was a sniper."

Tessa tugged at her braids.

"Sounds strange. I haven't heard anything about that. Why do you want to know if it isn't part of your job?"

"I'm just curious."

"Right," she said. "Just curious."

"Okay, the dead policewoman had complained about the poor equipment used by the Nepalis who were supposed to serve as their backup. Her friend believes she was killed in retaliation."

Tessa raised her eyebrows. "Are you going to look into it?"

"Yes, I'm going to Zam Zam in the morning."

"You are? Could I come along? I haven't been able to get inside that camp."

Vermeulen hesitated. That's what he'd been afraid of—Tessa taking advantage of him. She must have sensed his unease, because she sweetened her request considerably.

"Listen. Sami, my cameraman, has a knack for finding decent booze. Are you interested in a nightcap?"

Chapter Eleven

———◆·———

Diary of Ritu Roy

Some of the UN personnel have such a bad attitude. We're all here to help. Aren't we? Maybe not everyone volunteered like we did in our unit. But they're here anyway, so why not do their best?

Priya and I are patrolling Zam Zam every day, sorting out arguments, helping families access services, breaking up fights, and listening to women. It's hard. It's depressing. But we keep at it as best we can. And we smile. Well, maybe not smile, but we put on a good face. Some of the other units just seem to lounge around and not do anything.

Take the Nepalis. They are supposed to be our backup. But they're never around when we need them. We start late so often because of them. If we ever got in real trouble, we'd be on our own.

Wednesday, March 17, 2010

The village of Zam Zam lay at the southern edge of the camp named for it, just a half hour drive from El Fasher. Vermeulen sat in the rear of the Nissan SUV with Tessa. Sami rode up front with Wambui. They made it across the foothills without any incident. Wispy strands of cirrus clouds covered the sky. Despite the early hour, the sun shone hot. The dry season was just getting started, so there was still plenty of green grass to graze cattle. In one valley, Vermeulen saw his first camel herd.

These impressions didn't register quite as clearly as they would have ordinarily, because Vermeulen was tired and nursing a bit of a hangover. Tessa had brought him to the Crimson Lights hotel, where he met Sami—no last name provided—her laconic Kenyan cameraman with a knack for finding alcohol in a Muslim country. That night he'd procured a no-name brandy. They sat and talked about their jobs, Africa, the UN.

When the conversation became more personal, Sami took the hint and disappeared. Vermeulen wasn't surprised by how different he and Tessa were. He'd assumed as much after the meal together. It made her interesting.

She didn't drink coffee. Vermeulen couldn't imagine functioning without it. She hated punk rock. Vermeulen thought of the Clash as the epitome of human musical achievement. She thought *The Reader* should have gotten the 2008 Oscar, while he had rooted for *Frost/Nixon*. They continued sparring until the brandy had done its damage. It was two in the morning when he finally got back to his room.

As they descended into the village of Zam Zam, he saw craggy peaks loom in the distance.

"Is that Jebel Marra?" he said.

"It is," Tessa said. "Isn't it a majestic range? The mountains are an important symbol to the Darfuris. The upper reaches are also very fertile and have plenty of water. Prime land for agriculture and grazing."

"And, no doubt, a source of conflict."

"Like so much in Darfur."

A Nepali officer stopped them when they pulled into the UN police post outside the village of Zam Zam. After checking their IDs, he directed them to his commander. Their tents were the same he'd seen in El Fasher. Here there were no concrete pads, and the bottom panels were red from the splattered mud left by the rain. A fence surrounded the compound. Three armored personnel carriers and two SUVs were parked at the center. They were painted white.

The commander of the unit, Superintendent Dilip Jirel, a short man with a weaselly face, greeted Vermeulen with a curt handshake and nod. He radiated the impatience of someone living in a constant state of annoyance.

"I'm sorry for barging in unannounced," Vermeulen said, presenting his credentials. "It's part of a routine audit. I need to check the paperwork on the armored personnel carriers that were delivered several months ago."

He'd given Tony Gianotti the same reason. It was a weak excuse. He had no good reason to visit the unit. All the relevant paperwork was either in Nairobi or in El Fasher. Any expenditure at Zam Zam was the UN equivalent of petty cash.

The superintendent had lived his entire professional life in a hierarchy, and in hierarchies nothing mattered more than a piece of paper signed by someone at the top. Jirel studied Vermeulen's ID and the authorization signed by the Under-Secretary-General. He was properly impressed.

"Welcome, Mr. Vermeulen. How can I help you?"

"I'll need to see the delivery papers. Anything you signed when the APCs were delivered."

Jirel frowned.

"I don't think I signed anything."

"You must at least have a receipt. It's part of the protocol for direct deliveries to units in the field. Would you mind checking? I have to make sure all the paperwork matches."

There was no chance they'd have any paperwork, but while they looked for it, Vermeulen could check things out.

Jirel nodded. Protocol needed to be followed.

"I'll look into it."

"No problem. Since I have to wait anyway, I thought it'd be a good opportunity to see the camp. Could you have someone show us around?"

The request wasn't part of the protocol. But Vermeulen wanted to find Amina. Not surprisingly, Jirel didn't like the idea. His face was unambiguous. He also didn't know what to make of this stranger with papers signed by the Under-Secretary-General.

"We don't conduct tours. We're rather busy policing here."

"I understand. We could just go on our own. I'm sure we'd be all right."

"No, I can't allow that. The security situation is very tenuous. You'll need an escort."

"Tenuous since the murder of Constable Roy?" Vermeulen said.

Jirel flinched at the word *murder*.

"A very unfortunate incident. Have you been here before?"

Vermeulen shook his head.

"It's a large camp," Jirel said. "About fifty-three thousand displaced persons. The camp is divided into four sectors—South, North, Jaffalo, and the New Arrivals section. The South sector is the oldest and looks not much different from the village. The same is true for most of the North and Jaffalo sectors. People built more permanent structures as they realized that returning home wasn't in their immediate future. We have two schools, four clinics, two mosques, a lot of shops. It's really like a city—"

"I do know the basic statistics for Zam Zam. I'd just like to see a UN mission in action."

Jirel gave up.

"One of my officers will give you a short tour."

The clouds had merged into a thin sheet covering most of the sky. The light was hard on Vermeulen's eyes.

He walked over to the APCs. Each vehicle had six oversized tires, slanted metal surfaces, and a small turret with a heavy machine gun. Close up, they loomed large and menacing.

Other than the black UNAMID letters and a small license plate with a five-digit number, no other labels or insignia were visible. Up close, the paint job looked sloppy. Someone had just sprayed everything white. Many drips had dried hard on the metal surface. He found a manufacturer's plaque on the nearest vehicle, but it was coated thickly with paint and unreadable.

Shadows of overspray exaggerated the worn look of the tires. The last time Vermeulen had seen such big chunks of rubber missing from a tire was after his father's tractor had tumbled down a ravine on their farm. Either the terrain in Zam Zam was really hard on tires, or these were very old.

Hearing a voice calling, he saw Jirel gesturing for him to come back to the tents.

"Anything special about these APCs?" Jirel asked.

"No, nothing at all. Just curious. Never been close to one of them. Where are the other five?"

"On patrol in the camp."

So there were eight, total.

"What kind are they?"

"These are Pandur armored personnel carriers. They're made in Austria."

Bingo. The ones delivered by Assured Sovereignty.

"That's odd, the paperwork I've seen said they were shipped from the Czech Republic."

"I don't know anything about that. Here's Inspector Gupta." Jirel pointed to another policeman in camouflage who hurried across the yard. "He will join you in your vehicle for a quick tour. One of the APCs currently on patrol will meet up with you at the New Arrivals section. If you'll excuse me, I have to look for your paperwork."

Jirel disappeared into his tent. Gupta saluted and shook Vermeulen's hand. He was a tall and dark-skinned man with a longish face and bushy eyebrows that gave him a stern expression. Vermeulen pointed to their Nissan SUV. "That's our car, Inspector."

After a short drive, Gupta pointed out that they had entered the Zam Zam camp. The camp did indeed look like a regular village: squat, single-story homesteads surrounded by walls or fences, children loitering at a corner shop, a man pushing a wheelbarrow laden with sacks, three women carrying plastic water containers on their heads. A teenager passed them on a noisy moped, stopped and stared until they drove by him, then revved his bike and passed them again.

"It doesn't look any different from the village we just left," Vermeulen said.

"Yes," Gupta said. "These people have been here for more than seven years. They built houses and fences. Basically replicating their old life in a new place. The locals have gotten used to their presence because the refugees contribute to the local economy."

The camp was laid out on a grid, and they followed the main road, a compacted dirt track with plenty of potholes. Small shops sat between walled compounds. Empty lots held surprisingly green gardens. Vermeulen saw why. Water pumps dotted the camp at regular intervals. Women and children congregated around them. One building bore the sign of a Danish nonprofit organization advertising a women's activity center. A white Toyota had stopped next to the building, and two Nepali policemen waved at them.

Using a small recorder, Sami had started filming through the window.

"What happens there?" Tessa said.

"Training workshops for women to learn new skills that are marketable. You know—handicrafts, weaving, that sort of thing."

Gupta told Wambui to turn left, and they passed a large structure that turned out to be a hospital run by Mercy Malaysia.

"How many hospitals do you have here?" Tessa, the reporter, was in her element.

"One. There are three clinics for outpatient treatment. This is the only place where people stay overnight. By the way, we are now in the Jaffalo sector. It is named after the small hamlet you see over there."

Gupta pointed to their left. Again, Vermeulen couldn't see any difference between the village and the camp. He saw one of the APCs several blocks over. They passed another larger building. A sign indicated it was a school.

"Who runs the schools?" Tessa said.

"They are funded by the United Nations Children's Emergency Fund. The teachers are mostly locals or qualified refugees. We want to keep the surroundings as close to normal as possible."

The track became rougher and the buildings sparser as they reached the end of the Jaffalo sector. A half mile later, there were no buildings left. A sea of shacks made of sticks and straw and topped with white or blue tarps covered the area as far as the eye could see.

"This is the New Arrivals section," Gupta said. "And there's our escort."

Wambui drove to the APC standing near a borehole where two men had brought their goats. One of the crew stood bent over a hatch near the rear of the vehicle; the rest, five officers in camouflage uniforms, loafed in the shade. Gupta checked in with the policemen.

"Lots of questions," Vermeulen said to Tessa.

"It's my first visit to Zam Zam. Journalists don't usually get into this place.

I've been making mental notes. I want to come back for in-depth reports. In the meantime, this will do."

Gupta came back to their truck. "The engine won't start."

That confirmed Priya's claim that the Nepalis often arrived late because of engine trouble.

"Does that happen a lot?"

Gupta hesitated and looked away. He hadn't received any instructions on how to deal with this stranger and probably didn't want to highlight their problems.

"It happens more often than we'd like," he said finally.

"What's the problem? Do you need parts?"

"I'm not a mechanic. I don't know. These are old vehicles. They wear out, just like any old car. The conditions here aren't the best for motor vehicles."

Vermeulen looked at the tires and noticed again how worn they looked.

"How long have you had these?"

"About ten months."

"Were the tires new when they arrived?"

"No, they looked just as bad as they do now."

Vermeulen nodded. They did receive used vehicles, no matter what the invoice stated. And the UN was paying for *new* vehicles. Now he had to find Amina.

"Can you show me where the Bangladeshi policewoman was killed?" Vermeulen said.

Gupta hesitated again. His guest was turning out to be much more trouble than he'd expected.

"I don't know where that happened."

"Could you ask one of your colleagues?"

Gupta turned and said something to the officer in charge. The officer looked at Vermeulen, then back to Gupta. He nodded and said something. Gupta turned back to Vermeulen.

"They know. They were there. It's far, and their APC won't start. We can't go there by ourselves. It's too dangerous."

"We can fit one more into the third-row seat. With Wambui and you, that makes three armed people. That should be enough. Let's go."

"No, we can't. It's against regulations. The APC has to accompany us."

"Inspector Gupta, I'm sure your regulations have their place. This is just a quick trip. It'll be much easier to just go than to explain to the superintendent how you refused a direct request from a representative of an Under-Secretary-General of the United Nations. Just think of the report you'll have to submit."

Gupta gave in. He commandeered one of the policemen to join them.

They drove past a group of boys playing soccer with a ball made of wadded-up plastic bags. Women cooked whatever meager rations they had on small fires. Four men shooed a few sad-looking goats into a pen made of dried sticks stuck into the ground. A row of girls waited at a borehole. The trickle of water dripping into the container made watching paint dry seem an exciting adventure.

They had reached a spot located between two rows of huts when the policeman signaled Wambui to stop.

"This is where the men found the dead policewoman."

They got out and looked around. There was nothing special about this place. The shacks were no different from the hundreds they had passed on their way here. Three paths converged at the spot where Roy had been killed. He looked around and saw the outcropping.

"Where was the APC when that happened?"

Gupta asked the policeman, who pointed to the left path.

"It stood about five hundred yards away in that direction."

"Ask him if he remembers anything particular about that day."

The two men talked back and forth.

"He says there wasn't anything different," Gupta said finally. "When they came here they found the other policewoman holding a bandage against the wound in the neck of the first one."

"Any different faces in the crowd, anyone who doesn't live here running away?"

More exchanges.

"Nobody was here when they came. They'd all run away."

Three children came out of the closest shack, having heard the car arrive. They stood at a safe distance and stared.

"Maybe they know Amina," Vermeulen said to Tessa. "Could you ask them?"

Tessa shouted in their direction. The little ones inched back to the shack. But the tallest girl, maybe ten, remained where she stood. Vermeulen pulled an energy bar from his bag and held it out to her. She looked at him with her dark eyes but didn't come closer.

Tessa walked over to her, and Vermeulen followed.

"You should stay with the vehicle," Gupta said. "Zam Zam can be dangerous."

Tessa spoke to the girl. At first she seemed reluctant to speak. Vermeulen handed her the bar. It broke the ice. She said something. Tessa followed up. The girl turned and pointed.

CHAPTER TWELVE

———◆———

THE SKY HAD BECOME OVERCAST. THE air stood still, and sweat beaded on Vermeulen's forehead. He didn't care. The mix of nervous energy and anticipation he knew from his previous cases was back.

"We must head back. It's too dangerous without backup," Gupta said.

"Come on, man," Vermeulen said. "The Bangladeshi women patrol on their own."

"Yes, and one of them is dead now. Zam Zam is always unpredictable."

"We'll leave after I speak to Amina."

Wambui inched the Nissan along the bumpy dirt until they reached the end of a row.

"Now where to?"

"Turn left," Tessa said. "Amina's family lives three rows over."

Before they reached the third row, they saw people run toward them. Wambui nosed the car to the corner and stopped, half concealed by a hovel. Three hundred feet down the row stood two pickups with heavy machine guns mounted on their beds. Several men stood near the trucks. One of them leaned against the gun on the first truck. Wambui stopped.

"Shit!" Gupta said. "Those are technicals. We gotta get out of here."

"Technicals are the preferred fighting vehicles of the rebels," Tessa said, as if Vermeulen didn't know that already.

"What are they doing here?" Vermeulen said.

"That could be Amina's place," Tessa said.

"It doesn't matter!" Gupta said. "We have to leave. Now."

Wambui put the Nissan in reverse.

"Wait," Vermeulen said. "If that's Amina's place, I want to see what's going on there."

"No! We can't go against two technicals. Those are .57-caliber machine guns," Gupta shouted.

"He's right," Sami said. "They'd tear us to shreds in seconds."

"Who said anything about shooting?" Vermeulen said. The men with the technicals weren't shooting. They weren't even brandishing their guns. They just stood there. It wasn't an ambush. "You stay here. I'm going to speak with them."

"Are you crazy?" Specks of saliva flew from Gupta's lips. "I forbid it. I'm in charge here and we are going back."

"You can go back if you like, but you can't forbid me to speak to anyone."

Vermeulen climbed from the Nissan and walked slowly toward the men. Their guns hung from their shoulders. One gestured to another, and he heard laughter. The machine gunner's arms and head rested on the gun. They were relaxed. The trick was not to surprise them. He shouted "Hello!" and waved. The gunner on the technical looked up, saw Vermeulen, and cocked his head. Taking his time, he swung the long barrel toward the stranger. The other men turned to look at him. Two pulled their rifles from their backs, also moving at a leisurely pace. They didn't look like AK-47s, not that it mattered. At this distance even an old hunting rifle would do serious damage.

It was too late to turn around now. That much was clear. The fifty yards between him and the pickups seemed much longer. Raising his hands in the international sign of surrender, Vermeulen kept going. The sweat on his forehead rolled down toward his eye and stung. He resisted the urge to wipe the eye. No sudden moves. The sound of a slide being pulled and snapping back into place cut through the silence.

As Vermeulen saw it, the men had two options, shoot at him or talk to him. They hadn't used option one so far because they were curious about the lone European walking toward them. That meant they weren't going to shoot now either.

"I'm looking for Amina," he shouted. They probably didn't speak English. He should've thought of that. Tessa had better translate once there was a chance to talk.

The man behind the machine gun shouted something into the shack. That produced more men. There were at least eight now, all heavily armed. They stared at him. A sturdy man wearing a red beret led a girl, two boys, and a woman to the second pickup. He opened the door and the three climbed into the cab. The men climbed onto the beds.

Vermeulen stopped. They were taking Amina. That was an option Vermeulen hadn't considered. He shouted for them to stop and started running. The man with the red beret looked at Vermeulen. He shook his head and shouted a command.

One of the men lifted his gun. Vermeulen still didn't think they would shoot him point-blank, but felt considerably less certain. Since there was no place to hide, Vermeulen kept running. He had to talk to Amina.

The burst of gunfire came when he was fifty feet away from the technicals.

He dropped to the ground. The bullets whistled far above his head. The pickups sped off, spewing a cloud of dirt in Vermeulen's direction. A rock bounced off his forehead, leaving a bloody mark.

"You are a crazy man," Tessa shouted, running toward him. She helped him up.

"Not really," he said, and brushed the dirt off his jacket and pants. "They weren't going to shoot me. But I didn't get to talk to Amina."

"Was it worth the risk?"

He nodded. "It wasn't as risky as you think. This wasn't an ambush or battle. These guys looked relaxed. They didn't have any reason to kill me."

"They shot at you."

"Yes, but way over my head. Just telling me to stay away."

"Will you?"

"Of course not."

Their Nissan stopped behind them and Gupta jumped out. He was livid.

"Into the car. Now. I'm not going to be responsible for your death."

"Inspector Gupta, you have an exaggerated sense of your power. You can't order me to do anything. I'm the one who's in charge. My authority comes directly from the Secretary-General and I'm telling you to get into the truck and wait for me."

Gupta stood in shock, swallowing repeatedly. He opened his mouth, but no words came.

"Walk with me," he said to Tessa. Out of Gupta's earshot, he stopped. "I told you about Priya's suspicion. There's more. According to the invoice, the APCs are supposed to be new. You've seen them. They obviously aren't. Something is going on here. Ritu Roy had complained about the vehicles, since they were supposed to protect her. Two weeks later she was killed."

Tessa examined his face. "I'm beginning to see."

"See what?"

"Nothing. What do you want to do next?"

"If I had my way, I'd follow those rebels. But I'm sure Gupta wouldn't let us. Besides, I have no idea where they went."

Tessa looked at the horizon. The sky had turned gloomy, and he could feel the air pressure increasing. The wind had picked up, and little dust devils danced around the shacks.

"Listen, I haven't been completely straight with you," she said after a moment. "I'm after a different story. Reporting on UNAMID is a cover."

"Why am I not surprised?"

"I need to know I can trust you."

"You can trust me until you start breaking the law. I can't speak for Wambui, but I believe he's happy to tag along and won't say anything unless a superior tells him otherwise."

Tessa looked back to the Nissan, then at Vermeulen.

"I know I'm going to regret this, but here it is. I'm here to get an interview with Commander Hammed Masaad of the United Justice Movement. So far he has refused to join the Doha peace negotiations. He's an elusive character who rarely appears in public and makes even fewer statements."

Vermeulen considered this. It seemed more likely than her previous story of reporting on gender empowerment issues.

"Why so much subterfuge to talk to a rebel leader?"

"Don't be dumb. I'd never get a visa to enter the country if I told them what I really wanted."

"Why is Masaad so important?"

"Because everybody thinks he's a maximalist, that he won't settle for anything short of independence for Darfur. I think he's more flexible. I want to give him a chance to get his side across."

"And it's got nothing to do with you landing a major journalistic coup?"

A flash of anger lit up her eyes.

"You really can be an asshole, you know that? Masaad is highly educated, a smart and wily leader. The media ignore him because they think the UJM is too small to be important. I think he could be the one to break through the stalemate. If, that is, he has a chance to lay out his position."

She spoke with conviction, and Vermeulen almost believed her. But something told him to be wary.

She saw the doubt on his face. "What?"

"I must admit, this save-the-world attitude is a new side of you. What happened to getting the story?"

She shook her head.

"Don't play the cynic. It doesn't suit you. Yes, getting the story is what I do. It's possible to do that and do the right thing at the same time."

She was correct, of course. He felt the same way about his job. It was an opportunity to do what needed to be done, to set things straight.

"What do we do next?"

"I believe those technicals were from the UJM," she said.

"How does that help us find Amina?"

"I have some GPS coordinates for a place where he supposedly hides out."

"So let's drop off Gupta and go."

"It's over twenty miles over hard terrain. We can't make it today. Look at the weather." She stared up at the sky.

"Come on, we've got an almost full tank of gas and it's only one p.m. It can't be that difficult."

She looked at him with so much pity that he cringed.

"You really don't know a thing about Darfur, do you?" she said.

"All I know is that we need to find Amina. She's the only one I know who might have seen who killed Constable Roy. If you're not coming, give me the coordinates and I'll go on my own."

* * *

THE DIRT TRACK HAD BEEN CARVED by many trucks before them. It led first northwest and then west. It didn't look as if the Darfur highway department— if there was something like that—had played any role in its construction or maintenance. The Nissan's GPS indicated they still had to cover fifteen miles to reach the coordinates Tessa had programmed. At their current speed, that would take about an hour. Despite the early afternoon, the horizon had turned into muddy gloom.

"Man, I can't believe we're doing this," Sami said from the passenger seat. "I was looking forward to a cool beer in El Fasher."

"There's beer? In Sudan?" Vermeulen said.

"Of course. You can't deploy a Kenyan contingent without their Tusker." He turned to Wambui. "Am I right, Winston?"

"I'm glad to know that," Vermeulen said. He turned to his driver. "What other hidden talents do you have?"

Wambui just grinned.

The gloomy horizon seemed to close in on them. The sun had long since disappeared.

"I thought the rainy season was over," Vermeulen said, pointing out the window. "That sure looks like rain."

Concentrating on the track, Wambui hadn't looked north for a while. He peered past Sami's head and stopped the car.

"That's not rain. That's a dust storm. We'd better find cover. It'll be here in no time."

Vermeulen scanned the surroundings. The area was as flat as the Flanders marshes. The occasional clump of trees provided the only relief in the tableau of orange dirt and gray rocks.

"Where might we find that?"

"I don't know. Check the map, the GPS, there's gotta be a place around here."

Vermeulen turned to Tessa and Sami. They shrugged. He turned back to Wambui.

"Just keep going. Maybe we'll come across a settlement."

Wambui sped up. The SUV almost immediately bottomed out with an ugly grinding sound. He slowed down again. The brown cloud to the northeast grew in size. It rose to the gray sky and billowed like a massive curtain covering a long-forgotten stage.

A clump of trees in the distance indicated a source of water. Wambui veered off the track and bounced over the rocks toward the trees. The terrain dropped suddenly, giving way to a hollow. A small pond fed the trees and other grasses. A large rock sat on the other side. Wambui maneuvered around the pond, careful to avoid treacherous mud, and parked the car so close to the rock that Vermeulen could no longer open his door.

"It's the best we can hope for," he said. "Let's get ready."

He opened the rear hatch of the SUV, took out several bottles of water, and passed them to Tessa. Then he grabbed two short-handled spades and handed them to Vermeulen and Sami.

"To dig out," he said in response to Vermeulen's look.

CHAPTER THIRTEEN

———————◆———————

THE AIR GREW THICK. VERMEULEN LOOKED through the windshield and saw a wall of brown race toward them like a tsunami of muddy water. He'd experienced the gales from the North Sea battering his father's farm in the winter. Gray clouds pelting the shutters with sleet and rain. This storm looked different. He didn't get around to sorting out the differences, because the wall reached them and what light there was faded to a gloomy sepia. The world outside disappeared. Sand blew past them in horizontal squalls as if someone were aiming to blast every last bit of paint from the Nissan. The car shook violently. He was thrown against the door, then against Tessa. She swore. Vermeulen managed to fasten his seatbelt before another gale almost tipped the car over.

Yellow dust spread through the cabin. It coated Vermeulen's mouth, grated against his eyeballs, and gave the rest of his body a powdered feeling. The loose layers of clothing worn by many Sudanese men were beginning to make sense. He took a swallow of water and tasted mud. The car yawed and lurched like a rag doll in the fangs of an enormous dog. Bad memories from amusement park rides made bile rise from his stomach. Despite the drop in temperature, he felt sweat pearl on his forehead. His armpits turned muddy.

A loud crack cut through the howling storm. A second later, something smashed the roof of their SUV. A crack appeared in the window next to him. It spread from one edge to the other like ice on a lake not quite thick enough for skating. Hairline cracks appeared immediately, turning the pane into a myriad of pieces. Two bits of glass hit his face, cutting his cheek. He flinched. Despite the force of the wind, the pane stayed in place. He pushed his hand against it to stabilize it.

The intensity of the storm lessened for a moment, giving him a quick view of sand piling up in the lee of the car. Without the shelter offered by the rock, the car would have been tossed about like a tumbleweed. Three dark shadows loomed behind them. Remainders of the trees? One of them must have landed on their car.

The hole in the window let more dust into the car. His nostrils were clogged with dirt. He saw Tessa pressing a cloth against her nose and mouth. She gave him an angry look. *You've gotten us into this mess*, it said. *We should have waited for another day.* There was nothing he could do about it now. He breathed through his handkerchief and waited.

Two hours later, the storm ended abruptly. The wind ebbed, then stopped, and the air cleared. Wambui had to push hard to open the door against the sand that had piled outside. They climbed out and sank into the soft piles. The air smelled fresh. The sky had turned midnight blue. A star twinkled above the faint line of mountains still visible to the west. Vermeulen swished water in his mouth and spit out the grit. Splashing some onto his handkerchief, he cleaned the caked blood left by the glass splinters. His cheek stung. The cut had better not get infected.

Wambui shone a flashlight at the tree on the Nissan. The roof and rack toward the rear were dented. Except for the one window, nothing else was broken. Nobody spoke, which was just fine as far as Vermeulen was concerned. He didn't need to hear the others' complaints.

The three men struggled to lift the tree trunk off the roof. Tessa grabbed one of the spades and began clearing the front wheels. With a collective heave, the men managed to push the trunk behind the car. Sami grabbed the other spade and cleared the sand from the rear. Once the wheels were cleared, they got in. Wambui started the engine, turned on the high beams, engaged the low four-wheel drive, and eased the car from behind the rock. They drove four yards before the front wheels sank into a rut filled with soft sand.

"Fuck!" Wambui's curse, so unlike his usual reserved self, broke the tense silence.

"You said it, bro," Sami chimed in. "It's a fucking mess."

Vermeulen expected Tessa to chime in as well, but she remained silent. Wambui reversed and managed to pull the SUV back out of the dip.

"You two have to walk ahead and test the ground until we get back to the road," he said.

Vermeulen and Sami jumped out, grabbed two lengths of corrugated metal from the trunk, and laid them across the furrow.

The high beams of the Nissan showed a landscape dramatically changed by the storm. The sand had shifted. Bushes had disappeared. Familiar landmarks were gone. Without the GPS, they would have been lost.

Lugging the sheets of metal from the rear to the front of the car was more exercise than Vermeulen needed at that moment. He was breathing heavily. His body felt gritty with dust and sweat. The mile back to the road took almost thirty minutes.

The road was covered with sand drifts, making driving in the dark difficult. The ruts were also filled with sand but provided enough traction for a reasonable speed. A half-hour later, they reached a fork and stopped.

"Okay, we're about twelve miles from Masaad's location," Tessa said, consulting the GPS and her map with a flashlight. "Alternately, we're about three miles from the paved road to the north and then another fifteen to get back to El Fasher. I think we should go back and try again tomorrow."

"I'm ready for that beer," Sami said. "Let's go back."

Wambui also nodded.

Vermeulen wanted to keep going. He was worried about Amina. It wasn't clear why the rebels had taken her. He needed to speak to her soon. The more time passed, the more she'd forget. It had already been more than a week, and the rebels might not stay wherever the GPS coordinates were leading them. But he knew better than to insist on continuing their trip.

A sudden flash of bright light flooded the inside of their car. Shielding his eyes with his hand, Vermeulen turned and looked into the headlights of a vehicle behind them. None of them had seen the car approaching.

"Bandits! Quick! Step on it!" Tessa shouted.

Wambui reacted immediately. The engine whined at a high pitch and their SUV shot forward. It was too late. The other car sped past them. Vermeulen saw the machine gun mounted on the back. A technical. Several men in uniforms huddled in the bed. Another pickup followed. A burst of gunfire shattered the windshield. Wambui screamed and grasped his left arm. The Nissan lurched to a stop.

The doors were pulled open, and Vermeulen looked into a dark face partially covered by a head wrap. The man wore a camouflage uniform and pointed a rifle at him. Another man holding a flashlight joined them. They yanked Vermeulen out the door. The strike of a rifle butt coaxed him against the back of the car. On the other side of the Nissan, Tessa emerged into the beam of light. The man holding the flashlight shouted something in Arabic. Tessa answered. The others on the pickup shouted back and laughed.

"What are they saying?" Vermeulen asked.

"They're not bandits. They're Masaad's men. They know me from TV."

"Is that good?"

"We'll find out."

* * *

IN THE FLICKERING LIGHT OF FIRES, Vermeulen saw the outlines of drab military tents standing under trees. The sound of a generator filled the night air. UJM soldiers sat around the fires. They got up when the convoy arrived. The four were pulled from their Nissan. Outside, Vermeulen saw that the convoy consisted of two technicals followed by a large truck and two more technicals. The rebels seemed elated. They patted their returning comrades on the back, laughed, and shouted. He assumed that the convoy had returned from a successful mission. The truck was the prize.

Two soldiers used their rifles to prod Tessa and Vermeulen to one of the tents. Inside, a man sat behind a field desk littered with pieces of paper. He had a dark, round face with a bushy black mustache and intelligent eyes. Round glasses gave him an owlish air. His uniform looked well used. An old tin can overflowed with cigarette butts.

"The United Justice Movement welcomes you. I'm Hammed Masaad," the man said. He spoke English with a slight accent.

Masaad didn't show any of the glee exhibited by his men outside. *An earnest man*, Vermeulen thought. The cigarette butts and the strewn papers reminded him of his own desk. Organized chaos. But serious. Masaad could be a formidable opponent.

"It's not like we had a choice," Vermeulen said. "Your men wounded our colleague."

"Sometimes, the best choices are the ones made for you. The man is being taken care of as we speak." He turned to Tessa. "We are especially pleased to welcome Tessa Bishonga into our midst. We follow your Darfur reports with great interest."

"Thanks." She smiled.

Vermeulen had no time for small talk.

"I'd like to know what happened to Amina."

Masaad looked at Vermeulen with a mixture of surprise and irritation.

"Who are you?"

"Valentin Vermeulen. Lead Investigator, Office of Internal Oversight Services." Vermeulen showed him the authorization from the Under-Secretary-General. Unlike Superintendent Jirel, Masaad was not impressed.

"You know, of course, that it doesn't mean anything here." He turned back to Tessa. "My men radioed me when they found you. Four strangers in a UN vehicle. I asked myself, what are they doing in my territory? A nuisance, to be sure. Maybe even trouble, given that we just completed a successful operation. Then they told me that Tessa Bishonga was among them. That was a surprise, but also an opportunity."

He paused, a smug smile on his face. When neither Tessa nor Vermeulen took the bait, he continued,

"So far, we have avoided television. It never told our story properly. Since the beginning of the peace negotiations in Doha earlier this year, our attitude has changed. We've learned that a large part of the battle is fought in the media. We've come to realize that without media presence, we're just a bunch of ragtag fighters in the middle of nowhere. The government can attack us without repercussions, and the world doesn't care. So, we must get our side out to the world. And you, Ms. Bishonga, will help us."

Tessa's smile widened. "I think I can do that."

"Before you continue hammering out your media strategy, tell me where Amina is!" Vermeulen said.

"It would behoove you to show some manners," Masaad said. "One doesn't barge into someone's home and issue orders."

"One does if that someone has taken an innocent girl. Let me see her."

"You are in no position to demand anything. Why do you want to speak to her?"

"She has information crucial to my investigation. Why did you bring her here?"

"Zam Zam is no longer safe for her."

"Why?"

"I assume it's related to the information you desire."

"She saw who killed the UN policewoman?"

"She was present," Masaad said.

"I must speak to her."

"All in due time. We've heard reports of a stranger appearing in the camp around the time the UN policewoman was killed. Nobody wanted to tell us about him. When we found Amina, we thought she was safe because nobody notices a child. That changed when we heard someone was asking for her."

"Who was that stranger?"

"We are investigating. Since Zam Zam lies in our territory, we must know who comes and goes. There are too many of al-Bashir's spies around." He spat out the name of Sudan's dictator with disgust. "It is late. My men will show you to your quarters. We will speak in the morning."

One of Masaad's men took them to a tent that contained four cots. It must have been vacated in a hurry. A pair of sunglasses lay on the table and a bag leaned against the rear canvas. Someone had already brought their things from the Nissan and piled them into a corner. Sami's camera equipment constituted most of it. Wambui sat on a cot. A bandage covered part of his left arm.

"It's nothing," he said in response to Vermeulen's raised eyebrows. "A scratch from flying glass. I'm all right."

Vermeulen plopped down on a cot and let out a long breath. The routine audit had quickly turned into a complex case with more twists than a Rubik's Cube. Being held by a rebel group had definitely not been part of the plan.

"So, are we prisoners or guests?" he asked no one in particular.

Sami pointed to the tent entrance. "See the guard outside? We're prisoners. Masaad is going to milk us for what it's worth. Ransom, guarantees from the UN, and whatever else he can get."

Wambui nodded in agreement.

"Let's not be so gloomy," Tessa said. "Masaad wants publicity. I can give him that. If we play our cards right, we'll be out of here in no time." She smiled and stretched out on another cot. "This trip turned out to be a great stroke of luck. Masaad practically begged me for an interview."

"Well, bully for you!" Vermeulen said. "It's not going to be anything like you expect. Sami's right. He's going to use us to get whatever ransom he can get. Your interview is just part of his plot. But, hey, it'll get your face on TV."

He lay down on the cot. He knew the last bit was harsh, but she'd asked for it. She was no different from all the other news hounds he'd known.

"You calling me a media whore?" Tessa jumped up, her eyes fierce with anger.

"Your words, not mine. But if the shoe fits—"

"Do you really think I'd let Masaad pull the wool over my eyes?"

"You won't have a choice. He won't let you go unless you record what he wants."

"You don't know shit about broadcasting, do you? He gets to say what he wants, but we do the editing. I thought I could trust you. I guess I was wrong."

"Will ya quit bickering?" Sami said. "I know we are stuck here and it sucks. We need to stay together. Also, Tessa is right. Once we edit the interview, Masaad won't recognize himself."

The tent door was pushed aside. A man carried a tray with four bowls to the table and left without saying a word. The stew barely qualified as edible, just a few gristly pieces of meat floating in a thin broth. But Vermeulen remembered the destitution of the New Arrivals section of Zam Zam. The line about a lot of people not getting supper from the Clash's "Justice Tonight" seemed more than apt.

The meal calmed the atmosphere. Afterwards, Sami messed around with a laptop he'd pulled from one of their bags. A few minutes later, he closed the computer with a loud snap.

"No damn signal. I wonder how Masaad communicates."

"He probably has a satellite phone," Wambui said. "I sure wish we had one."

* * *

THAT EVENING, THE *GLORIA* DOCKED AT Container Terminal 2 of the Jebel Ali Free Zone in Dubai. Comparing the Dubai Container Terminal to Umm Qasr was like comparing Grand Central Terminal to an Amtrak stop in Montana. Not even in the same category. It's the largest free zone in the world and the largest container terminal on the Persian Gulf. Huge container vessels crowded the quays. Equally huge cranes collected containers, two at a time, and deposited them on the front apron. A cacophony of beeps filled the air as straddle carriers, reach stackers, and tractor-trailers zoomed back and forth, following an intricate plan determined by computers in the Dubai Port Authority's offices.

Following standard practice, the owners of the *Gloria* had forwarded their bay plan to the port authorities, indicating which bays were to be loaded in Dubai. Halfway through the loading process, the crane operator was surprised to find that the bay designated for the orange container labeled 'ACME' hanging from the spreader was already occupied by a blue container. There must have been a mistake with the bay plan. He hesitated for a moment, checked the plan again, and noticed that the space next to the blue container was not scheduled for any cargo. Deciding to make the mix-up someone else's problem, he deposited the orange box next to the blue one. One extra container wasn't going to upset the vessel's balance. He'd notify the proper individuals once the ship was loaded. If he got around to it. Which he didn't.

Chapter Fourteen

———◆———

Diary of Ritu Roy

WE STARTED OUR PATROL LATE AGAIN. That's the fourth time in a row. We had to wait for forty-five minutes until the Nepalis got their stupid APC started. I just got out of our SUV and walked over. The guys standing by the rear door were friendly enough. I asked what the problem was. They just shrugged. They said they'd never had such bad equipment at home. They were kind of embarrassed.

We can't go into Zam Zam unless the Nepali contingent provides a backup team. Too many incidents, we are told. I'm sure they don't mean the women who are abused.

There was a short battle with some bandits who came to steal food and supplies that had just been delivered. It happened at the other end of the camp. I heard the gunfire and a few explosions. The fight ended quickly. The Nepalis took credit.

Amina told me later that the Nepalis never showed up and that UJM rebels sent the bandits packing.

Thursday, March 18, 2010

MASAAD HAD BOTH VERMEULEN AND TESSA brought to his tent first thing the next morning. In the light of day, Vermeulen saw that the camp lay nestled against the outcroppings of three hillocks that dotted the land like camel humps. Compared to the sandy terrain they drove through the day before, the area was lush with trees, bushes, and grass.

He saw ten tents scattered under trees. A primitive wooden latrine stood apart, toward the hills. Their tent sat close to the center of the camp. Four others occupied the expanse between them and where the UJM's technicals and the large truck were parked. Several men were unloading wooden boxes from the truck and lugging them to the pickups. Their own SUV was easy to spot with its white paint. He saw machine gun emplacements near the entrance of the camp, one almost across from their tent and another one farther up on the hillside. All three were occupied. Between them, they covered any possible escape route.

They might get as far as their Nissan, but they would have to cover quite a stretch of open space before the track disappeared behind a hill. Any halfway-competent gunner would destroy their truck. Not a good prognosis for escape. Their best chance would likely be stealing a technical. The machine gun crews would take a moment before recognizing that the wrong people were driving away. That might give them enough time.

Masaad seemed hostile when they entered his tent. A tray with a pot of tea and three glasses sat on his desk. He didn't offer them any.

"Why were you looking for me?" he said.

Vermeulen looked at Tessa, surprised. She shrugged.

"We were looking for Amina," Vermeulen said. "We saw your men take her."

"The GPS in your car was programmed with the coordinates for my camp. Who gave them to you?"

This was Tessa's terrain, and she answered without hesitation. "A contact gave them to me."

"A contact in El Fasher?"

"No, a contact in Kenya."

"His name?"

"I'm a journalist. I don't reveal my sources. Valentin is right, though. We came because we were looking for Amina. We saw your men take her from Zam Zam. We decided to come here."

"You put us in danger," Masaad said, shaking his head. His face was difficult to read. "This location is secret."

"It obviously hasn't been secret for a while, or my contact in Nairobi wouldn't have known about it," Tessa said.

"I'll have to find that leak. Still, you put us at risk. Who knows you are here?"

"No one," Vermeulen said. "We left from Zam Zam without telling anyone."

"I don't believe that."

"I can't help you there. But I assure you that you have at most a day before the UN will mount a search and rescue mission."

"That's the least of my worries. We ambushed a government convoy and liberated a truckload of ammunition yesterday. Al-Bashir's forces are out there looking for us. If you know how to find us, the army won't be far behind. We'll have to move soon. Dealing with you just adds complications."

So that's where the truck came from, Vermeulen thought. It would be quite a firefight if the army should show up. Dangerous, but also a chance to escape.

"About your media exposure," Tessa said. "I thought an interview would be best. It'll allow you to present your ideas to the world."

They hadn't really spoken since the argument the night before. Vermeulen had hoped Tessa would reconsider the interview idea. He couldn't see any benefit coming from it.

"Ah, yes, an interview," Masaad said, stroking his mustache. "Yes, that would be good. Too bad we don't have enough time."

"We could be set up in thirty minutes," Tessa said.

Masaad pursed his lips and looked up at the tent ceiling. *He's in more trouble than he admits*, Vermeulen thought. *Otherwise he wouldn't hesitate.*

"Okay," he said after a moment of reflection. "Tell your cameraman to set up here."

"We need to take some shots around your camp. It adds context, credibility, and color."

Masaad shrugged. "I'll tell my deputy. You can't film any faces. That would compromise my men's security."

"Now that you've sorted out the media campaign for the United Justice Movement, maybe you could let me speak to Amina," Vermeulen said.

Masaad's eyes flashed with anger.

"Don't overestimate your importance, Mr. Vermeulen. More significant people than you have disappeared in Darfur."

"I'm going to speak with Amina and then I'm going back to El Fasher. You don't want the UN as an enemy. So let's go."

Despite the bluster, he wasn't sure the UN would do much if he did disappear. But it was his only card, and he decided to play it as often as needed. With government troops after him, Masaad was in a bind. He didn't need UN troops joining the pursuit. Masaad must have made the same calculation, because he took Vermeulen outside.

The rebels had finished unloading the ambushed truck. Vermeulen wondered if all their ammunition was stolen from the government. The rebels were well armed. They all carried assault rifles. He recognized the curved magazines of well-used AK-47s. Others carried more modern weapons with black plastic stocks, a pistol grip closer to the front, and shorter barrels. After seeing how blatantly the government violated the arms embargo, he wasn't surprised that the rebels did likewise.

"What kind of guns are these?" he said, pointing to one hanging off the shoulder of the closest soldier.

"Tavor assault rifles. Made in Israel. They are very good."

"How did you get them?"

Masaad ignored the question.

They entered a tent sited near the rear of the camp. It must have been the kitchen tent. A large propane stove stood in the center, surrounded by prep tables. A woman, probably younger than she looked, stood bent over a plastic tub, washing bowls. A tall girl stood next to the woman, wiping the washed bowls with a rag. Two boys, maybe five and seven, sat on the ground rolling a small ball back and forth.

Masaad greeted the family and said something in Arabic. The woman nodded.

"This is Amina," Masaad said. "Ask your questions."

She eyed Vermeulen with curiosity.

"Hello, Amina. I spoke with Priya Choudhury, who told me that you were a good friend of Ritu Roy."

Amina smiled and nodded.

"I'm so sorry your friend was killed. I want to find out who did this, and I'm hoping you can help me."

She nodded again but didn't smile anymore.

"I know Ritu sent you home when the mob came. Did you go?"

"No," she said in English.

"I didn't think you would. What did you see?"

"Many angry men. By Ritu. And another man."

"Was he with all the other men?"

"No."

"Where was he?"

She said something in Arabic to Masaad.

"She says he hid behind rocks," he said.

That must be the outcropping, Vermeulen thought.

"Okay. Did you see him shoot Ritu?"

Amina shrugged and said more to Masaad.

"She saw him go behind the rock, then she heard the shots, then she saw him leave," Masaad said.

"What did he look like?"

"He was big."

"What did he wear?"

She spoke again to Masaad.

"He wore jeans, boots, and a khaki shirt. No uniform." He sounded impatient. "Listen, I've asked her this already. He was European, he was tall, and he had a goatee."

"I want to hear it from her." Masaad's interference annoyed him, but he didn't want to anger the man.

"So the European had a beard like this?" He stroked his chin.

She nodded. "And sunglasses."

"Did you see where he went afterwards?"

She nodded again.

"Could you tell me?"

"He go away in car."

"They had a car?" Masaad sounded surprised. Obviously he hadn't asked that question.

Amina nodded.

"What kind of car?" Vermeulen said.

"White car. Toyota."

"A white car like Ritu's?"

"No. No U-N-A-M-I-D car." She pronounced each letter of the acronym individually.

Vermeulen looked at Masaad, who seemed just as surprised.

"Did you see a license plate?" It was a long shot, but to his surprise, Amina nodded.

"KH"—she pronounced each letter slowly—"143. I no read all."

* * *

DURING THEIR ABSENCE, SAMI HAD CONVERTED Masaad's tent into a makeshift TV studio. Two director's chairs stood in front of an easel holding a large map of Darfur.

Civil war managed as a media event, Vermeulen thought. The interview might buy them time, but it wouldn't get them back to El Fasher. Escape was their only option.

Sami had put the camera on a tripod, positioned two bright lights, and strung the cords for two lavalier microphones. No wonder he had so many bags.

Masaad entered his tent, surveyed the arrangement, and nodded with satisfaction. He wore a clean, crisp uniform and his green turban. He took his seat. Vermeulen was struck by the surreal quality of the occasion. They were being held by a rebel group in the middle of nowhere, all the while Masaad and Tessa pretended to be on a TV set.

Tessa wore the same pants, but she'd switched to a well-tailored jacket that must have been in one of her bags. A scarf with an intricate pattern reminiscent of a Moorish mosaic he'd once seen in Spain was carefully arranged to cover her hair. It was the first time he'd seen her with makeup. She looked good, really good, and she knew it as she took the chair opposite Masaad.

"Are we ready?" she asked Sami.

"I'm all set."

Masaad pulled a sheet of paper from his jacket. "Here are your questions," he said.

This is where the charade begins, Vermeulen thought. It was going to be a publicity stunt for Masaad and the UJM. He couldn't believe that Tessa had fallen for this trick.

She took the sheet and barely glanced at it.

"Sorry, Commander Masaad," she said. "If you want this interview to have any credibility, you've got to let me ask my questions my way. If I sit here reading from a piece of paper, everybody will know this is a staged event. They'll tune out."

There was an indulgent smile on her face when she handed the paper back.

Masaad was taken aback. He looked at the paper in his hand, then at Tessa. Vermeulen saw the arched eyebrows and readied himself for a tirade. Masaad's men obviously didn't contradict him. And here this woman dared to challenge him in front of everybody.

Tessa jumped in before the explosion happened. "Please," she said, "I'm the media professional here. An interview has to flow naturally, just like a conversation. You want to come across as an engaging, popular leader with a serious agenda. Otherwise we can just set up the camera and you can read a prepared statement."

She's good, Vermeulen thought. Masaad seemed to think so, too. His eyebrows flattened out again.

"Maybe you are right."

A bemused smile played around the corners of Masaad's mouth when he ordered his assistant and the guard out of the tent. Vermeulen caught it and knew that all wasn't settled yet.

"Let's go," Masaad said.

Sami counted down from ten, replacing the last three numbers with hand signs.

After opening the interview with a quick intro, Tessa waded right into the fray, asking Masaad why the UJM had so far refused to participate in the Doha peace talks. Masaad was smart enough to take the question not as a challenge but as an excuse to outline the group's opposition to any collusion with the illegitimate regime of al-Bashir. He presented himself as a maximalist for whom compromise was a dirty word.

Vermeulen had heard such statements before, and they usually fell into two categories. Either they were used to stake out a negotiating position or they were the pronouncements of a deluded individual. In Masaad's case, it was obviously the former.

The interview unfolded quite differently than Vermeulen had expected. Tessa asked tough questions regarding the tactics used by the UJM—the civilian casualties, the direction of the peace process. Masaad returned the volleys, sometimes with anger, sometimes with charm, but always with the confidence of someone who knew his strategy would, in the end, be successful. He seemed to enjoy the verbal sparring as much as Tessa did. His maximalist position became more nuanced as the interview continued. In response to concrete scenarios, he advanced more accommodating opinions on how to settle the conflict. What had begun with a demand for independence slowly changed to acceptance of autonomy, devolution of power from Khartoum, withdrawal of Sudanese troops, establishment of a regional police force recruited from all sectors of Darfur, and finally, elections for an autonomous Darfur.

The interview ended after forty-five minutes. Tessa detached the microphone from her jacket, got up, and looked at Vermeulen. *See*, her eyes said, *I know how to do this.* She most certainly did, and he felt sheepish about having doubted her.

Masaad stood as well and stretched out his hand to Tessa.

"Thanks," she said as she shook his hand. "A great interview. It will establish you as a credible leader in Darfur."

"Yes, it was a good interview," Masaad replied. "Of course, it will never be broadcast."

Tessa frowned, not sure she'd heard right.

"Do you think I'd let my people, or the world for that matter, see my participation in a debate club? I enjoyed the discussion with you, but nobody else can ever see it. My credibility would be destroyed. I've just outlined the compromise I would accept. If al-Bashir and his minions see this, they will use it as a starting point for negotiations. Please give me the tape. Then, as you suggested, we will record my official statement."

Tessa stood speechless. Seeing her deflate, Vermeulen guessed nobody had pulled that kind of switch on her before.

"Commander Masaad," she said, grasping for words. "That wasn't what we agreed on. Besides, you are wrong. The rest of the world will accept you as a credible representative of the people of Darfur. That's what matters, not how al-Bashir might twist your words." She said the name of the dictator with the same venom Masaad had used earlier.

"I can't take that risk. I applaud your skill, though. You are a great—"

A loud explosion interrupted Masaad. It was followed by four more in rapid succession. Sami dove to the ground, and Vermeulen followed suit.

The staccato sound of automatic weapon fire cut through the air. The deputy appeared in the tent door and shouted something. Masaad responded with rapid-fire commands.

He turned to them. "It appears al-Bashir's soldiers have already found us."

* * *

Campbell parked his white pickup under the same acacia tree near El Fasher Lake. He dialed the same number.

"Yes," Houser said.

"There's been a new development."

"Yes?"

"Some kind of UN investigator arrived three days ago. Tuesday night, he went to the Bangladeshi quarters and spoke with the cop's friend."

"What's his name?"

"Vermeulen. I checked. He's supposed to do a routine audit. I don't know why he's paying attention to a dead peacekeeper. He went to Zam Zam yesterday."

"He went to Zam Zam?"

"Yes."

"Why?"

"To poke around," Campbell said. "I talked to Jirel. First he was checking out the APCs, then he wanted to see the spot where the policewoman was killed."

"Where is he today?"

"I don't know. He didn't come back to the Nepali post. I thought maybe he drove back to El Fasher, but I checked his living quarters and he isn't there. Maybe he stayed somewhere in Zam Zam."

"There's no place to stay in Zam Zam. Talk to Jirel again. He must be somewhere."

"Will do, boss. Oh, that reporter Bishonga went with him."

"Find him. Now. This is high priority. We can't afford any scrutiny at the moment."

CHAPTER FIFTEEN

———◆———

"THE TAPE, PLEASE," MASAAD SAID. HE seemed calm despite the explosions outside.

Sami opened the video recorder, extracted the digital videotape, fished through his bag for a case, inserted the tape, and handed it to Masaad.

"You'd better stay here," he said. "It's too dangerous out there. We will repel them, of course, but it might take a while. No need for you to become a target."

After Masaad left the tent, they stood and looked at each other. That wasn't a turn of events Vermeulen had expected. A loud burst of gunfire nearby reminded him that a tent was no place to sit out an ambush.

"We gotta get out of here. Now!" he shouted.

High-pitched barrages indicated that the machine guns he had seen earlier now engaged the attackers. Tessa didn't seem to hear them. She walked to Masaad's desk and riffled through the papers lying next to a laptop computer. She found a small book, paged through it, and slipped it into her bag. Her calm seemed entirely inappropriate to Vermeulen.

Once she finished examining the desk, she said, "Okay, let's go."

"What about Wambui?" Vermeulen said.

"He'll know what to do," Tessa said. "He's the pro."

"I'm not leaving him."

A mortar round exploded nearby, and the pressure wave squeezed the breath from Vermeulen's lungs. Two more followed in rapid succession. He pressed his hands against his ears and swallowed to equalize the pressure in his ear canal. A piece of shrapnel sliced through the tent and let in sunlight. Sami took the camera from the tripod and began filming the holes in the tent. *What a crazy thing to do*, Vermeulen thought.

"Ready?" Tessa looked at Sami. He nodded and turned the camera off. "Let's make a run for the car," she said.

"Won't they shoot at the car?" Vermeulen said.

Sami nodded. "You're right. The white Nissan couldn't be a better target. We'd better find a place to hide."

"Where?" Tessa said.

Vermeulen replied, "In the hills behind the camp. I saw trees there this morning. It's as good a cover as we're going to find."

Tessa scratched her head. "I bet the rebels are thinking the same."

"You have a better idea?"

She shook her head. The stuttering of guns, the boom of explosions combined into a clamor of destruction. Masaad's fighters shouted to each other. An agonized scream pierced the racket. A volley of bullets whistled through the tent, ripping the fabric and leaving the three pressed to the ground. The ominous thudding of a helicopter penetrated the battle noise.

Vermeulen crawled to the door and lifted the flap just enough to peer out. Two tents to the right were burning, as were two vehicles near the entrance of the camp. A group of Masaad's fighters had thrown together a barricade of tables, sandbags, and other junk next to the burning tents. While two kept firing in the direction of the entrance to the camp, four others hurried to assemble a mortar. They had already placed the barrel and were adjusting the leveling gear. Minutes later, one of the fighters dropped a round into the barrel. The mortar sounded like a shotgun. An explosion followed almost immediately. The attackers returned fire, and the ground near the barricade was plowed by bullets. The helicopter circled above, muzzle flashes flickering when its guns fired.

Sami stood next to him, pointed the camera lens through the slit, and trained it on the rebels with the mortar.

"This way is blocked," Vermeulen said.

Tessa joined them and nodded. "You're right. Those chaps have attracted too much attention. Let's try the rear."

She pulled a knife from her bag and sliced the fabric at the opposite side of the tent.

"I think it's clear here," she said.

Vermeulen saw the trees on the hillside. They seemed close enough. A trail led past another burning tent and the latrine, wove around several car-sized rocks, and then disappeared into the woods.

"Okay," he said. "Let's go."

Before he could move, Tessa dashed across the open space, dodging the burning tent, racing past the latrine, and diving behind one of the large rocks. Her movements were graceful and swift, like a dancer crossing a stage.

Vermeulen followed, running in a crouch to keep low. The wind shifted when he reached the burning tent. Acrid smoke made his eyes tear up, and for a moment the world blurred into an ugly watercolor painting. He pushed ahead. There'd be time to rest in the woods.

Next thing he knew, his face lay in the dirt. He'd tripped over a root. Good thing, too. A salvo of bullets stitched a seam across the ground he'd just covered. Bits of gravel hit his face. This wasn't a random barrage. Somebody must have seen Tessa dash across the open space and was waiting for the next sprinter. His stomach clenched, and he remained on the ground, breathing hard. The noise of the battle, pushed into the background by the blood rushing through his ears, muscled its way back to the foreground.

The rebels had recovered from the surprise of the ambush and were mounting a fierce defense. The low tack-tack-tack of AK-47s dominated, interrupted by bursts of machine gun fire and mortar explosions. Somebody was using a large-caliber gun as well. He looked back and saw Sami filming everything as if he were wearing an invisibility cloak.

Another volley sprayed more sand into his face. He couldn't stay in that spot. But running farther would expose him even more. "Should I stay or should I go?" The Clash had a song for even this situation. He decided to go.

Following Tessa's example, he just ran for it. He propelled himself forward with all the force he could muster. Abreast with the latrine, he turned for the rock that sheltered Tessa. His lungs burned. He gulped air as fast as he could. He didn't make it to the rock. The shockwave of an exploding mortar round smashed him against the latrine. The wood planks splintered under the impact, and he tumbled onto a heap of lumber, barely avoiding the holes in the ground.

The stink of shit mixed with the reek of burnt gunpowder. Tessa waved to him, urging him to come to what little shelter the rock provided. He pushed himself up, dashed the twenty yards to the rock, and dropped into its shadow.

"Are you okay?" Tessa said.

He nodded, unable to speak for lack of air. Sami, camera in hand, followed him, moving swiftly with experience and foresight and without drama.

"Is he still filming?" Vermeulen said, breathing hard.

"Yes, he is. He's getting great footage. His basic philosophy is that you can't beat a bullet. You can only act with care and hope for the best. So far, it's worked for him."

Once Sami had made it to the rock, Vermeulen plotted their way into the woods at the foot of the hills. The initial section of the path was easy, since they were moving away from the battle and the rocks provided cover. Between the last of the rocks and the woods, they'd have to sprint across fifty yards of open space.

As Tessa got ready to move, he heard branches crack. Somebody was coming. Tessa had heard it too. She hunkered down low to the ground. Quick steps approached the rock from the other side. Sami put down the camera and picked up a good-sized stone. Vermeulen did the same. He heard deep breathing and the clanking of metal against stone. Whoever was coming carried a weapon. A rebel fleeing? Sami raised the hand holding the stone. Vermeulen positioned himself a little to his left, giving Sami a better opportunity to strike. The steps came closer. The tip of an RPG launcher appeared. Sami waited no longer. He grabbed the tube and yanked it forward. Wambui tumbled into their midst.

"Am I glad to see you," Vermeulen said.

"And I you," Wambui replied. "I figured you'd be heading for the hills. There was no other way out."

"What's with the launcher?" Sami asked.

"One of the rebels got killed and dropped it just a few feet from me. I also got his Tavor assault rifle."

He handed the RPG launcher to Vermeulen. Vermeulen hesitated. It seemed too complicated a weapon.

"It's easier to handle than the Tavor," Wambui said.

"Are these the government troops we saw at the El Fasher airport?" Vermeulen said as he shouldered the RPG.

"It wouldn't surprise me. Why else bring in reinforcements in violation of the embargo?"

They crept to the next rock. The battle continued to rage behind them. Vermeulen looked back and saw the olive helicopter circling closer. A soldier knelt behind a machine gun at an open door, firing at targets on the ground. The chopper followed a spiral pattern, its gunner targeting whatever rebels he could see. With each turn it came closer to the rock.

"We gotta move," Sami said. "The gunner in the M-17 will spot us on its next turn."

Tessa, again, ran first. She moved easily to the last rock, then whirled across the open space. The gunner in the chopper must have seen her, because Vermeulen saw the telltale clouds of dirt bloom behind her. The M-17 changed course and flew closer. A salvo hit the corner of their rock and bits of stone flew through the air. Ricochets whined into the trees. The helicopter came so close, the jets of the engine drowned the thudding sound of the rotor. Dirt raised by the downwash blew into their faces. With the chopper hovering right above them, the gunner could not shoot at them, but Vermeulen saw a face looking at them through the glass at the bottom of the nose. The pilot inched the M-17 around, giving the gunner a better sight of their position.

The staccato of the machine gun ripped through the air again. He pressed against the rock, feeling the grit and dust in his face.

The helicopter's tail twisted into view.

"You've got to take it out," Wambui shouted. "There's no other option. Flip up the sight, aim, and press the trigger."

Vermeulen shouldered the RPG launcher and stepped from behind the rock. He aimed the tube, focusing on the little square of the metal sight. His vision narrowed to a tunnel. A monstrous dragonfly, the M-17 moved slowly into the square. The din of the battle receded. He felt the turbulence of bullets whizzing by him but only heard the blood coursing in his ears.

Through the sight he saw the details of the aircraft in exquisite clarity, the treads on the tires, the airspeed nozzle, the riveted segments of the undercarriage. He saw each of the five blades motionless against the hazy sky. Some part of his brain told him that was impossible. But it was the fuselage that was turning, not the rotor. A thought materialized from somewhere, suggesting that he might want to pull the trigger. It was an interesting idea. The fuselage kept turning inside the square as he contemplated it. The open cabin door moved past the sight. A man kneeling next to the machine gun, pulling a new belt from a box. The machine gun appeared next, the gunner sitting behind it. He saw the barrel. It was aimed straight at him.

The black eye of the muzzle staring at him shattered the silence. The howl of the engine above him, the tack-tack-tack of automatic weapon fire, Wambui shouting, the cries of the wounded, the whole clamor of battle engulfed him. Somewhere in all that racket, Vermeulen thought he heard Joe Strummer sing, "Go straight to hell, boys." He pulled the trigger.

There was no recoil. A white jet trail rose into the sky. He couldn't see the machine gun anymore. The trail led straight into the open door. The charge slammed into the fuselage. The chopper bucked like a wounded deer, but it kept turning. Had he fired a dud?

A fireball burst from the helicopter's fuselage, painting the sky the color of a fiery sunset. A deep boom sent shockwaves in all directions, pressing on his ears and quieting all other battle sounds. The chopper disintegrated into large chunks that tumbled to the ground.

Vermeulen stood next to the rock. The empty tube of the RPG lay next to him. He stared at the burning wreckage of the helicopter. Had he really just done that? The jumble of steel, glass, and smoldering rubber seemed entirely out of proportion to the slight pull on the trigger that caused it. Sami pulled him away from the rock and to the shelter of the trees.

The loss of the helicopter turned the battle in favor of the rebels. They pushed forward and recaptured the area where their vehicles were parked. The government troops fell back, unable to regroup and regain their momentum.

Motionless bodies lay scattered around the camp. The screams of the wounded became more pressing as the battle noise ebbed.

"Are you okay?" Tessa asked Vermeulen.

He sat down. Every bit of energy had left his body.

"We should wait here until this is over," Tessa said.

"No," Wambui said. "It's not safe. The rebels may have the advantage now, but I bet the army will radio for reinforcements."

"What are our options?" Sami said.

"We need to find a car and drive away."

"Right," Sami said. "We'll just walk down there, get in the car, and say 'toodeloo.'"

"Of course not." It was the first time Vermeulen had seen Wambui angry. "There will be a lull in the fighting. The army has lost its main asset. Their soldiers will retreat to a more defensible position and wait for reinforcements. The rebels know they can't rout the attackers. They don't have enough men here. They'll leave. We have to take advantage of that confusion."

Vermeulen forced himself up again. "He's right, we have to get out of here. I shot down their helicopter."

The fighting slowed down. Each side was tending to its wounded. The machine gunners mounted their weapons on the beds of pickups. They loaded boxes, guns, ammunition.

"This isn't their main camp," Wambui said. "They'll retreat to their headquarters before the government can reinforce its troops."

A convoy formed below: two technicals in the lead, followed by a line of pickups. Vermeulen saw their white SUV fourth in line. The rebels had requisitioned it. More technicals brought up the rear. As the rebels drove off at high speed, the gunfire increased in intensity. Mortar rounds exploded near the convoy. It was clear that the government troops didn't have the stomach for a pursuit.

"Let's move," Wambui said. "The army will come and search the camp. We have to be ready to drive while they do that."

Vermeulen looked back. Soldiers were approaching the burning remnants of the helicopter. The heat of the fire prevented them from recovering the remains of those who had been aboard.

He'd killed people before. It wasn't something he was proud of. On each occasion, it had been a reflexive rather than a premeditated act. An immediate arithmetic of life or death that made contemplation impossible. Shooting down the helicopter was different. It felt more deliberate, even cold-blooded. Sure, the gunner had been aiming for them. He had no choice. It didn't make the hollow feeling in his stomach go away.

Sami saw him lingering. "No time for sentimentality," he said.

Vermeulen hurried to catch up with the rest. The path wove through the woods until they reached the parking area. A dead rebel lay near a tree. Spent casings lay scattered on the ground near the body. Vermeulen picked up several. Their head stamps could tell him where they'd come from.

Two battered pickups and the burnt shell of the truck the rebels had captured the day before were the only vehicles left in the parking area. The stink of burning rubber was overwhelming. Vermeulen put his handkerchief in front of his mouth and nose. The others did the same. Only Wambui seemed impervious to the acrid smoke.

"I'll go and check if one of these works," Wambui said. "Wait here for my signal. Once I wave, run as fast as you can. Sami, you drive. You two"—he pointed at Tessa and Vermeulen—"sit in the cab. I'll be on the back with the gun."

He disappeared.

Since they first met, Vermeulen had thought of Wambui as the consummate assistant—competent, courteous, unassuming. During the battle, he'd seen the real Wambui for the first time—a well-trained, skilled soldier.

He watched Wambui take the long way around, ducking behind any cover he could find. The government soldiers were already searching the camp. Vermeulen couldn't see if there were more of them outside the perimeter. Once Wambui had gotten as close to the trucks as the trees permitted, he stood up and walked to them as if he were one of the soldiers. His green-brown camouflage uniform looked similar enough.

Wambui opened the door of the first pickup. His head disappeared behind the dashboard. A couple of minutes later, he exited and walked to the second truck. Vermeulen wondered if those vehicles had been left behind because they were unusable. Wambui followed the same routine. A moment later, the engine sputtered to life. A cloud of blue-black smoke came from the exhaust. *Bad rings*, Vermeulen thought. Not the best getaway car, but it would have to do.

Wambui waved and they raced across the empty lot. Sami aimed for the driver's side. Tessa and Vermeulen headed to the other side and jumped in. Wambui hunkered down on the bed.

"Don't kill the engine, Sami," he shouted.

Sami nodded, revved the engine, jammed in the first gear, and drove off.

Their sudden exit roused the attention of the soldier standing in the shade near the entrance. He fired a couple of shots and missed. Sami skidded around a bend, trying to keep the truck's rear wheels from sliding into a bush. They cleared the shrubs and found themselves facing a row of trucks and armored vehicles. *Damn*, Vermeulen thought, *from the frying pan into the fire.*

He heard shouts. More gunfire. Loud pings told Vermeulen that at least some rounds found their target. Wambui returned fire with the Tavor. Sami accelerated along a straight stretch of the track. Vermeulen looked back and saw the machine gun in one of the pickups turning toward them. Clouds of dirt shot up next to the pickup. Then the dust obscured everything behind them.

* * *

BEFORE THEY REACHED THE TARRED ROAD to El Fasher, the stink of burnt oil was impossible to ignore. Vermeulen, sitting in the middle, pointed to the oil pressure gauge. The needle hovered in the red zone.

Sami shrugged. "What do you want me to do? Stop?"

"Yes. We're not being pursued anymore. Let's check the engine."

They rolled to a stop.

"Don't turn it off," Wambui shouted from the back. "I don't know if it will start again."

Vermeulen lifted the hood and a cloud of blue smoke engulfed him. Just as he had expected—bad rings. They were burning oil. The hot vapors made his eyes tear. He turned to catch a breath of fresh air. When he knelt to check under the engine, he found more bad news. A telltale black spot had formed under the engine block. Maybe it wasn't bad rings after all. He examined the engine compartment. An old six-cylinder block, nothing special. The head gasket seemed fine, no seepage there. He examined the engine. There it was. A ragged hole, not very large at all, and a small trail of black oil running down the engine. A bullet or a piece of shrapnel had pierced the aluminum.

"We're losing oil because the engine's been hit. I can't tell how much we've lost already, but we have to assume that we won't get much farther."

Wambui jumped from the rear and joined him.

"That's bad news. It'll be dark soon. We have no food, no water. We are at least twenty miles from El Fasher. "

"We should drive until the engine ceases," Vermeulen said. "Get as close to El Fasher as possible. That increases our chances of being found by a patrol."

Wambui nodded.

The engine lasted another four miles after they reached the tarred road. It gave up its ghost with the sickening grind of metal against metal.

CHAPTER SIXTEEN

———◆———

Diary of Ritu Roy

IT WAS AN AWFUL DAY. THE worst. A woman died today. She didn't have to. We started late again because the APC that was supposed to accompany us didn't show up. We finally got a replacement and then we went on our way. An hour into our patrol, a woman pulled us aside. She pointed to a large shack and urged us to check it. We went there and came across another woman, who had a broken arm. Her face was full of bruises. Priya and I set the arm as best we could and took her to the clinic by the water tank. They had a line; the wait was long. We waited with her, and she told us that her husband had beaten her and broken her arm.

We left her there and went to speak to the husband. He denied it all, claimed that she'd fallen. I could tell he was lying. We told him that we could arrest him for assault. We told him that we'd keep an eye on him. It didn't seem to faze him one bit.

During our lunch break, we got an urgent radio message about a fight where we had picked up the woman earlier. Halfway there, the APC stalled and the Nepalis couldn't get it started again. We wanted go on our own but weren't allowed to. By the time the replacement came and we made it to the location, the woman lay dead on the path. The neighbors told us that her husband had beaten her to death. He was long gone.

Tonight I sat down and wrote a letter of complaint to the head of mission. I told him that the Nepalis were violating UN policy by not having proper equipment. I told him that it had cost a woman her life today. That it had probably cost lives before and will again until somebody does something about that.

Things have to change.

Friday, March 19, 2010

THE DEPUTY FORCE COMMANDER OF UNAMID, a Rwandan brigadier-general, was too busy to spend much time with Vermeulen. Not only had the government of Sudan violated the embargo—that was well known—but now it had actually used those extra troops to attack a rebel group. That violated the ceasefire—a far worse offense, because it upset the routine. His boss, the force commander, had already gone to deal with the fallout of this flagrant disregard of the rules. Of course, there was little he could do. As usual, the violation highlighted the impotence of UNAMID, which was supposed to prevent such attacks. The last thing the deputy commander wanted to worry about was some OIOS investigator getting caught up in the incident and losing one of the vehicles.

Vermeulen had anticipated that reaction. He stayed as close to the truth as necessary, omitting Tessa and Sami's presence and of course, his downing the helicopter. If it ever came out that he'd done that, he'd be looking for a job the next day. So he kept it simple. They'd gotten lost in the sandstorm, were abducted by the UJM, and escaped during the firefight. Their vehicle was stolen. They'd caught a ride back to El Fasher. He concluded his report with a request for a new vehicle.

The brigadier-general nodded and dismissed him.

Outside, Vermeulen took a deep breath. The easy part was over. Now he had to break the news about the armored personnel carriers to Bengtsson in Nairobi. For that he needed a shower and a fresh change of clothes.

Back in the office, Tony Gianotti was predictably annoyed.

"You had no business driving down to Zam Zam. They don't have any paperwork there," he said. "What were you up to?"

Smart boy, Vermeulen thought. *You caught on faster than I expected.*

"Investigating," he said. "I unearthed a major fraud." He fished the invoice from the box on his desk. "See this invoice? What does it say?"

Gianotti read the paper and shrugged. "Delivery of eight armored personnel carriers."

"Come on, focus. What kind of APCs?"

"Pandur I models."

"And?"

Gianotti stared at the invoice, but didn't see anything else remarkable.

"They are new. See that box there?"

Gianotti nodded. "So what?" he said.

"Well, the APCs I found at Zam Zam were used," Vermeulen said. "So used, in fact, they were falling apart."

Gianotti sat down. "Really? Damn. That's just the kind of trouble we don't need."

Vermeulen stared at him. "And why is that?"

"Because it means a lot of extra work."

Vermeulen had seen that attitude many times before. It didn't make it any more tolerable.

"It's our goddamn job! That's why we're here. That's why we're checking all those numbers. To find fraud and stop it."

"You don't have to shout," Gianotti said. "I'm just saying—"

"Don't worry. You just stay here and complete the rest of the audit. I will investigate who is involved. That means I'll be gone on and off."

"Oh no, you won't. You're not going to dump all this crap in my lap while you gallivant around doing who knows what."

Vermeulen didn't bother to reply. It was time to pull rank. He dialed Bengtsson's number. The regional director answered on the third ring.

"Vermeulen here."

Bengtsson didn't sound too happy. "Where the hell have you been?"

"What do you mean?"

"You were gone two days without explanation."

"It was only one and a half days. How did you know?"

"How do you think?"

Vermeulen glanced over at Gianotti, who was suddenly very busy cleaning his pen.

"I've uncovered a major fraud. One unit here received a field delivery of eight APCs. The invoice states they are new and the UN is paying for new vehicles. Except they aren't. I saw them at the Zam Zam post. They are old. Practically unusable. They break down, have bad tires. You get the idea."

Bengtsson was quiet. Vermeulen waited. He heard papers being shuffled. A couple of minutes passed before Bengtsson spoke again.

"Are you sure? Of course you are." As usual, Bengtsson answered his own question. "You know what this means. Fraud at this scale can only work if people at the highest level are involved. What unit is it?"

"A Nepali police unit stationed in Zam Zam."

"The unit's commander must be involved. I'm sure that the commander's superiors in Nepal are also in on the scam. This is going right up the chain."

There was another pause. *I've just ruined his day*, Vermeulen thought. *Why is it that everybody at OIOS hates doing the job they were hired to do?* Whenever he uncovered illegal doings, he got excited. Finally, some real work to do. Everyone else just got annoyed. More work, diplomatic troubles, the usual claptrap.

"You still there, Vermeulen?" Bengtsson asked.

"Yes."

"Here's what I want you to do. Check out the unit's commander. Where does he go? What people does he meet? Are there follow-up meetings with the supplier? Be very careful. Don't, I repeat, *don't* step on anyone's toes. Who's the supplier, by the way?"

"Assured Sovereignty, a British company."

"Good. I'll inform the Under-Secretary-General. We'll take it up on this end. Remember, Vermeulen, tact is the best tool in your box. Understood?"

"Understood. One more thing. Tony here doesn't seem too pleased with my investigating this matter. Said something about not wanting to do the crap work while I gallivant around."

"Put him on."

Vermeulen handed the phone to Gianotti, whose face was red as a beet.

He listened for a long while, nodding, getting even redder. Finally, he said, "Yes, sir. I'll do that. Thank you, sir."

He ended the call and handed the phone back to Vermeulen. His eyes spoke murder, but he contained himself and went back to his desk.

Vermeulen's mobile rang. It was his daughter. He stepped out of the shed. No need for Gianotti to overhear this conversation.

"Hi, Gaby. How are you?"

"Fine. Things are a bit slow at the moment. Anything new with you?"

He decided not to tell her about the last two days. No need to worry her.

"I may be on to something, but tell me, what've you got?"

"I have some information for you. It took me a while to dig it up. Assured Sovereignty is a shady company. They are incorporated in the Turks and Caicos Islands. They have offices in London and Vienna. I asked one of our guys in Vienna to check out the address. It's just a letter box at some lawyer's office. When I hear something about the London office, I'll let you know."

There was excitement in her voice, and that made him happy.

"Wow, thanks. I didn't mean for you to do all that. I just wanted some names."

"No worries, Dad. I've got the resources, so why not use them? You would have asked for all that, anyway. I know you."

She had him there.

"What about Assured Air Services?"

"Different company, but using all the same addresses. They have the same owner."

"Who's that?"

"A Brit named Dale Houser. A bit hard to pin down. Not much public information available about him. Maybe you can use your sources. I'll message you his picture."

"Great. I have another question. Don't all weapons sales have to be registered someplace?"

"There is no central registry, if that's what you are asking. The UN encourages all members to submit weapons sales information for their database. But it's voluntary. Most countries require export licenses and end-user certificates to make sure the weapons are delivered to the intended customers. Which country are we talking about?"

"Not sure. The armored personnel carriers were made in Austria, but they were exported from the Czech Republic."

"I have a contact at the Czech Ministry of Industry and Trade. Want me to check with him?"

"Hold off for now. I'm supposed to proceed carefully."

Her laughter rang across the phone. "You, careful? Do your bosses know you at all?"

"Thanks for rubbing it in. I'll check a little more and get back in touch. Don't forget to send the picture."

"Will do. Take care of yourself there."

Gaby sounded as excited as he was. Maybe investigating ran in the family. He stepped back into the shed with a smile on his face.

His phone made a sound and the display indicated an incoming picture message. He waited for the image to download and pressed a button to view it. A tan, longish face with a narrow chin looked back at him. Dale Houser sported a neatly trimmed Van Dyke and had a mop of dark blond hair that covered most of his forehead. His pale blue eyes looked at the camera with irritation. Someone had caught him unaware, and he didn't like it. The annoyance gave the face a hard edge.

As he looked at the picture on his phone, he remembered Amina's description of the European she had seen in Zam Zam. He was tall and had a goatee.

* * *

GIANOTTI AVOIDED LOOKING AT VERMEULEN, BUT he wasn't doing any work, either. He was probably still angry that Vermeulen had ratted him out to Bengtsson. That was his problem.

Vermeulen sat down behind his desk, took a piece of paper, and sketched out what he knew. Assured Sovereignty (Dale Houser) buys used Czech APCs and sells them to the Nepali police unit in Darfur. Somewhere along the way, the paperwork is altered to turn used APCs into new ones. The UN reimburses the Nepalis for new vehicles. Someone pockets the difference. A nice little scheme.

He drew a small box and wrote 'Houser' in it. He had to be involved. That was a given. Who else? Somebody at the top of the Nepali command structure. He drew another box. Was that person in Darfur or in Nepal? For now he entered Jirel's name. According to Amina, the man had been European, so Jirel didn't do the shooting.

Gianotti got up and left the shed. He didn't say a word. Vermeulen looked up, shrugged, and went back to his papers. A third box represented the armored personnel carriers. How did those vehicles come to Darfur in the first place? By sea, obviously. He checked the end-user certificate attached to the invoice. It listed Port Sudan as the port of entry. From there they were trucked to Darfur.

Any scheme this scale had to involve more than two parties. At a minimum, the customs officials in Port Sudan had to look the other way. Export control personnel in the Czech Republic could be involved, too.

He took a new sheet of paper and listed everything he knew about Ritu Roy's death. There were two links that connected the papers. Ritu had complained about the lousy APCs, and according to Amina, she'd been shot by a European man with a goatee, driving a white pickup.

He got up and took a Gitane from the pack. Reaching into his pocket for the lighter, he felt the casings he'd picked up at the UJM camp. That was another lead he had to follow up on. He laid the casings on the table, pulled out his mobile, and took a picture of the heads, making sure the stamped codes were in focus.

Hans Reiker, a former colleague who last year quit OIOS to work as researcher for the UN Panel of Experts Concerning Sudan, would be able to identify their origin. His new job focused on small arms and ammunition that reached Darfur despite the embargoes. Vermeulen messaged the photo to him and followed with a text message asking Reiker if he could identify the origin of the cartridges as well as the head stamp 'L45A3 RG 09' Priya had given him.

Back to the pieces of paper on his desk. There was another, bigger connection—he knew that—but it eluded him. What was he not seeing? He had to speak to Priya. Maybe there was something she hadn't told him.

His phone rang again. Gaby. She told him that she'd contacted her friend in the Czech Ministry of Industry and Trade.

"Gaby, I asked you to wait. It's all very sensitive," he said.

"I didn't mention you at all. I just asked for a favor. He checked. It was easy. They've computerized all records. It was just a question of searching their database. He found the sale in question. You're right, the vehicles were used, and they were declared as such. The end user on the certificate was the Nepali police."

"Didn't he ask any questions? Seems like an odd favor to ask."

"Don't worry, Dad. I just told him that a client had asked for a shipping quote and had mentioned that sale as a reference price. My friend wasn't suspicious at all. The Czechs sell a lot of weapons, and it's all legit. Just more paperwork. Did you get the picture I sent?"

"Sure did. Thanks. Can you find out where Mr. Houser hangs his hat these days? Does he live in the Turks and Caicos or does he maintain a residence elsewhere?"

"People like him always have several places to live. I'll poke around. Don't get your hopes up."

"Listen," he said, "I just had an idea. I'll be back in touch. And, Gaby?"

"Yes, Dad?"

"Thanks for your help. It's lovely talking to you."

"You're welcome. It sure is more fun than what I'm doing at the moment. It's lovely talking with you, too."

He opened the web browser on his computer. A few keystrokes later, he looked at a row of pictures of Dale Houser that his search had produced. Most showed him at one Caribbean locale or another. Vermeulen found a photo that appeared more businesslike, then used its URL for a reverse image search. The screen displayed more information about Dale Houser and links to visually similar images. Each led to an article featuring Dale Houser, the businessman, in different locations. One showed him shaking hands with a short man in a white uniform shirt. The caption of the picture was in Arabic, as was the webpage that displayed it. That was of little use. Another picture on the same page showed a port city. He copied the URL of that picture, reverse-searched again, and found that the city in question was Port Sudan.

Had Dale Houser been to Port Sudan? It was a stretch. For all he knew, the picture of Port Sudan had nothing to do with Dale Houser. He needed more evidence. The computer was no help. No matter which combination of Houser and Port Sudan he entered, the search results did not yield any indication that Houser had been in Sudan. A reverse image search of the picture with the uniformed man was just as frustrating. Hundreds of photos of men in uniform. None depicted the man shaking Houser's hand in the original. A dead trail.

Assured Sovereignty sold weapons. That much was clear. The UN arms embargo banned supplying weapons to Darfur. That meant selling weapons to the rebels or selling weapons to the government for use in Darfur was not allowed. If Houser was doing that, he'd be eager to find a cover. Could the APCs be that cover? No, it didn't make sense. The APCs were delivered to peacekeepers. Those deliveries were exempted from the embargo. It was perfectly legal.

He stopped himself. His imagination was running wild. He only had a simple case of fraud and an Arabic language website that displayed a picture of Houser and of Port Sudan. That wasn't much to go on. His gut told him that Houser had something going in Port Sudan, and he was going to get to the bottom of it, even if it meant going there.

Gianotti came back and made a face when he smelled the smoke. Vermeulen ignored him and focused on the sheets. Looking at the papers on the desk, Gianotti said, "Why did you scribble the name of the dead policewoman on that paper? Are you now investigating a murder, too?"

All Gianotti wanted was to climb the hierarchy. At the same time, he didn't want to stick his neck out for fear that he'd be implicated if something went wrong. He also didn't want to miss an opportunity to shine. Bengtsson had upbraided him. Which made him angry and unpredictable. Vermeulen didn't need that. He had to involve Gianotti, if only peripherally, to keep him from sabotaging the whole investigation.

"Listen, Tony. For starters, everything I'm going to tell you is confidential. The only person who knows this is Bengtsson. Don't breathe a word of it to anyone. Okay?"

Gianotti nodded eagerly. Vermeulen then told him everything he'd collected about the used APCs, the falsified end-user certification, the possible role of Dale Houser and his company. He only mentioned Ritu Roy because she had complained about the rotten APCs. He left out everything about meeting Masaad, Tessa's interview, and the helicopter.

"Here's the most important issue. We've got to pretend everything is normal. Go about our work as usual. Of course there will be some deviations. We have to be certain that we don't arouse suspicion."

Gianotti nodded, but his enthusiasm faded. It probably dawned on him that there wasn't going to be a change in his routine at all.

"I'll have to go to Port Sudan and check out what happened there. In the meantime, you continue with the audit. But"—he waved off Gianotti's protest—"I also want you to create a dossier for the commander of the Nepali police contingent at Zam Zam. His name is Dilip Jirel. Who is he? What's his background? Did he travel recently? I don't have to impress on you how important discretion is. You are not to contact him or his unit. Use UN information only. We have access to plenty of that."

* * *

PRIYA CHOUDHURY LOOKED BETTER THAN AT their last meeting. Her face seemed less drawn. She even smiled when she saw Vermeulen enter the canteen that evening.

"How are you coping?" he asked.

She shrugged. "I take it a day at a time. My colleagues have been wonderful. They make sure I don't spend too much time alone. The best thing has been going on patrol again and helping the women."

Vermeulen nodded.

"Do you have any news?" she said.

"It depends. Do you want me to tell you, even if it's bad news?"

"You didn't find anything?"

"No, I did. I found Amina. It was a bit involved, but I did. She didn't run away after Roy told her to leave. She saw the man who killed Roy. He was a European and came in a white pickup."

"That's good news, isn't it?"

Vermeulen wasn't sure that was the right description, but from her perspective, he supposed it would be good news.

Priya pulled her chair closer. "I also have some news. You asked me to go through her things. I didn't want to at first. Just opening her footlocker was painful. Too many reminders of how much I miss her."

Her eyes teared up again. Vermeulen put his hand on her arm. Choudhury swallowed and wiped her eyes.

"Seeing that you took my concern seriously, I decided that I could do my part and help you. I took everything out and put it back, one item at a time. That's how I found this."

She pulled a small book from her pocket. It was covered in maroon fabric.

"It's Ritu's diary. I felt very uneasy reading it. These were her most private thoughts. She didn't even share them with me. I feel even worse about sharing them with a stranger. But she's dead. She can't be hurt anymore. Please treat it with respect and don't show it to anyone else."

Vermeulen swallowed. "I can't promise that. If there is an entry that is crucial to the investigation, I might have to show it to others. I will make a copy of that entry and keep the rest of the diary private. I hope that's acceptable to you."

Priya thought for a moment. Then she nodded and pushed the book across the table.

He took it. "Thanks. I appreciate your trust, and I want to assure you that I'll do my best to find out who fired the bullet that killed your friend. I'm going to Port Sudan tomorrow for just that purpose."

CHAPTER SEVENTEEN

———◆———

Saturday, March 20, 2010

CAMPBELL PARKED HIS PICKUP NEAR THE souk of El Fasher and dialed Houser's number.

"Yes," Houser said.

"This UN investigator, Vermeulen? He's coming to Port Sudan. He's on his way already … should land there in three hours."

"Okay. Did you find out where he was?"

"No. He definitely wasn't in El Fasher on Wednesday or Thursday. Now he's back. That's all I know."

"Find out."

"He met with the woman cop last night."

"If you hadn't left the casing, I'd feel a lot better," Houser said. "Well, what's done is done. Do you have a contact in the woman's unit yet?"

"Yes, I do. Chatted up a girl in the mess hall. She's the one who told me that Vermeulen had been there again."

"Okay. Find out where the dead woman's things are. Get them. I want to make sure there's not a trace of anything that can point back to us. Got that?"

"Will do."

"So let's move on. Who else has he talked to?"

"He talked with Jirel."

"We know that. Anyone else?"

"Not to my knowledge. But that doesn't include those two days."

"Good. Keep me informed. In the meantime, we'll give Mr. Vermeulen a proper reception in Port Sudan."

* * *

CAPTAIN MANSOUR, THE HARBOR MASTER OF Port Sudan, rose from behind his desk. Vermeulen recognized him immediately. He was the same man who stood next to Houser in the photograph on the Arabic language webpage.

"Welcome, Mister …" he hesitated and looked at the card Vermeulen had handed the secretary.

"It's Vermeulen," Vermeulen said. "It's a Flemish name."

Mansour's lips curled in a feeble attempt at a smile. He was a short man with a big, round head. The black-rimmed glasses were too small, and the temples were bent out to reach his fleshy ears. Like his head, the captain's epaulettes on the white shirt seemed too large for his slight stature. Except for a mustache, his light-brown face was clean shaven. It had that stony expression of bureaucrats who compensate for their short stature by their use of power.

"Have a seat, Mr. Vermoolen. We don't often get visitors from the United Nations. What can I do for you?"

The man was already lying. His way of avoiding Vermeulen's eyes made it clear that he had no intention of doing anything for his visitor. Vermeulen had met enough of these characters to fill a field guide to bureaucrats. Usually the best strategy was to flatter them.

"Thank you for making time on a Saturday to see me."

"A port doesn't take the weekend off."

Vermeulen sat down. The chair was old but comfortable. The entire office looked a bit like the high-end antique shops he'd seen in Brugge. Dark wood paneling with matching desk, shelves, and furniture. *Just like a club*, he thought. *The only things missing are the cigar smoke and the glasses of sherry.* Mansour kept a neat desk. Two telephones and a radio transceiver took care of his communication needs. There were two trays, one to the left and one to the right of the blotter. Each had a stack of paper in it. A closed laptop sat on the right side of the desk.

"I'm here to follow up on a delivery of armored vehicles to one of the UN contingents in El Fasher. They arrived about ten months ago. I'd like to see the bill of lading and the end-user certificate."

The glint of recognition that flashed in Mansour's eyes was so short, Vermeulen almost missed it. Mansour knew why he was here.

The captain rubbed his earlobe and looked out the window at the harbor. "Ten months ago, you say?" He emitted a weary sigh. "That will be difficult."

"The shipper was a British company, Assured Sovereignty. The vehicles were shipped to a Nepali police unit."

"Assured Sovereignty? Never heard that name." Mansour moved a folder from the right stack to the left stack. The man was a terrible liar. "Is there any special reason for this request? I'm a busy man, you know."

No, Vermeulen wanted to say. I just came all the way to Port Sudan because I've got nothing better to do.

"I'm doing a routine audit," he said instead. "It's a small discrepancy. Probably just a mistaken transcription. A quick look at the paperwork is all I need."

Mansour leaned back in his chair. He sighed again, shook his head, and gave Vermeulen a bored look.

"What does your agency do?" Mansour lifted the card lying on the desk. "I've never heard of the Office of Internal Oversight Services."

"OIOS is a bureau at the New York headquarters. Sort of an in-house watchdog, making sure that everything is on the up-and-up. With the Americans always screaming about waste at the UN, we're trying to make sure there isn't any. Or at least fill out the proper forms to that effect. In the end it's all paperwork. I bet you have more than your fair share."

The harbor master's lips curled again. Another hint of a smile.

"Will you have some tea?"

Vermeulen didn't want tea, but he nodded anyway. No reason to annoy the man. Mansour lifted one of the telephone receivers.

"Bring tea," he said and put the receiver down. "Yes, paperwork, the bane of my existence." He moved the folder from the left to the right stack. "It would be nice if we could dispense with it. Alas, it's the way of the world. Do you have the date?"

"Yes, I do." Vermeulen handed him a sheet of paper that contained only the minimum information—date, name of shipper, name of agent.

"What kind of vehicles were these again?"

Vermeulen had the distinct feeling that the man was playing for time. Either that, or he was very slow on the uptake.

"Armored vehicles for the police unit."

"Yes, so you said." If Mansour had noticed Vermeulen's agitation, he gave no indication of it. "What about make and model? Were they new, used? All that would help us find the right paperwork."

"I'm sure that's all on your computers."

Captain Mansour attempted another smile. His tongue dashed out to moisten his lips.

"I'm afraid you've come a little too soon. Maybe a few more months and we will have computerized everything, but so far ...." He shrugged.

A knock on the door interrupted them. An assistant appeared carrying a tray with two glasses, a container of sugar, and a pot of tea. He placed the tray on Mansour's desk and poured tea. The man was in his early forties and had a narrow, brown face with a salt-and-pepper full beard and a sharp nose that gave him a hawkish appearance. He wore a double-breasted suit with peaked lapels that had gone out of style with the British Empire. Just like the office, he looked like he came straight from colonial times.

"Would you like sugar, sir?" he asked Vermeulen.

"Yes, one spoon, please."

The assistant stirred the tea with great deliberation. *Like a bloody Japanese tea ceremony*, Vermeulen thought. He felt the stare of the man's eyes. A quick glance confirmed the feeling. It was just a glance, but it made the hair on his neck rise. Behind the servile mask of the assistant loomed something different, something menacing. The man handed him the glass of tea on a saucer. Vermeulen caught the scent of rose oil. The man turned to Mansour and repeated the process. Finally, he withdrew.

"As I said," Mansour continued after taking a sip of tea, "the container port is newest, and all records there are computerized. The bulk freight and goods port is still a little behind. We'll have to search our records. So anything you can tell us about the shipment will speed up that process."

Mansour's posture still radiated bureaucratic indifference. But Vermeulen noted an edge to the man's voice. Was it hostile?

"They were Austrian-made armored personnel carriers, Pandur I, and they were shipped from the Czech Republic."

"So they were used?"

"Yes, they were."

"Good, I will direct my staff to find the relevant documents. Please come back Monday afternoon."

"Thank you, Captain Mansour. I appreciate your help. Is there any chance your staff might retrieve the paperwork sooner?"

Mansour's lips finally managed a real smile. Vermeulen had seen it on the faces of bureaucrats the world over.

"I'm afraid that is not possible. This is the weekend. Why not enjoy your time in Port Sudan? We have a bustling waterfront, and there are wonderful restaurants. You might find some compatriots at the International Club. Where are you staying?"

"The Hotel Mercury."

"Excellent choice. If you'll excuse me, I have work to do. I'll expect you Monday at fourteen hundred hours."

In the secretary's office sat a European—bald, with a ruddy complexion and big mustache. He was a big man, muscles tending toward fat, with a thick neck, broad shoulders, and a wide chest. He wore the kind of khaki outfit, part uniform, part casual, that had become the quasi-uniform of private military contractors during the second Iraq war.

The man checked him out. Vermeulen looked back and nodded. The man's eyes were pale and blank, no emotion, nothing. Not someone you'd want to meet alone in a dark alley.

* * *

VERMEULEN TOOK A TAXI BACK TO the Port Sudan Hotel. He didn't know why he'd given the harbor master the wrong hotel name. Was it the searching look of the assistant? The edge in Mansour's voice when he left? The fact that the harbor master had lied about not knowing Assured Sovereignty? Whatever it was, he might need the extra time the lie bought him.

He was prepared for the wait. It gave him the opportunity to make other inquiries. After taking a shower and changing into fresh clothes, he called room service and asked for beer. The steward informed him politely that the hotel only offered nonalcoholic beer. He bit his tongue to keep from swearing. Of course! He was still in Sudan. For a moment, the décor had fooled him. He checked with the concierge and yes, the International Club had a restaurant that nonmembers could use. He decided to go for a stroll first.

Since the days of British colonial rule, the coast around Port Sudan had been called the Red Sea Riviera. It still was a destination for holiday makers, but the international sanctions had cut down on foreign tourists' travel. The once-splendid corniche along the water's edge, with its benches, palm trees, and open-air restaurants, had the dispirited atmosphere of a seaside town in winter.

Sunlight twinkling on the wavelets, a blue sky stretched to the horizon, warm weather: a perfect afternoon to be by the sea. He'd always preferred the shore. The salty air, the breeze, the squawking of gulls usually brightened his mood and lifted his spirits. Not this time. A dull sense of menace hung in the air. Vermeulen was convinced that Mansour knew why he was there. He'd seen it in his eyes. The authorization from the Under-Secretary-General was useless here. Especially if there was trouble.

He strolled toward the city, drifting past buildings from the British colonial era interspersed with new construction. The grandeur of the colonial buildings had faded—the whitewash no longer white, the window frames peeling and crooked. Still, they were more attractive than the newer structures.

Late-afternoon traffic flowed by with the usual din of cities where horns substitute for brakes. He passed a park and a building with Arabic and English signs designating it as the Legislative Council. An imposing monument stood in the middle of an intersection. He turned right and was surprised to see two steeples of a good-sized Coptic Christian church.

A pleasant breeze blew from the Red Sea, bringing with it the smell of salt and fish. It reminded him that he hadn't eaten since a meager snack on the plane from El Fasher. He continued past the College of Engineering and reached another quay facing the old port area. A rusty bulk-goods freighter had docked across the water and was being unloaded. Probably the same place where the APCs had been lifted to shore.

On his side of the water, an open market hall displayed the day's catch spread out in plastic trays and buckets. Having grown up near the North Sea, he'd been around fish markets for most of his life. This one was no different. The salty, tangy smell of fresh fish and the slippery shimmer of scales transported him back home. Except here, the fish were colorful—blue, purple, and pink hues along with the usual shades of steel he remembered from Antwerp.

Outside the market, a man stood by a hut tending several charcoal braziers. He gestured. It took Vermeulen a moment to understand that he was to pick out a fish and bring it over to have it cooked. He chose a fish, paid for it, and brought it to the man. With deft movements, the man sliced, gutted, and filleted the fish. He pointed to two bowls with different colored marinades. Thinking that red would be the hottest, Vermeulen chose the greenish one. The man dipped the fillets into the marinade and slapped them on the grill. Five minutes later, Vermeulen sat on a concrete bench, paper plate in hand, and ate the best fish he'd had in a long time.

He watched the freighter being unloaded across the water. It occurred to him that coming here hadn't been such a smart decision. All he'd get would be some doctored paperwork. The harbor master had no reason to give him anything that might help this case. He'd already disavowed knowing anything about Assured Sovereignty, which meant that he had to find what he needed a different way. The International Club, if it lived up to its name, would be the place to find journalists and other expats hanging out. Maybe they knew something.

He strolled along the corniche until the sun painted the clouds over the Red Sea the color of blood oranges. The pedestrians seemed in a hurry. White-collar employees wore the usual dark trousers and white shirt uniform. Those employed in less remunerative settings wore blue overalls; sometimes jeans and a T-shirt, and occasionally, a *jalabiya* and *kofia*. The women's dress varied from long gowns that showed nothing but their face to jeans and shirts with just a thin scarf to cover their hair.

He stopped to look at the window of an appliance store. The shop was closed, but the display offered well-lit machines for modern living. Most of the stoves and washers were Chinese-made. More expensive models came from Germany and Sweden.

In the reflection in the window, he saw pedestrians walk past him. About to turn back into the flow, he saw Mansour's assistant pass behind him. The old-fashioned suit was unmistakable. He froze. That couldn't be a coincidence.

CHAPTER EIGHTEEN

———◆———

THE SIGHT OF MANSOUR'S ASSISTANT RATTLED Vermeulen. The weary feeling of being on a futile mission disappeared. Adrenaline took its place.

He crossed University Street and walked toward the city center. Nobody followed him. He stopped at random moments, looked back, continued again. Still no suspicious characters. Twice, he doubled back suddenly. No suspicious faces hurriedly looking the other way. He dashed across the street and ducked into a dark passage. From behind the stone wall, he watched people pass by, committing every face to memory. Five minutes later, he continued around the block. A man came toward him. He recognized the face. The man had walked by the passage only a few minutes earlier. They were after him. He shivered, despite the warm air. The meeting with Mansour had stirred things up. He wasn't sure whether that was a good thing or not.

Once he knew who to look for, the surveillance was obvious. At least two men followed him to the waterfront. They stopped when he stopped, even if there was nothing to see, but were careful about it and kept their distance. At one point, just a block before the corniche, one of the watchers talked on his mobile phone. As Vermeulen crossed University Street again, he saw the bald European he'd seen in Mansour's office standing at the railing, staring at the water.

The International Club stood right on the water's edge where the quay curved to the west. It occupied a surprisingly large area. Next to the building, a large veranda offered spectacular views of both the old port and the container port. Vermeulen went inside.

The restaurant wasn't busy. Only three tables were occupied. Two waiters stood by the bar, looking bored. Cigarette smoke hung in the air. There were no women in the room. Vermeulen didn't know if they were prohibited or if they had better places to go. A group of expatriates occupied a large table in the rear. Their conversation was noisy. The very people he was looking for.

Virgin cocktails dressed up like the real thing were the drink of choice as far as he could tell. He ordered orange juice.

A ruddy-looking man with blond hair and mustache joined him at the bar.

"Gimme another of these daiquiris," he said to the bartender. "Bloody country," he said, turning his head. "Bad enough to be reporting from such a stinking hot place. But they gotta rub it in by banning booze. It's what's wrong with this place, if you ask me. Wouldn't be shooting at each other if they sat down and had a drink together." He stuck out his hand. "Luke Waters, Evening Standard."

"Couldn't agree with you more. Valentin Vermeulen." He shook Waters' hand.

"What brings you here? Newshound like the rest of us?"

Vermeulen hesitated a moment. Should he be open about why he was here? Better not. A cover would be useful.

"Yeah. Freelancer. Doing a piece on the UN mission."

"A bit far from the action, aren't you?"

"Nah. Just checking the supply lines. You know, the nitty-gritty that makes everything go 'round."

Waters nodded.

"Why don't you join us? We usually complain, argue, and shout at each other. It's the best fun in town."

"Sure."

They picked up their glasses and walked over to the table. Waters pulled up another chair.

"Listen up, folks, this here is Valentin. Poor sod is a freelancer."

A collective groan rose from the table.

"It's people like you who take our jobs," a dark-haired man with a sharp nose said.

"Shut up, Tito," Waters said. "Valentin's just trying to make a living like the rest of us." He turned to Vermeulen. "Tito here is always complaining, but never about the right things. It's the bleeding bean counters at our head offices who are killing our jobs."

Everybody nodded in agreement. Waters introduced the rest of the group.

"Over there's Shawn." He pointed to a large man with the ruddy face of a heavy drinker, wearing a vest with many pockets. "He's a photographer and all-around factotum from the *Daily Mail and Guardian* in Jo'burg. He can get you anything, if you know what I mean. Next to him sits Max, the fading

Africa star of the *Frankfurter Allgemeine*." Max had the unhealthy pallor of someone who hates being outside. He seemed an unlikely candidate for an Africa correspondent.

"You've already heard from unfriendly Tito. He represents *El País*. There's Antonio, *Corriere della Sera*. He's a man with the endless enthusiasm of youth. Don't let him talk you into anything. It'll wear you out and probably get you into trouble." Antonio did indeed have the rugged good looks of an outdoorsman—tan face, dark blond hair.

"And then there's Basil from the *Independent*. He's been around since Kitchener defeated the Mahdists at Omdurman." The man had a weathered face of indeterminable age. He wore a light suit, cut as old-fashioned as that of Mansour's assistant; a white shirt with tie; and sturdy shoes. Add a pith helmet and he could indeed have accompanied Kitchener at Omdurman a century ago.

"Hand over your drink," Shawn said.

Vermeulen was confused.

"I'm assuming you'd really like some vodka in your OJ." Shawn held his hand out.

Vermeulen grinned and handed over his glass. Shawn poured a healthy portion of vodka from a bottle he kept in his bag. No wonder the group was so boisterous.

"Valentin is here to cover the nuts and bolts of the UN mission. Tell us about it," Waters said.

"Not much to say. It's a background piece. All the things that go on behind the scenes of a peacekeeping mission that usually don't make the news."

"Because it's boring!" Tito shouted. "Who wants to read about a bunch of bureaucrats shuffling paper?"

"Will you just shut up, you Spanish hack," Basil said. "It can't all be bullfights. There's news everywhere. It's just that none of you sons-of-bitches know how to write about it. What brings you this far north, Valentin?"

"Supply lines. Everything going to Darfur and the South comes through Port Sudan. I'm talking to the harbor master. You know, can the port handle all that cargo? What are the bottlenecks? That kind of thing."

"Good old Mansour," Max said. "Always with that Sphinx smile on his fat face. Notice how he never actually tells you anything. A year or so ago, I was following up on the story of Chinese helicopters that came here despite the embargo. He gave me the runaround without ever being rude. Had to bribe one of the freight handlers to get the scoop. Then my editor spiked the story."

"I'm supposed to come back Monday for whatever information he can dig up," Vermeulen said.

"Good luck with that. I bet you a week's worth of rum that he won't have anything. Just an apologetic smile."

"How did those Chinese helicopters get here?" Vermeulen asked.

"Well, China sells them, of course. But they don't want to annoy the rest of the Security Council too much, so they use intermediaries for the actual delivery."

"Would you know who those middlemen are?"

"Your usual crop of crooked operators. They create a new company in some tax haven just for one transaction, if it's big enough."

"Was Assured Sovereignty one of those involved with the helicopters?"

Max shook his head and took a long swallow from his daiquiri. "I'm not sure, would have to check my notes." Valentin saw Basil examine him and turn away when he noticed Vermeulen's glance.

"What about the peace talks at Doha?" Waters said, shifting the conversation to a new topic. "Movement toward peace or more of the same?"

"That's just talk," Antonio said. "In the meantime, al-Bashir's been shifting troops into El Fasher. Rumor has it that he's just attacked the UJM."

"Where'd you hear that?"

"You gotta keep your ear to the ground."

"Nonsense, it would have been in the news here. There was nothing."

"Maybe it didn't go as they hoped. My sources confirmed the attack. Masaad and most of his men got away."

"This is big," Tito said. "They really tried to catch Masaad?"

"They did," Vermeulen said and instantly regretted having opened his mouth. All faces turned to him.

"Our new friend seems to have the scoop," Basil said. "Pray tell."

"The attack took place three days ago. And, yes, the UJM got away with minor casualties. The army lost a helicopter in the process."

"Ouch," Antonio said. "That's gotta hurt. With the embargo and all."

"He'll get another one from his friends in Beijing," Max said.

"Who needs a refill?" Shawn said.

Vermeulen wanted to avoid further questions and went to get another glass of juice. While he waited for the bartender, Basil joined him.

"You, my friend, seem to have access to unusual information," he said.

"Oh, it's nothing special. I've been hanging around the UNAMID headquarters in El Fasher for the past week."

"Strange, the UN hasn't released any statement related to the clash. They usually do when there's a violation of the ceasefire."

"Hmm. Maybe it's still coming. That's where I heard it."

"I don't believe that, and I don't believe you're a freelancer, either. What are you after?"

There was no hint of a threat in Basil's voice. Vermeulen was not sure what there was, and he didn't want to find out.

"I don't know what you're talking about."

Basil raised both hands, palms out.

"I'm just curious. Port Sudan is a small place when it comes to foreigners. Every new arrival is of interest, especially when they have knowledge not available to mere mortals."

The bartender brought them their drinks, orange juice for Vermeulen and tonic water for Basil.

They walked back to the table.

"I've been in Sudan for a while now, and I know my way around," Basil said. "Maybe I can help. Let's talk."

He slipped his card into Vermeulen's jacket pocket as they reached the table.

Was Basil a spy? Maybe he was just full of himself.

Vermeulen excused himself and meandered to the veranda. The security lights twinkled on the dark waters, giving the harbor a festive appearance. He chose a table concealed from the street and ordered lamb chops with rice and vegetables. The plate arrived rather quickly. As he began to eat, Basil joined him, carrying a bowl of hummus in one hand and a plate of flatbread in the other.

"So tell me what you are really looking for," he said, a smile playing around his lips. He dipped a piece of bread into the hummus, popped it into his mouth, and chewed.

"Why don't you tell me who you really are?"

"Fair enough. I'm Basil Macklevore, just as Waters said. I write for the *Independent*. I also gather information. Like your information about Masaad getting away and the army helicopter being shot down."

"What do you do with that information?"

"I give it to my friends."

"And these friends are?"

"Knowing too much is often a burden. Let's just leave it at that."

"No, let's not. Are you MI6, CIA? What?"

"My friends work closely with both. That's all I can say."

So Basil was a spy. But who was he working for? Until Vermeulen knew that, there was no upside to telling him the truth.

"Just as I said, a freelancer working on a UNAMID story," Vermeulen said. "Looking for background, details, whatever I can find."

"What kind of details?"

Vermeulen took out his phone, found the photo of Dale Houser, and showed it to Basil.

"Like who this fellow is and if he's been here lately."

Basil's smile faded as he stared at the picture. He took another dip of hummus, leaned back, and looked out at the harbor. Vermeulen sliced off a piece of lamb and chewed. The lights of the freighters across the water sparkled against the dark sky.

"I would be careful showing that picture around," Macklevore said. "Dale Houser likes his privacy."

"Who doesn't? What do you know about him?"

"Depends. Why are you looking for him?"

"His name came up in conversations."

"What kind of conversations?"

"Logistics. That's all I can say. How do you know him?"

"It's hard not to. His services are indispensable to many parties."

"Why?"

"Many reasons."

"Is he here?"

"Yes. Are you sure you don't want to tell me why you're looking for him?"

"No offense, Basil, but I don't know you from Adam. I just came here to eat, then you show up and start asking questions."

* * *

VERMEULEN TOOK A CAB BACK TO his hotel. No need to give someone an opportunity to drag him into a dark corner. He checked frequently to make sure nobody was following. The streets weren't empty, but traffic was light. He saw nothing. The watchers had gone home.

The night porter nodded when Vermeulen crossed the lobby. The elevator dinged its way up to the fourth floor. Turning into the corridor leading to his room, Vermeulen heard music, which surprised him. The hotel had been very quiet when he checked in. The volume of the music increased as he approached his door. Just his luck. A whole hotel full of rooms and his had to be next to some backpackers who got their hands on smuggled booze and decided to party. He hesitated a moment and thought of going down to ask for a different room. It seemed too much of a hassle.

He inserted the key card into the slot over the door handle. A little green light blinked. The lock clicked. He pushed the door open. The music was suddenly loud and familiar. It came from his room.

Had he forgotten to turn off his iPod? He'd played "London Calling" while dressing after the shower. He was sure he'd turned the music off. And he hadn't played it this loud.

The room was dark.

He didn't remember closing the curtains. Maybe the maid did that after she turned down the bed. She could have left the music on as well. But there hadn't been any maids about when he checked in or when he came back to shower. This wasn't the kind of hotel where they turned down the bed. Besides, if they did, they'd leave on a light, wouldn't they?

The Clash opened the next song. "When they kick at your front door, how you gonna come? With your hands on your head or the trigger of your gun?"

Neither, he thought. *I'm going to run.*

It was too late.

Two hands grabbed his arm and yanked him into the room. The door fell shut. A different arm closed around his neck from behind, choking him. He opened his mouth, gasping for air. A hand forced a gag into his mouth. He retched. The arm around his neck loosened a little. The scent of rose oil was in the air. Mansour's assistant, and someone else.

Vermeulen's first assessment was that they weren't out to kill him. They could have done that on the street. Less messy and easier to get away. And they wouldn't have needed a gag.

That meant fighting back was an option. He jammed his right elbow back. It smashed into a rib. The man behind him grunted and hissed something in Arabic. The arm around his neck fell away. He spun around and followed with a powerful roundhouse. His fist struck a face. Someone screamed. He turned to face whoever else was in the room.

That was a mistake.

A fist hit his stomach, burying itself deep in his gut. All the wind left his body. He folded at the hips. He wanted to scream, but with the gag only managed a muffled sound. He fell to the floor. He retched. The half-digested lamb dinner rose up his gullet. It got stuck in his throat, where it burned like acid. Choking to death on your own vomit. What a pathetic death. He swallowed desperately to clear his throat. There was no saliva.

He should have stayed in El Fasher. What had he expected, waltzing into Mansour's office? That the man would cooperate, turn over the evidence? Waving the authorization from the Under-Secretary-General in people's faces had given him a false sense of security. He should have turned around the moment he recognized Mansour's face.

Before he could spin that thought further, a vicious kick hit him in the ribs, sending fireworks through his left side. Another kick hit his kidneys and a red-hot wire seemed to cut his lower body in half. He curled into a fetal position, sucking air through his nose like a desperate cocaine addict.

Two hands pulled him up and twisted his arms back. The pain was worse than he imagined pain could be. He tried to shout against the gag. Again, to no avail. He sensed a face next to his ear. The rose oil scent became overpowering.

"Mr. Vermoolen. Do you hear me?"

Vermeulen couldn't answer.

"Mr. Vermoolen, stop asking questions. Go back home. Or you will die like the policewoman."

They tied his arms together, then let him fall to the floor. When his head bounced on the carpet, he managed to spit out the gag. Vomit trickled down his cheek and neck. A last kick into his groin drove home the point of the visit with terrible efficiency.

* * *

WHEN HE REGAINED CONSCIOUSNESS, THE CLASH were singing something about having been beaten up but not being down. Nothing could have been further from the truth.

He lay in the dark on his right side, his head on a damp circle of carpet, his hands and feet tied, his knees pulled to his chin, pain flashing through his body like a massive atmospheric disturbance. A roll call of body parts confirmed they were all present, albeit not functioning properly. He tried to roll onto his back. He might as well have tried rolling onto a bed of hot coals. He was definitely down.

He remained on the floor, drifting out of consciousness whenever the pain grew overwhelming. His iPod had long since reached the end of the playlist. The illuminated digits of the alarm clock on the bedside table kept track of his meanders along the edge of awareness. At two in the morning, his brain asserted a bit more control and he assessed his situation.

They didn't kill him. Which meant that they didn't want the trouble of having the UN investigate the death of one of its employees.

He'd gotten close enough to attract their attention. But not close enough to find the evidence.

He needed proof.

To do that, he had to free himself. He could scream or kick against the door to attract the attention of his neighbors. The night porter would come, then the police. There'd be an investigation. They'd ask him what he was doing in Port Sudan. The UN would be contacted. Bengtsson would have a fit.

He decided to leave his neighbors alone and started rubbing the rope tying his hands against the corner of the bathroom wall.

CHAPTER NINETEEN

───────◆───────

Sunday, March 21, 2010

Along shower and a hefty dose of painkillers made it possible to move again. The toll on his body was mixed. Oddly, his attackers had left his face alone. The midriff had taken the brunt of the attack. Intricate purple blotches bloomed all over. Maybe he'd cracked a rib. His groin pulsed with a dull ache in the rhythm of his heartbeat.

He took his penknife, cut a long strip from the sheet, and tried to wrap it around his chest. He groaned when the arm movements caused new flashes of pain to breach the barrier of the painkillers. It had to be tight to do any good. When he finally knotted the ends, he sank onto his bed, drenched in sweat again. Twenty minutes later, he put on a fresh shirt.

So much for the easy part. The difficult part was figuring out what to do next. Half-sitting, half-lying on the bed, he sorted out what he knew. Mansour was involved. There was no other way to explain the attack. That meant the harbor master had the documentation for the APC fraud. He didn't look like the kind of man who'd do his dirty business from home. He didn't need to. It had to be in his office.

Vermeulen tried to recall what security features he'd seen at Mansour's office. Nothing stuck out in his memory. No number pads on the wall requiring codes, no readers through which one slid ID cards. Just a plain old building. Solid construction, to be sure, but nothing that was designed to keep out intruders.

The night porter was surprised by his early checkout, but for a generous tip, was more than happy to store his suitcase.

A taxi trolling for early customers dropped him at the entrance to the old port at four thirty in the morning. A little shack did brisk business peddling black coffee to day laborers. Apparently, ships arrived at all hours and needed to be unloaded. The first hit of the acrid brew threatened to turn his stomach again, but then the caffeine kicked his circulation into gear. A sweet roll, a second cup, and another analgesic later, he felt somewhat restored.

The workers headed for the hiring hall eyed him with curiosity. Europeans usually didn't come this early. He ignored the looks and hoped they'd forget him. When he could make out the harbor master's building, he stopped. The yellow glow from the sodium-halogen security lighting showed the peeling paint and a gutter hanging down from the edge of the roof.

Seeing the structure gave him second thoughts. Back at the hotel, breaking and entering had sounded like a reasonable idea. Maybe it was the painkillers talking. Now, it seemed preposterous. He only had his penknife and lighter. If caught, he'd have no protection whatsoever. He could imagine the headlines. *Rogue investigator caught in burglary. UN disavows any relationship.*

A small lamp lit a desk inside the main entrance. A guard dozed in his chair. Vermeulen thought about blustering his way past him using his UN credentials. That might get him inside. Without a key to Mansour's office, he'd be stuck inside, and the guard would be able to identify him later.

He circled to the back and found a rear door. It was unguarded, but locked. No good. Finally, along the port-facing side of the building behind a row of bushes, he found a steel trapdoor leading to the basement. The hinges and latch were rusted. He tried the handle. It barely budged. The effort made the dull pain of the bruised kidney and ribs flare red-hot. He stopped, breathing heavily. Gritting his teeth, he tried again. The pain in his side made him want to scream. He clamped his lips tight.

A rusty groan sounded through the still morning air. He stopped and listened.

Nothing.

He stepped on the brick frame and grabbed the handle with both hands. Slivers of rust dug into his palms. His last tetanus shot had better still be good. He yanked the door the rest of the way open. The mournful screech of the door covered his moan of agony. It echoed across the water. He clambered into the darkness beyond and lowered the door slowly.

A dank, dark space lay below. He flicked his lighter and saw the outlines of a low basement. Moldy boxes were stacked along one wall. The flame of his lighter didn't illuminate anything else. He inched forward, hoping to find a door. The flame showed the outlines of a staircase. He eased up, one step at a time. At the top, he bumped into a pile of boxes that blocked the way to the door. *Great.* Some lazy clerk had just left them there. He tossed the boxes down the stairs. The door at the top of the stairs opened without objection.

He found himself in a dark corridor. There were no lighted exit signs or other indicators. The day before, he'd walked straight from the front entrance to Mansour's office. This hallway branched off from the main one. He felt his way forward until he reached the corner of the main hallway. Far at its right end, he could see the lamp on the guard's desk. The guard was not sitting there. Vermeulen turned left and found Mansour's door.

He had no tools to pick a lock, and even if he had, he wouldn't have known how to use them. He fingered the door handle. Nothing more than a simple Yale lock. Since he had no key, it was enough to stop him. The door felt solid, not one of those thin, chipboard jobs. Feeling along the edges, he noticed that it opened inward. If the doorframe was as old as the building, there was a chance of breaking it open. He knew enough not to use his shoulder. The movies had it all wrong. He took a step back, aimed, and gave the door a sharp kick just below the handle. It sprung open with the sound of wood being wrenched from nails.

He peered around the corner. The guard was still away from his desk. The outside doorframe looked unharmed. Nothing appeared to be amiss.

Vermeulen stepped into Mansour's office and closed the door. He pushed the pieces of the doorframe back into shape as well as he could and dropped the splinters from the floor into his pocket. He checked his watch. Five thirty. He'd better hurry.

The colonial feel of the room was just as strong as the day before. Dust motes danced in rays from the security light filtering through the wooden slats of the blinds. He closed them and turned on the desk lamp. The work surface was as neat as he remembered. The two trays with papers, the telephones, and the marine radio sat as if aligned with a ruler. The laptop was gone.

The trays on the desk seemed unchanged from the afternoon before. Except that a familiar-looking document lay on top of the left one: the paperwork for the armored personnel carriers. The word 'NEW' in the box specifying the vehicles' condition looked just as doctored as it did on the copy he had in El Fasher. But this copy clearly showed that someone had applied correctional fluid and typed the word. It was a shoddy job. Still, without the original, he had nothing.

On the walls behind the desk stood bookshelves covered by glass doors. Behind those doors he saw ancient tomes with gold-lettered backs. Some had English titles, others sported Arabic script.

Solid doors concealed the contents of the bottom shelves. He opened one of them and found large binders. The one he pulled out held documents in Arabic script. He put it back.

He stood back and let his gaze wander around the room. As important as Mansour's job was, this office was decidedly low tech. Paper was still the primary means of communication. So the original document had to be somewhere. But where? A safe. Vermeulen lifted the large framed photograph of General al-Bashir on the wall behind the desk. No safe. The remaining walls were bare, and it didn't make sense to put a safe behind the bookshelves.

The harbor master had acted like a man fully convinced of his own importance, the kind of boss who'd tyrannize those working for him. They might mock him secretly but would never dare to disobey him. Mansour had no reason to hide things, because he knew no one would dare snoop in his office.

Vermeulen sat behind the desk and tried the drawers. They were locked. The keyholes looked like they would take simple skeleton keys. The blade of his penknife did the trick.

The first drawer contained more folders in Arabic script of no use to him. The second drawer offered a more useful bounty—a fat folder full of documents in English. At the top lay the same form he'd found on the desk tray. Except this one specified the condition of the APCs as 'USED.'

That's when he heard steps outside the door.

It was six o'clock. Office hours shouldn't begin this early. Was the guard making his last round? A rivulet of sweat ran down his back. The antique furniture in the room offered no hiding place. He tiptoed to the door leading to the reception area. It was locked. The desk was the only option, and not much of a cover at that. Anyone stepping around it would see him immediately. He ducked under it.

A key turned in the lock. The door opened. Light from the hallway flooded the room. Steps approached the desk. The scent of rose oil filled the air. Vermeulen held his breath. Of all people, the assistant had to show up now. As much as he wanted to tackle him, he was in no condition to do that.

The man dropped something on the desk. The steps retreated to the door, then stopped. Vermeulen heard him suck in a breath and mutter what sounded like an Arabic curse. He must have seen the broken doorframe. The assistant shouted something into the corridor. Vermeulen heard him running away.

Vermeulen crawled out from under the desk. He grabbed the folder from the drawer, slipped the doctored copy into it, and shoved it under his shirt and into his pants. At the door, he peered around the corner and saw the assistant shouting at the guard at the entrance. The guard wasn't taking it and shouted back.

There would be no better time to leave. Vermeulen crossed the corridor with three large steps. In the side hallway, he stopped and listened. The shouting at the entrance had stopped. They'd noticed his escape. Someone ran toward him.

The side corridor was still dark, but he knew the basement door was too far. He opened the closest door and slipped inside. It was a small space. The odor of industrial cleaners told him that he'd found a janitor's closet. There was a vent grille in the door. The corridor lights came on. He peered through the slits and saw the assistant come to a stop on the other side of the door.

The man looked back and forth, searching. Then his face turned toward the closet. He reached for the door handle. The handle moved down slowly. When it was down all the way, Vermeulen pushed the door open with all his strength. It wasn't as much of a surprise as he had hoped for. Still, the door slammed into the man on the other side and sent him tumbling backwards. Vermeulen dashed toward the basement door. The assistant scrambled forward and tried to block him. Vermeulen stopped, turned, lowered his shoulder, and gave the man his best rugby tackle. His bruised side complained bitterly about this sudden exertion, but it did the job. The assistant landed on the floor again.

Before Vermeulen could turn toward the basement door, the assistant's hand grabbed his foot and yanked him off balance. He crashed to the floor. His sore rib sent a firestorm through his chest. It took his breath away.

The assistant saw his chance. He jumped on top of him.

A knife gleamed in the light.

He drove it into Vermeulen's gut.

Chapter Twenty

---◆---

Vermeulen saw the knife coming. He tried to roll away. The assistant on top of him was too heavy.

The blade struck.

Vermeulen felt the impact. But instead of slicing through his stomach wall, the knife stopped with a dull thud.

He remembered. The folder. The knife was stuck in the papers Vermeulen had stuck down his pants. The assistant tried to yank it out. It took some effort. That gave Vermeulen the chance he needed. He jammed his knee into the man's gut. The assistant groaned and fell to the side. Vermeulen jumped up and kicked the knife away. The assistant raised himself onto his hands and knees and crawled toward the knife. Vermeulen kicked him again, this time in the groin.

Outside, he ran until he found a taxi that brought him back to his hotel. The night porter at the Port Sudan Hotel had been replaced by the regular day staff. They eyed Vermeulen with suspicion when he walked into the reception area, his jacket and pants filthy from the basement of the harbor master's building.

He ignored their stares, traded the receipt for his suitcase, and left the hotel. A small restaurant two streets farther offered a more substantial breakfast. He put the document folder into his bag, found Macklevore's card in his pocket, and called the number. Despite the early hour, Macklevore answered on the second ring.

"It's Vermeulen. I need to get out of Port Sudan, fast."

"I take it your visit didn't go as planned."

"No, I was ambushed in my hotel last night."

"Where are you?"

Vermeulen gave him the name of the restaurant.

"Look for a blue Datsun taxi. It'll be there in fifteen minutes."

That was fast. A little too fast. How could Macklevore organize a getaway so quickly? Okay, so Macklevore was a spook, but even spooks needed lead time to organize escapes.

Exactly fifteen minutes later, a battered blue Datsun drove up. Vermeulen grabbed his roll-on and hurried to the cab. The driver took off before Vermeulen could close the door. He sped around the next corner, darted between two cars, crossed an intersection, passed a bus, and almost immediately braked hard before swerving into a courtyard. There, a black Peugeot 408 with tinted windows waited, its rear door open.

"This way, Mr. Vermeulen," Macklevore called from the backseat of the Peugeot.

He hauled his carry-on into the Peugeot and settled on the rear seat. The car took off immediately.

"What happened?" Macklevore said.

"I have a few questions first. Let's start with who you really are."

"I'm Basil Macklevore, just as I told you. I'm a journalist and collector of information."

"And the employer you mentioned last night?"

"A private concern. That's all you need to know at the moment."

"How did you organize this pickup so quickly?"

"I had you watched since you left the club last night. Yes, I know you ventured into Mansour's office at some ungodly hour and broke in. I was pretty sure that afterwards you'd need to get out of town fast. I was the only contact you had in Port Sudan, so I was prepared. You want to tell me what's going on?"

Vermeulen gave him a quick summary of the attack.

"Ouch. My condolences," Macklevore said. "I knew Fareed had a nasty disposition, but this is by far the worst."

"That's Mansour's assistant?"

"The very same. What were you doing at Mansour's office?"

He told him about the burglary, omitting the fact that he'd taken a whole folder rather than just the documents related to the APCs.

"Sounds like Fareed has finally gotten his comeuppance." Macklevore laughed. "I've been wanting to kick him in the nuts for a long time. He acts so damn superior. Breaking into Mansour's office is a different kettle of fish, though. They know who you are, and they are going to arrest you the moment they get their hands on you."

Vermeulen figured as much. He looked out the window.

"I need to know more about Dale Houser," Vermeulen said.

"There isn't much to know. Dale Houser is a businessman and a British subject."

The Peugeot stopped at a traffic light. Vermeulen didn't know where they were driving, whether Macklevore was just giving him a tour of the city or headed to a specific destination. He looked around for familiar landmarks. There weren't any.

A black SUV waited behind them. In the passenger seat of the car sat a man wearing a double-breasted suit with peaked lapels.

"We're being followed," he shouted to Macklevore. "Fareed is in the car behind us. I don't think he's here by accident."

Macklevore turned around and shook his head. "These guys have no tradecraft. Who'd pull up directly behind the car they're supposed to follow?" He turned to the driver. "Lose them."

The driver didn't wait for the light to change. He accelerated without warning and turned right. Not buckled in, Vermeulen was thrown against Macklevore. The Peugeot bumped the corner of a vegetable cart. Looking out the rear window, Vermeulen saw tomatoes rolling on the street and the vendor shaking his fist. He found a new target for his anger when the SUV behind them squished the tomatoes as it tried to catch up.

Port Sudan's streets were laid out in a grid, which made dodging the pursuer a question of speed or trickery. Macklevore's driver chose speed. Vermeulen struggled to insert the flat end of the seatbelt into the buckle. At random intervals, the driver slammed on the brakes and squealed into a cross street. Each turn pressed Vermeulen's bruised body against the belt or the door. The painkillers had worn off, and he felt as sore as he had when he woke up that morning.

The driver's racing through Port Sudan didn't help. He swerved into the oncoming traffic lane to pass a delivery van. A car came straight at them. The driver didn't care. Vermeulen's panic made his pain seem trivial. He wanted to shout at the driver, tell him to turn back into their lane. His mouth was dry, the only sound coming out a croak. He could see the eyes of the people in the oncoming car widen with fear. They were only inches away. Vermeulen braced for the impact. It didn't come. The driver threw the steering wheel to the right at the last possible moment and slid back into traffic.

Macklevore talked into his mobile as if he had no concern in the world. Twice he gave the driver new directions. They meant nothing to Vermeulen. At the last instruction, the driver threw the Peugeot into a sudden U-turn. More distraught car horns. The face of a woman in another car flew by his window. It was twisted with fear. Vermeulen knew exactly how she felt. They crossed another intersection.

"Now!" Macklevore shouted into his phone.

A cacophony of honking rose behind them. Vermeulen turned and saw a large truck pull into the intersection. It stopped. Its driver got out and lifted the cover of the engine compartment as if he had no other worry in the world.

"Finally," Macklevore said. "It took a while to coordinate that maneuver."

* * *

AT SUNRISE, THE *GLORIA* DOCKED AT the container wharf of Port Sudan. Dock workers threw the rope loops over rusty bollards; the sailors aboard the *Gloria* tightened them. Then all activity ceased. As in Umm Qasr, the crew was given shore leave, but only four hours. It was enough time to get into town and find a decent breakfast. The cook on the *Gloria* wasn't what one would call good.

At eight o'clock, the crane operator began his long climb to the cab some fifty yards up. Several Port Corporation trucks were lined up, idling. A little to the side, a Volvo truck without the Port Corporation signage waited, the empty trailer's kingpin securely locked in the fifth wheel coupling. Its driver had very specific instructions.

At eight thirty, the crane came to life. The trolley moved above the *Gloria*, the spreader descended, its twistlocks attached to the four corner castings of the first container. The rust-orange steel box rose thirty feet into the air, traveled back toward the front apron, went down again, and hit the first trailer with a bang. The operator released the spreader, and the trailer's suspension groaned as the full weight of the cargo hit the springs. The driver engaged the trailer's twistlocks and drove off.

The next ten containers were deposited on the quay, where a reach stacker picked them up and brought them to stacks near the rear of the dock. After that, a few trucks were loaded again.

The radio in the Volvo's cab crackled and a voice said something in Arabic. The driver navigated past several waiting trucks and stopped under the crane. A blue box labeled 'Excelsior' came down to the trailer. The bang and groan repeated themselves. The driver secured the container and drove off.

The container port was surrounded by a tall security fence topped with razor wire. Pilfering was a bane of shipping everywhere. The fence and two guards at the gate were supposed to prevent that. The driver showed his ID and the paperwork for his cargo. Everything was in order. He drove off.

From the port he headed south, out of town toward the airport. He'd done this run before. Nothing special, except it netted him a little extra cash, which came in handy now that his wife was pregnant again.

He'd prayed that his second child be a son, a strong boy who'd make something better of his life. But his three-year-old daughter was such a delight, he sometimes forgot why he wanted a son. Until he thought of her marrying some man fifteen years down the road. Then his insides got all twisted up. He lit a cigarette to dispel such thoughts. It was a long time until then. Times change. Women did things these days. Maybe she'd be successful and take care of her parents when they got old.

In the meantime, the extra money was welcome.

About halfway to the airport, the city limits behind him and the desert ahead, he turned into the yard of a gray aluminum warehouse. There was a series of such warehouses on either side of the road, all equally unremarkable. This one sported a small sign: Assured Logistics.

The gate, a tall steel- and razor-wire contraption, matched the fence that surrounded the warehouse. It had been rolled to the side. A guard raised a red-and-white boom when he saw the truck slowing down.

Once past the entrance, the driver turned toward the wall and backed the trailer against the tall door in the long side of the warehouse. The air brakes vented with a loud sigh. He switched the engine off.

A bald European approached the cab. He wore the usual European uniform of khaki trousers and shirt.

"Any problems?" the man said.

The driver shook his head.

"Okay, then."

CHAPTER TWENTY-ONE

———— ◆ ————

MACKLEVORE'S DRIVER DROVE THEM OUT OF town to a warehouse. It was surrounded by a tall fence topped with razor wire. A large metal gate stood open, but a metal boom blocked the entrance. A guard hurried from a small shack and raised the boom. They turned into a dusty yard.

The warehouse was just like its neighbors, a gray aluminum structure with a door and three windows facing the street and a loading dock at the side. A trailer with a blue container was backed against the dock. A large panel truck was parked to the side near the fence.

There was a sign on the warehouse.

It said 'Assured Logistics.'

Vermeulen did a double-take. No, he'd read it correctly.

That's when he knew he'd gotten it all wrong. Macklevore worked for Houser, who was a private military contractor for MI6 or the CIA or both. He obviously also had other business his employers didn't know about. Which meant there was lot more at stake than eight shoddy armored vehicles. That's why Houser had killed Ritu Roy. She had drawn attention to the illegal side of his business.

He took a deep breath. Dwelling on his mistakes was useless. It wouldn't change anything.

The car stopped near the front entrance. They got out.

"I assume Assured Logistics is a subsidiary of Assured Sovereignty," Vermeulen said.

"Sister company would be the better term. They operate independently of each other."

"Just like Assured Air Services?"

"Exactly. Mr. Houser finds that keeping his different undertakings at arm's length serves his overall business interests best."

"Why did Fareed pursue us? Aren't you working with him?"

"We don't work with Fareed. Nobody in his right mind would. The man is dumber than a bag of hammers. We use Mansour when necessary and pay him accordingly. For reasons that I fail to understand, he uses Fareed to do his dirty work. I'm sure the car chase was Fareed's idea. You shouldn't have kicked him in the balls."

Macklevore opened the warehouse door and stepped back to let Vermeulen enter.

The inside was just a large space. The air felt hot and stagnant. Rows of crates and pallets occupied half the area. The tall overhead door to the loading dock was closed. A forklift moved crates from near the door to their assigned spaces. The bald European supervising the unloading was the same man Vermeulen had seen the day before.

The area to the right of the entrance had been partitioned into two offices. Macklevore led him to the first.

The office wasn't much. A file cabinet against the rear wall stood alongside a door leading to the next room. Two grimy windows—one solid, one louvered—let in pale light from the outside. A desk stood in the middle. Papers that looked like bills and receipts lay strewn across the surface. Near the center sat a phone and an open laptop. A chair stood behind the desk, with two in front. A portable air conditioner blew cool air into their faces.

Macklevore waved to the European in the warehouse, then closed the door.

"Mr. Houser should be here in a moment. Have a seat. Ben Tower here will keep you company." He left the office again.

Tower came in and positioned himself next to the door. He wore the same clothes he'd worn the day before. He had the red face of someone whose approach to hot climates involves imbibing quantities of alcohol. He was big, six and a half feet tall. What must have been muscle at one point in his life had gone to seed with drink and other indulgences. Still, he'd be a formidable opponent.

"You like working for Houser?" Vermeulen said.

Tower shrugged. "It's okay." Not a talker, then.

"See much action?"

"No."

"So you do … what? Manage the warehouse? Babysit visitors? Anything more exciting?"

"This and that."

"Ever go out and shoot policewomen?"

"Shut up."

"Well, it wasn't you. Takes skill to shoot straight over six hundred yards. You strike me more like an automatic fire kind of guy. Just pull the trigger and mow 'em down."

"I said, shut up."

"So who killed the policewoman? Not you, and definitely not Macklevore. Maybe Houser is a hands-on kind of executive ... does the dirty work himself."

Before Tower could react, the door opened. Dale Houser entered the room.

He looked older than in the photo Gaby had sent him, more drawn. His face was just as tan, the shock of blond hair as unruly. His cheeks were hollower, his mouth tighter. His clothes, a beige suit with a light-blue shirt, were much more formal than those in the photo.

"Mr. Vermeulen, pleasure to meet you." His Newcastle accent was strong. He stretched out his hand as if Vermeulen were a new business contact. Vermeulen shook his hand reflexively. Then he remembered that Houser had shot Ritu Roy.

"So," Houser said. "We've got ourselves quite a mess here. Mansour is upset. His nasty sidekick Fareed is after you. You got yourself on the wrong side of the law. How'd you manage to do all that in less than forty-eight hours?"

Houser's smile radiated like high beams. Vermeulen understood why the man seemed to have such an active social life. He was personable, came across as genuine, and radiated confidence. Whatever problems one might have, Houser would take care of them.

"You seem to have a lot to do with that mess."

"I do? How?" Houser sounded genuinely surprised.

"Eight Pandur I armored personnel carriers, bought used in the Czech Republic and sold as new to the Nepali police unit at UNAMID, for starters."

"I remember those Pandurs. The Nepalis showed up bare-assed and needed equipment fast. I was able to help. But I never pretended they were new. Did Jirel say I sold them as new?"

"Not as such, but the paperwork at the UN lists them as new and the UN's reimbursing the Nepalis at the rate for new vehicles."

"That Jirel." Houser shook his head as if Jirel were his wayward son. "He's a wily fox. I'm afraid he's taken the UN for a ride. Sorry to hear that. I assure you I had no part in it."

"I don't believe you. The paperwork for the APCs was altered here at Port Sudan. Jirel never got his fingers on the paperwork. Mansour may be happy looking the other way in exchange for cash, but he's not the kind of person to initiate this kind of fraud. That leaves you, Mr. Houser."

"That's quite an accusation. Something you shouldn't make unless you have proof."

"I do."

"You do?"

"Two copies of the end-user certificate. The original lists the condition of the vehicles as 'used,' while the doctored copy lists them as 'new.' "

Houser's smile grew a little thinner.

"Admirable detective work, but not what I'd call proof."

"On March tenth, you killed a UN policewoman at Zam Zam," Vermeulen said.

"From fraud to murder. That's quite an escalation. Are you just throwing things against the wall to see what sticks, or do you have any evidence?"

"I talked to a girl who saw you. You fired the shots that killed Ritu Roy."

His face showed clear surprise. Then he shook his head. "I wasn't even in the country on March tenth. I couldn't have been at Zam Zam. Besides, I've got more important things to do than take potshots at UN personnel."

"She described you down to your neatly trimmed beard."

"I'm telling you I was in Basra. The girl is mistaken." Houser's protestations seemed genuine.

Could Amina have been mistaken? It did seem far-fetched that a man running three companies would bother organizing a small riot to track down Ritu Roy and kill her.

The smile had disappeared from Houser's face. Vermeulen had hit on something. Houser may not have pulled the trigger, but he was involved.

"You are definitely barking up the wrong tree," the man said. "I can prove that I was in Basra. I have my tickets, and you can check the hotel. I stayed at the Basra International Hotel." He turned to Tower. "Make sure our guest is comfortable. I've got to make a call."

Houser left the office.

"Have a seat, Mr. Vermeulen," Tower said. "Can I get you something to drink?"

Vermeulen shook his head. Things didn't add up anymore. Houser had probably orchestrated the APC fraud so that the blame would fall on Jirel. But had he killed Ritu Roy? Vermeulen was no longer certain. Who else could have done it? His initial doubts when Priya told him her story came back in full force. Yes, the UN got ripped off, but was it enough to warrant killing Ritu? That seemed to be an extreme response to a complaint from a lowly policewoman.

Unless there was more at stake. Much more.

He glanced at the freight stored in the warehouse. There were pallets wrapped in netting that looked like cargo he'd seen at other UN operations.

Then there were crates. They were smaller, which meant heavier. The answer to his questions was in the warehouse.

Five minutes later, Houser came back. His face telegraphed bad news.

"Mansour wants you arrested. Breaking into his office really upset him. Fareed has his own axe to grind. And don't think for a moment that your UN credentials will make a difference. You're too far off the reservation."

"So get me back to El Fasher," Vermeulen said. "Once I'm back with UNAMID, Mansour can't do a thing."

"You're wrong. He'll issue an arrest warrant and the police will follow you to El Fasher. I doubt the UN will protect you. Breaking and entering isn't in your job description."

He nodded to Tower, who left the office.

"Here's what I can do for you," Houser said. "I can get you out of the country. It's really the best solution all around."

Vermeulen didn't buy it. Sure, Mansour was a bureaucrat on the take. He might have influence and connections in Port Sudan. Vermeulen doubted that it extended to the rest of the country. Even authoritarian governments didn't tolerate corrupt minor officials. Men like Mansour were perfect patsies to show the public that the government was serious in its fight against corruption. He had every reason to stay quiet once he realized that Vermeulen was beyond his reach.

Houser was trying to get rid of him.

He pushed a lock of hair from his forehead. "I'm not going to leave. I will finish the investigation, and that involves finding the person who killed the UN policewoman."

Houser shook his head. "It doesn't. I checked. You have no orders to investigate the death. The UN already closed that file. Mob violence. Just leave it at that. You can complete your investigation of the APCs back in New York and deliver Jirel as the culprit. Everybody will be happy."

Vermeulen shook his head. Making people happy was definitely not in his job description.

"There's a parliamentary delegation leaving for London tomorrow," Houser said, ignoring him. "They just came from the south and stopped for a little R and R in Port Sudan. Their chartered plane leaves at nine in the morning. You'll be on that flight. One way or another."

"You're not shunting me off to London. I want to speak to my superiors."

"You can, when you arrive in London. Of course, once you are there, you are also subject to the Official Secrets Act. Assured Sovereignty has a contract with the British Ministry of Defense to provide a number of services, the nature of which is classified. All I have to do is declare that your actions compromise British national security. You tell any of this and you'll go away for a long time. Your superiors will be most eager to distance themselves from you. So spare yourself the trouble."

Tower came back into the room.

"Give Ben your phone," Houser said.

"I'm not going to give him my phone."

"Come on, Vermeulen," Houser said. "Don't make a scene. It'd be tedious. Just give him the phone."

"Fuck you, Houser. I'm going to make a scene. Everything you're doing is outrageous. I can't wait for the world to hear that Her Majesty's Government is in bed with an arms dealer who's violating the UN arms embargo."

Houser shook his head, looking disappointed. "I was afraid it would come to this."

Tower stepped forward and grabbed Vermeulen's arm. A syringe gleamed in the overhead fluorescent lights. Vermeulen jerked the arm away, but Tower held on to it with the power of a vise. The needle plunged through the fabric of his jacket and shirt and pricked his skin.

The sting conjured up a childhood memory for Vermeulen. When he was just seven, the school nurse had tried to give him a shot, some standard childhood vaccination. Back then he hated needles, and he wasn't going to let her do it. He'd twisted his arm just before the plunger came down, and half the liquid squirted around when the needle slipped out from under the skin. The nurse, tired of putting up with him, let it go.

Now he tried the same trick again. It didn't quite work. The needle did slip out, but only after the plunger was more than halfway down.

A comfortable drowsiness descended on him. It had been a long time since he last rested. Too much had happened in the last forty-eight hours. His body needed rest to recuperate from the beating it had sustained. Sleep struck him as a wonderful idea. An instinct deep inside him urged him to fight the drowsiness, to run away. His body obeyed reluctantly. He tried lifting a leg. It wouldn't budge. His foot seemed bolted to the floor. He tried the other leg. It, too, was stuck to the floor. *Get out of here*, his brain shouted. The message disappeared into the ether without an echo.

CHAPTER TWENTY-TWO

———◆———

Monday, March 22, 2010

VERMEULEN'S HEAD RESONATED WITH THE RUMBLINGS of a hangover when he woke up. They had a chemical quality, not at all what one would expect from a decent binge. Besides, the last thing he remembered was the bright midday sun. Too early to be drinking. His brain began to pull the events of the past twenty-four hours from whatever recesses it had buried them in.

The International Club, the attack, the break-in, Macklevore. Houser!

Then he remembered the syringe.

He was lying on a cot. The ribs and kidney on his right side were still sore. The room was dark, but yellow sodium-vapor lights shone through the venetian blinds. The cot was the only piece of furniture in the room. There was a door. It probably led to the office where Tower had administered the drug. His carry-on bag stood next to the cot. A dark box with green lights was attached to the wall above the door. Maybe a smoke alarm.

His watch told him that it was three in the morning. He'd been out for about fifteen hours. The flight Macklevore wanted to put him on was supposed to leave at nine. Six hours to devise a plan. He got up and pushed down the door handle slowly. The door was locked.

He opened his bag. The folder with the documents he'd taken from Mansour's office still lay nestled among his clothes. The gash left by Fareed's knife winked at him like an evil eye. Houser must have been certain of the drug's effectiveness; otherwise, he wouldn't have left all his things here.

His iPod Touch and speaker were in the bag, too. At least he could listen to music while he waited for the inevitable. Except he wasn't going to wait. Going to London was out of the question.

There was only one option. Get back to El Fasher and complete the investigation. He owed it to Priya and to himself. That much was clear. What wasn't clear was how he'd make that happen. Flying was out of the question. Houser and Fareed would be waiting for him at the airport. Which left ground transportation. By road, Port Sudan was about eleven hundred miles from El Fasher. The air-conditioned first-class buses were off limits for the same reason as flying. They were also expensive, and he had only six hundred Sudanese pounds and one hundred U.S. dollars in his billfold. The credit cards were useless because of the U.S. sanctions.

That left the rickety buses and *boksi* pickups that formed the backbone of the Sudanese transport system. The thought of having his bruised kidney shaken for eleven hundred miles sitting on a wooden bench in the back of a pickup made him shudder. Flying was really the only way. It just couldn't be a commercial flight.

He had to contact Tessa, who had the connections to figure something out. He searched his pocket for his phone and remembered that Tower had taken it. He checked the room again. Except for the box with the lights above the door, there was nothing. Was it really a smoke detector? That wouldn't have more than one light. He dragged the cot to the corner.

The box turned out to be a wireless router. It should work for his iPod. He got the device from his bag and scanned for a WiFi signal. The router showed up as ALLTD. It was password protected. He tried some obvious options. No luck. They had changed the default settings.

He checked his watch again. A quarter after three. Time was marching on. He could smash the window with the cot and get outside. Then he'd be stuck there. He needed help and Tessa was his best option.

He looked at the router again. Just a simple password stood between him and a plan. Had Houser chosen it? Whoever administered the office? It didn't matter. There were too many possibilities and he had no time to check them all. How did one change the default settings? Each router had a built-in interface for such changes. He remembered doing that on his own router. He also remembered resetting it after he'd forgotten the password.

The rest was easy. He removed the router from the wall. The rear had sockets for the power supply and network connections. Near the bottom edge, he found the reset switch. It was hidden under a tiny hole. He pushed the nib of his pen into the hole and held it for several seconds. The lights went off. He released the pen. They came back, blinking one at a time until they resumed their normal status.

The iPod no longer displayed ALLTD, but simply the name of the manufacturer. He pointed the iPod's web browser to the router setup page using the information conveniently printed on the back of the router. Two minutes later, the fan icon told him that his iPod was connected to the internet.

He tapped the Skype icon, entered Tessa's number, and tapped the dial button. It rang for a long time, and he was about to hang up when he heard her sleepy voice say, "Goddamn it, Valentin. This had better be good!"

"I need your help!" Vermeulen whispered.

"At three thirty in the morning?"

"Yes. I'm in Port Sudan and Houser, the guy behind everything, wants to ship me to London in five and a half hours."

"What?" She sounded wide awake.

"Listen, Tessa. I haven't got time for explanations. The Sudanese authorities are after me as well. I have to get back to El Fasher, but I can't take regular airlines. Do you know someone who can fly me?"

"Are you in a safe place right now?"

"No. I'm locked up in Houser's warehouse. I hacked their WiFi."

"Can you get away from there?"

"Yes." He wasn't at all certain, but didn't want his dithering to stop her from making a plan.

"I'll have to make some calls. Call me back in ten minutes."

Just hearing her voice and her matter-of-fact manner calmed him. He'd called the right person. He had no idea whom she was calling. Whoever it was would be woken at an ungodly hour. If she was calling someone in Europe, it would be even earlier. The ten minutes took forever.

"Okay," she said when he called her back. "Just past the edge of town, on the way to the airport, there's a bunch of warehouses. One of those is occupied by Global Relief. Get there by six. They'll figure something out."

"Thanks, Tessa. I owe you."

"I can't wait to hear how you got yourself into this. See you soon."

He was buoyed by her certainty. Get to the Global Relief warehouse by six.

Step one, examine the window. He raised the blinds. The right side was a solid pane of glass, no handles, no hinges. The other half was louvered, ten strips of glass set in three-sided aluminum frames all connected to a crank that opened and closed them. To facilitate removal and cleaning, each strip could be pulled from its frame. Vermeulen tried to turn the crank. It didn't budge. He pushed harder. No difference. The window hadn't been opened in a long time.

Step two, break the window. He folded the cot and jammed it against the window pane. It shattered. Still holding the cot, he positioned himself next to the door.

Just as expected, he heard movement in the next room. Keys fumbled in the lock. The door flew open. Tower rushed in, pistol in his hand, and tripped over Vermeulen's outstretched foot. He fell. His pistol slid across the floor. Tower's training kicked in. He broke the fall by rolling to the side.

Unfortunately for Tower, he rolled to the wrong side. Vermeulen had raised the cot up high behind him, and now he swung it against Tower's head like a cricket batter. Tower was out cold.

Vermeulen picked up the gun and peered around the door. The office was empty. He ripped the cord from the telephone and the wall and tied Tower's arms and legs together. He found a roll of sticky tape and taped Tower's mouth shut. Vermeulen's phone and two sets of keys were in Tower's pocket. He took both. One set was for the Peugeot, which was handy. It would make finding the Global Relief warehouse much easier. He stuck the pistol into his jacket pocket.

The warehouse was next. Two emergency lights at each end helped orient him, but most of the space was dark.

He turned back to look for a light switch and stood face to face with the guard from the gate.

Damn! He'd forgotten about the guard. The man must've heard the smashing of the window. He was medium-sized, shorter than Vermeulen, but stocky and solid. He held a nightstick in his raised hand. Without uttering a word, he swung it. Vermeulen ducked away, but the tip of the stick grazed his shoulder.

The flash of pain on top of all the other aches in his body made him furious.

He watched as the momentum of the swing carried the arm of the guard through an arc that left the man's right side open. Vermeulen jumped forward and jabbed his elbow hard against the guard's head. The man crumpled to the floor. His nightstick clattered into a corner. Before he could get up again, Vermeulen pulled the pistol from his pocket. He remembered that Glocks don't have safety levers. Just point and pull the trigger. He only pointed.

The gun changed the dynamic of the situation. The guard wasn't paid enough to get shot.

"Turn over." He motioned with the pistol.

The guard rolled onto his belly.

"Hands behind you."

The guard put his hands behind his back.

Grabbing the sticky tape, Vermeulen pulled the end loose with his teeth, stuck it to the man's wrist, and taped the wrists together. After the first few layers, he put the gun in his pocket and wrapped a thicker layer of tape around the wrists. The guard wasn't going to get that off. He did the same with the man's ankles. A final strip of tape over the mouth finished the job.

Back in the empty office, Tower was grunting behind the tape over his mouth. Vermeulen checked him and found that the telephone cord had loosened. He used the rest of the tape to make sure Tower remained immobilized.

It was four thirty. Not knowing how far it was to Global Relief, he gave himself a half-hour to explore the warehouse.

A little more than half of the cargo stored there consisted of ordinary supplies—dried foods, uniforms, soap, the sundry things that any army needs when in the field. He checked the manifestos attached to the pallets. The goods had no obvious destination. They could be going to any of the regular or irregular forces fighting in Sudan, since they weren't subject to any restrictions.

It was obvious that Houser and his companies straddled the line between legal and illegal. Unless Houser was lying, which he had no reason to do, Assured Sovereignty worked for the British government. That put it in the same category as Blackwater and all the other private military contractors that had popped up in the last couple of decades. War was a good business. It also meant Houser had connections to the top people in British defense and intelligence. He'd used those connections to hide his illegal activities right under the nose of the UN.

The evidence was in the wooden crates he'd seen earlier. The stamped information outside left no doubt. It specified the type of ammunition in clear black letters—7.62x39mm for AK-47s, 7.62x51mm for NATO rifles, 9mm for handguns and Uzis, even 5.56x45mm. He figured those were for the Tabor rifles he'd seen in the UJM camp. The crates came from all over the world: AK cartridges from China and Belarus, NATO and 9mm from the UK, and 5.56mm from Israel.

The consignees for the ammunition were contingents serving with UNAMID. That didn't make any sense. He'd seen the paperwork in El Fasher. Supplies came from all over. Houser couldn't have managed to get all the supply contracts for some 25,000 troops. He photographed a sample with his phone. Three of the crates were addressed to the Kenyan contingent. He'd ask Wambui about them.

Deeper in the warehouse, he came across different crates. They contained Belorussian rockets labeled SA8. These were air-to-ground missiles for fighter jets. Neither UNAMID nor the rebel forces had jets. They had to be for the Sudanese Armed Forces. Which was illegal. He took pictures of those too.

He checked his watch. Ten to five.

The blue container outside hadn't been unloaded yet. Its doors were padlocked. He tried the keys on the large ring he'd found in Tower's pocket. The fifth one fit. When he pulled the handle to open the doors, a loud screech sounded through the morning stillness. The door opened without much further trouble. The security lighting didn't help much inside the container. Using the flash from his mobile phone, he found more crates—longer than the ones inside the warehouse and not as tall. The stamped letters on the side designated the contents as eight 'AGM-114A.' He didn't know what that meant. He did know, however, that the container wasn't where it was supposed to be. The manufacturer listed was 'Lockheed Martin,' the consignee was 'Iraqi Air Force,' and the destination read 'Baghdad.'

He photographed several crates, took one picture of the container information, and headed for the Peugeot.

CHAPTER TWENTY-THREE

——◆——

GLOBAL RELIEF SHARED WAREHOUSE SPACE WITH a number of other companies. That made finding the place harder than he'd assumed. After driving past the entrance twice, he finally saw the small sign among many others attached to a fence. The gate was locked. A tall wall surrounded the entire complex. There was no guard to let him in.

He checked his watch. Five thirty-five. Too much time. Being on the road with a stolen car wasn't a good idea. Parking at the entrance and waiting was even worse. Better to find a place to dump a car. There had to be dark corners in this industrial area. He followed the wall and turned onto a side street. The farther away from the airport road he got, the more low-rent the businesses looked. A half a mile away, he found what he was looking for.

The junkyard was surrounded by a fence that had fallen down in many places. Vermeulen drove the Peugeot across one of the broken sections and parked it behind a stack of five wrecked cars. There was some paperwork in the glove compartment. He took it and left the keys in the ignition. It'd be stolen, resold, or chopped for parts.

He walked back to Global Famine Relief and arrived at the gate at five minutes to six. While he waited, he removed the battery from his phone. By now someone might be looking for him. No need to walk around with a homing beacon.

Three minutes later, a battered Land Cruiser pickup skidded to a stop at the gate. A woman got out, unlocked the gate, and hurried back to the car.

Vermeulen stepped out of the shadows and waved at her.

She stopped. "Are you Vermeulen?"

"Yes. Valentin Vermeulen."

"Close the gate after me and hop in."

She spoke with a Slavic accent.

He did as asked and climbed into the passenger side. In the glow of the instrument panel, he could tell that she had light hair, tied into a ponytail.

She drove around to the far corner of the warehouse and parked so the Land Cruiser couldn't be seen from the street. She motioned for him to follow her. They entered a dark, hot space that smelled of flour and rancid cooking oil. She closed the door. A light came on.

"You can't even imagine how much shit will hit the fan if whoever's after you finds you here," she said. "Non-governmental organizations like ours operate at the whim of the government. Any trouble at all, and we're shut down."

She had blonde hair and Slavic cheekbones. There was something asymmetrical about her face, which made it not so much good-looking as interesting. She wore jeans and a black T-shirt that looked a couple of sizes too large.

"I really appreciate your help."

"I'm Anya Selcovic. Tessa must really like you. She wouldn't get me out of bed at three-fucking-thirty-five in the morning for just anyone." She checked him out. "Hmm, I can see why. Let's go."

Vermeulen followed her to a small office.

"So, here's the deal," she said. "At seven thirty, we are delivering a load of food aid to the airport. At ten, it'll go to El Fasher. If all goes well, so do you."

"How big an 'if' is that?"

"Depends."

"On what?"

"Mostly on whether people are looking for you."

"They are."

"Already?"

He checked his watch. "Probably. If not, they soon will be."

"Who's after you?"

"Local authorities and British mercenaries."

"Shit. How'd you get here?"

"I stole their car."

"Where is it now?"

"At a junkyard nearby."

"Good. As far as they know, you could be driving or flying. That'll divide their attention. We need to make sure they focus on the right part of the airport. You flew here, right?"

He nodded.

"So you have a return ticket?"

"I do. It's for tomorrow."

"Just before we leave here, call the airline and rebook it for today. There's a flight via Khartoum at nine forty-five. It's all about diversion."

"They might be tracking my mobile."

"Use mine."

"Won't you get in trouble if they trace the call to you?" he said.

She shrugged. "It's a cheap prepaid. I'll get a new one."

"Sounds good. What then?"

"We've got to get you on that plane. Once you are in the air, nothing much can happen. I made up an ID for you. Since I didn't have your picture, I asked Tessa what you looked like. She described you with surprising detail. I found a picture in a magazine and laminated that."

She showed him a white ID hanging from a lanyard. The picture was so obviously not him, he had to shake his head.

"That'll never work."

"Don't worry. It kinda looks like you. The hair is the right color. The shape of the face is the same. Besides, the fact you that are wearing an ID means nobody will look at it. Here's one of our highly sought-after baseball caps. It'll complete the disguise."

* * *

FORTY MINUTES LATER, A TRUCK PULLED up to the warehouse. Selcovic talked to the driver, who remained in his cab. Then she jumped into the seat of the forklift and began loading the truck.

Vermeulen hadn't expected that. *A woman of many talents*, he thought as she whizzed by him. Her method spoke of long experience. Rather than climbing on the truck after depositing each pallet and moving it with a pallet jack, she used the pallet on the forks to coax the previous one forward on the truck bed. That day's load used up three quarters of the truck's space.

"Usually, our flights are later in the day. This one came as a surprise," she said after parking the forklift. "Our help doesn't show up until nine, if then. So I end up doing the grunt work. Then Tessa got me up even earlier. I had a damn short night."

"Thanks for everything you're doing for me. I really appreciate it."

She looked at him with a crooked grin. "Just promise me you're nice to Tessa. She deserves a good man for a change."

He was about to tell her that he and Tessa were only friends, but decided to leave it.

"Time to call and change your reservation."

She handed him her phone. He dialed the airline and changed the flight.

Compared to Europe and the U.S., where customer service had been all but eliminated, African airlines treated you well.

"Done," he said.

She pointed to the cargo bed. "Okay, hop on. I left a space in the front, right behind the cab. Duck in there and don't come out until I tell you so. We go through two checkpoints, and they may stop us and search the cargo. They never make it all the way to the front. So stay down. Not a sound until I call you."

He nodded, climbed onto the bed, and maneuvered his roll-on past the pallets until he found the space up front. There was barely enough space to sit.

The ride was bumpy. The driver didn't know he was in the back and thus didn't even try to avoid potholes. Vermeulen's bruised body made regular contact with pallets around him. Twenty minutes later, the truck slowed and turned right toward the airport. This stretch of road was newer, and the ride was smoother.

The Port Sudan airport was not much larger than the one in El Fasher. The influx of tourists probably made it busier. The access road led directly to the passenger terminal. He didn't remember if the cargo area was to the left or the right of the passenger terminal. In any case, he'd have to get off the truck and walk to the plane. That would be the riskiest part of the journey. If Mansour had watchers stationed there, it would mean trouble. Hopefully the ruse of changing his flight was enough to keep them off his trail.

The truck slowed, turned right again, and crept forward until it stopped completely. He heard voices outside. The tailgate crashed down, and the canvas cover was pulled back.

"Same as always, Mahmud," he heard Selcovic say.

"Got to check it, Miss Anya," a man said. "Extra security today."

Mansour had pulled his strings already.

The springs of the truck creaked, and he heard a man climb on. Mahmud had to be fat.

"How many pallets, Miss Anya?"

"Twelve."

The man counted in Arabic.

"Okay, twelve. Anything else on the truck?"

"Yeah, I'm smuggling a guy to El Fasher. He's hopelessly in love but has no money for a plane."

Vermeulen just about gasped. He wasn't in the mood for jokes.

Mahmud laughed out loud.

"Then I'd better check extra careful."

Vermeulen heard fabric scratching against the netting of the pallets. Mahmud was breathing heavily as he inched toward his hiding spot.

Vermeulen sorted out his options. There were two: give himself up and hope for the best, or subdue the man.

Option one was a nonstarter. That left neutralizing Mahmud silently. The only way to do that was to choke him. Get his right elbow around Mahmud's throat, clamp his hand over his mouth and hold until he passed out.

Mahmud took his time checking the manifest.

Vermeulen figured he was at the third row of pallets. Two more before he'd see him.

On second thought, option two wasn't any better. Neutralizing Mahmud wouldn't work. The guard wasn't alone. His buddies expected him to come off the truck again. They wouldn't let the truck through without getting the okay from Mahmud. Anya had said there were two checkpoints.

Sweat was running freely down his face. Mahmud's wheezy breath came closer. He heard the man mumbling to himself.

"Hey, Mahmud!" Selcovic shouted. "Are you jacking off in there? Do it on your own time. I've got a plane to catch."

Mahmud let out a bellow of laughter. "Such language, Miss Anya. That's not very ladylike."

"Ladies wouldn't have to put up with a fat paper jockey like you snooping through their cargo. So, are we all set here?"

"Yes, Miss Anya, we are all set."

Mahmud made his way back to the rear of the truck and jumped off.

They drove off and stopped again a short while later. The second checkpoint went much faster. No inspection, just a few words between Selcovic and someone.

The truck drove over bumpy ground until it reached a smooth surface and came to a stop. The rear gate crashed down and the canvas was pulled away. The whine of an electric forklift sounded. Someone stepped on the bed and dragged something with them.

"You okay, Vermeulen?" Anya said.

"Yes."

"Well, come out and make yourself useful. You got your ID around your neck? Good. When the first row has been unloaded, use this pallet jack to bring the others back so the forklift can reach them."

Vermeulen watched the first two pallets disappear. The pallet jack wasn't the newest. It didn't roll smoothly. He had to push rather hard to get the forks under the pallet. The jack itself didn't work properly. He pumped the handle up and down, but the pallet didn't rise. The forklift arrived. There was nothing to pick up. The driver beeped, impatient.

"What's the holdup?" Selcovic shouted.

"The damn jack doesn't work."

"You aren't holding the release lever, are you?"

He was about to answer with a choice curse, when he saw that the lever was stuck in the open position. He wiggled it, but it wouldn't budge. Only a hard push made it snap back into the closed position. The stuck lever made the jack a pain to operate, but Vermeulen managed to coax the freight to the edge of the truck, where the forklift picked up the pallets and brought them to the plane.

Selcovic came back and told him to get off the truck. Next to the truck stood a large four-propeller aircraft. Blue letters near the tail identified it as an Antonov 12.

"So far, so good," she said. "Let's go meet the pilot."

"Are we taking off soon?"

"No. They're still waiting for other cargo."

"More relief goods?"

"No. Just regular cargo. Global Relief runs on the begging principle. We contact all the air freight companies around here and beg for cargo space. The government-owned ones tell us to fuck off. Some of the private ones are nice enough. If they have empty space, they let us fill it. We've just got to make sure we get here first and get our stuff in."

"Who's operating today's flight?"

"Assured Air Services."

CHAPTER TWENTY-FOUR

———◆———

Dale Houser was surprised that the gate to his warehouse was already open at seven thirty. The missing guard turned the surprise into concern. That was not okay. Anyone could have driven into the yard. Then he saw the smashed window. His concern turned into alarm.

That was quickly replaced by anger when he found the guard and Tower tied up on the floor of the office and Vermeulen missing. He ripped the tape from Tower's mouth.

"What the hell happened?"

"He smashed the window. I thought he was trying to bust out, so I hurried into the room. He waited for me and knocked me out."

"He knocked you out? How?"

Tower's expression turned sheepish. "With the cot. He tricked me."

"And the guard?"

"He came, but by then Vermeulen had my gun, so it was no match."

"Two people with weapons done in by a pencil pusher." Houser shook his head. He untied Tower.

"Get rid of the guard," he said.

"Kill him? Why?"

"Not kill him, you bloody idiot. Just fire him. He's obviously useless."

Tower freed the guard and sent him away. The man tried to protest, but he read the expression on Houser's face correctly. No reason to stick around any longer. He left without another word.

"Vermeulen took the Peugeot," Tower said.

"I don't care about the damn car. It was banged up anyway. I care that Vermeulen got away."

"Do you think he'll drive to El Fasher?"

"Only if he's as stupid as you. Of course not. That's eleven hundred miles. He hasn't got time for that." Houser sat down behind the desk. "No," he said. "Vermeulen will fly. The only question is when."

"So, we can still catch him."

Houser looked at Tower and shook his head. "I oughta fire you, too. You are worse than the guard."

"No, Boss. Listen to me. All we have to do is put a few men at the airport. When he shows up, we'll grab him. No harm done."

"After you fought off Mansour's men? You know Fareed is going to be there, and he won't be alone." He took out his phone and dialed a number. "Yes, this is Dale Houser calling. Could I speak to the manager, please?" He waited for his call to be switched. "Good morning, Ibrahim, this is Dale Houser. I've got a problem. A friend of mine left an important document at my house. He's supposed to fly out today, but I don't know when. Could you check if a Mr. Vermeulen is booked for El Fasher today? It's really important that I catch him before he leaves."

He listened.

"He rebooked it? For nine forty-five? Great. Thanks for your help."

"We'll get him, boss," Tower said.

"Yes, we will, but not how you think. I bet Vermeulen rebooked the flight to throw us off his trail. It might fool Fareed, but it won't fool me. I want you to call a few of your regulars, go to the airport, and check each charter and transport leaving today. Look in the damn cargo bays if you must. Then bring him here. It's time Vermeulen learned his lesson."

At eight, three workers showed up. One of them started the panel truck and backed up next to the blue container. The other two went about shifting the cargo from the container to the truck. By eight thirty they'd completed their task. The truck left for the airport.

* * *

"YOU'VE GOT TO BE KIDDING," VERMEULEN said when he heard the name of the airfreight company.

"Why? Assured Air Services has been very supportive of our mission."

"It's owned by the man who kidnapped me yesterday."

"What?" For the first time since he met her, Selcovic looked perplexed.

"Do you know Dale Houser?" Vermeulen said.

"Not personally. Our headquarters deals with him. We just get instructions to deliver our cargo to one of his planes. What has he done?"

"He's an arms dealer, and a crooked one at that. Have you ever seen what his planes transport?"

"No, we just deliver our stuff and leave. Are you sure?"

"Of course I am. Yesterday he drugged me. I woke up earlier than they expected and fought my way out. That's why I needed to get away so urgently."

"Shit." She pronounced it "Shiiieet."

Vermeulen nodded.

"Maybe it's not so bad after all," she said. "The pilots don't know who you are. As far as they know, you work for Global Relief. I've never seen anyone named Houser at the airport. Usually it's just a few workers with a forklift. If you keep out of sight until takeoff, nobody's any the wiser."

Vermeulen pursed his lips. There were three other planes in the cargo area, ranging from large transporters to a single-engine Cessna. Two were owned by Azza Transport, and the Cessna sported the yellow colors of DHL International.

She saw his glance.

"You can forget Azza Transport," she said. "They are a government company. You know, the jerks I mentioned earlier. DHL is corporate—no hitchhikers, ever. I think you're stuck with this one."

Vermeulen nodded. She had a point. Unless Houser, Macklevore, or Tower came to the plane, nobody knew who he was. He relaxed.

"Okay, let's meet the pilot." He pulled the cap down into his face. The fake ID dangled from the lanyard.

They were maybe twenty feet from the door when a car came to a screeching halt next to one of the Azza Transport planes. Vermeulen saw a big bald man jump from the passenger door. Even though he couldn't see the man's face, he knew it was Tower. His blood ran cold. He stopped and turned toward the Antonov.

"They're looking for me," he said to Selcovic. "Over there, the bald guy. He's the one who drugged me."

Anya didn't miss a beat.

"Keep going, or you'll attract his attention."

"I can't go into the plane."

"You must. If you stay out here, fatso will spot you."

They climbed the stairs into the body of the Antonov. The inside was a typical cargo layout. Two sets of rails on which pallets could be moved and fastened. The Global Relief cargo was located only on one side of the plane, near the door they had just used. Toward the front were two rows of seats. They looked more comfortable than the one in the Buffalo he'd flown from Nairobi. Beyond the seats lay the cockpit. A partition separated the cockpit from the cargo area. Vermeulen could only see part of the instrument panel through the door.

"Hey, José, you up there?" Selcovic shouted.

A face appeared in the doorframe. José had dark close-cropped hair, brown eyes, a Roman nose, sensuous lips, and a two-day stubble. He could have stepped from the cover of a romance novel.

"Anya, the woman of my dreams. When are you going to ditch that girlfriend of yours and make me a happy man?"

"When hell freezes over, you wanker. Listen, I have an unscheduled passenger. Say hi to Valentin. He's here to check up on me, so be nice to him."

"Anya, you know we can't just take him along. You haven't filed the paperwork."

"Since when do you need paperwork? Our supplies are probably the only legit cargo on this rust bucket."

"No can do, Anya."

"I promised this man he'd get to El Fasher today. Don't make me look bad. There's a bottle of scotch in it for you and VIP passes to my next shindig. I know how much you like them."

"Make it four bottles. Two for me and two for Dragan, my co-pilot."

"Four it is. Thanks, José. If I were into guys, you'd be on the top of my list. Call me when you come back."

José came back and shook Vermeulen's hand. He saw the ID on the lanyard and didn't bat an eye. Anya had been right.

"Welcome aboard, Valentin. Have a seat. After we load the next batch of cargo, we're off.

Vermeulen looked out the porthole next to his seat and saw Tower climb from the cargo area of the Azza transport plane. He got into the car, which drove across the tarmac to the Antonov. José must have seen him coming, because he got up and walked back toward the door. He stopped next to Vermeulen.

"Get up in the cockpit. Take my seat. I shoulda never listened to Anya. Not a peep from you or you're gonna cost me my job."

Vermeulen stepped forward and sank into the pilot's seat. There wasn't a lot of ducking he could do. When you're six feet tall, there are limits to stowing yourself in a small space.

Dragan, the copilot, shook his head. He had a gaunt face with hollow cheeks and a patchy mustache. "José keeps thinking he's gonna get into that dyke's knickers if he's nice to her. So he does the stupidest things, like letting you on board."

Vermeulen heard voices from the rear. He couldn't make out the words. The plane shook a little. Tower must have come aboard. Steps were coming closer. His hand slid into his jacket pocket and closed around the Glock's grip. He wasn't going to leave this plane.

"You sure you haven't seen anyone?" Tower said, back in the cargo bay. "A tall guy, messy clothes? His name is Vermeulen."

"No, nobody like it," José said. "Anya was here, bringing her cargo."

"She come alone?"

"No, the truck driver was with her, the local guy she always uses."

"Did you see anything unusual, anything at all?"

"No. Same old Monday morning."

"What about Dragan?"

"Hey, Dragan, did you see a tall guy around here this morning?" José shouted.

Dragan turned in his seat. "Nothing. Just waiting for the cargo. Why are you looking for this guy?"

"That's Mr. Houser's business."

Tower's voice sounded very close. He couldn't have been more than three feet from the partition.

Dragan stood up and stepped into the doorway. "What happened to your face, Ben? Your girlfriend get mad at you?"

"Shut up, Dragan, or I'll send you back to your chickens in Serbia."

"Touchy, touchy. Was that the guy you're looking for? What did he hit you with? A pipe wrench?"

"I told you to shut up."

A panel truck pulled up to the rear of the airplane. It must have diverted Tower's attention. The plane shook again when he left.

Dragan looked relieved. "That was close," he said.

The next half-hour was taken up with loading. Vermeulen could hear the beeping of the forklift and the clicking of the tracks as the pallets were pushed into their spots in the cargo bay. Then the truck pulled away. A piercing whine indicated that the rear gate was being closed.

Vermeulen started breathing easier again.

José came back to the cockpit. "Who the fuck are you?" he said.

Vermeulen figured it was best to stay with the cover Anya had invented. "I work for Global Relief." He pointed to the ID on the lanyard.

"Don't give me that shit. Ben Tower wouldn't be searching the airport for you if that were true. That's not even your photo on the ID."

"Okay, you've got me there. I'm a journalist writing on the relief effort in Darfur. I don't have official accreditation, so Anya had the idea of passing me off as an employee of Global Relief."

"Who are you writing for?"

"I'm freelance. That's why I had trouble getting credentials."

The answer seemed to satisfy José. "You can take your seat now."

"Thank you both for not giving me up," Vermeulen said. "I really appreciate it."

"It didn't have anything to do with you. I love my job, and I don't want to lose it."

Vermeulen nodded and went back to his seat in the cargo bay. The new cargo looked familiar. He'd seen them last in the blue container outside the warehouse, the one meant for the Iraqi Air Force.

The roar of the engines starting closed off all other sensations. He sat down. It occurred to him that Assured Air Services' generosity was at least partly to serve as a cover for its illegal activities. A load of humanitarian goods took the scrutiny away from the other crates.

There was some talk in the cockpit. The four engines revved up and the Antonov taxied from the apron to the taxiway. The plane turned right, moved parallel to the runway, and picked up a little speed. Vermeulen saw the scrubland, bleached pale by the sun, move past his porthole. The air inside was getting very hot. No air conditioning.

They reached the end of the runway. The Antonov turned left and then left again. Just another minute and they'd be on their way.

That's when he saw the white and blue car with the red blinking lights through the porthole. The Antonov stopped.

CHAPTER TWENTY-FIVE

———◆———

VERMEULEN UNBUCKLED HIMSELF AND STUCK HIS head into the cockpit. José was busy talking to the tower.

"Is that car here for us?"

Dragan shot him a look of disbelief. "Of course. There's no other plane on the runway."

"What do they want?"

"We're gonna find out."

"Oh for Christ's sake," José said, taking his headphones off. "There are checking for unauthorized passengers. Two bottles of Scotch ain't worth this much hassle."

He set the brakes and turned to Vermeulen.

"Go hide way in back. Now! Duck behind the last pallet and don't move until I tell you so. This is the last time I let Anya talk me into anything."

Dragan rolled his eyes. As if that was going to happen.

Vermeulen hurried toward the rear of the plane and found a space between the last two pallets. He checked his watch. It was ten o'clock. Houser and Mansour knew he hadn't boarded the scheduled flight to El Fasher.

He heard José open the door. There was a shouted conversation that Vermeulen didn't understand. With a loud clank, José lowered the built-in stairs.

More voices. Then steps. Maybe two people. José and someone else. He fought the urge to peer around the edge of the pallet and find out who was there. Were they police? Airport officials? Mansour's goons? He had to trust José's ability to keep them at bay.

The steps seemed to move to the front, which was good. For the moment.

Then the steps came back again. Much closer.

"There's nothing back there," he heard José say.

The reply was a single grunt.

The temperature inside the fuselage had risen rapidly as the plane sat in the sun. Sweat dripped from Vermeulen's face. His shirt stuck to his skin. His right leg cramped and he desperately needed to stretch it.

The steps stopped at the pallet opposite.

"Just like I told you," José said. "Nothing back here either."

The steps came around the pallet. Vermeulen tried to crawl away. The leg refused to cooperate. He dragged himself across the floor. The space between the pallets wasn't wide enough to accommodate his body. There was nowhere to go.

He knelt and gripped the Glock for the second time that morning.

The man next to José wore a uniform Vermeulen hadn't seen before. He wasn't police or military. He looked like he had suddenly put on a lot of weight without having been issued a new outfit. Sweat beaded on his dark forehead and dripped past dull eyes. He was still breathing through his mouth, trying to catch his breath after the exertion of climbing the stairs.

"What is this?" he asked.

Vermeulen got up. He could tell that the man wasn't the sharpest knife in the drawer. He was the prototype for a whole category of bureaucrats who sat in their chairs so long that somebody somewhere decided to promote them because they were in the way of fresher blood, or it was embarrassing to the organization to have someone occupy the same seat for too long.

"I'm accompanying the Global Relief cargo to El Fasher," Vermeulen said, pointing with his left hand to the ID still hanging from the lanyard. The right still grasped the grip of the Glock.

"Highly irregular," the fat official said. "No paperwork for a civilian passenger was filed."

"I'm not a passenger," Vermeulen said. "I go with the cargo. That's different."

The man looked confused. "A person on a plane is a passenger, no?"

"Not always. See José here? He's a person on a plane, but he isn't a passenger, he's the pilot. I'm in a similar position. I accompany the cargo, so technically, I'm part of the cargo, which means I'm not a passenger. Therefore I need no paperwork."

"Yeah," José said slowly. "I'm sure it's in your regulations somewhere. It happens all the time. Didn't you know that?"

The airport official looked from Vermeulen to José and back. He'd heard the words but was unable to make sense of them. He scratched his head.

Vermeulen had seen it countless times before. Like all low ranking officials, he worried about being taken advantage of. At the same time he knew that raising a stink without knowing the regulations could make him look even more stupid, something he wanted to avoid at all costs.

It took a minute before he came to a conclusion. "Okay, you are not a passenger. But extra cargo cost extra airport fee." A big smile spread over his face.

If in doubt, demand a bribe, Vermeulen thought. He turned a bit so the man couldn't see the contents of his wallet. He pulled out two one-hundred pound notes and handed them to the man. The UN wouldn't reimburse him for the 45 dollars because the UN frowned on bribes, but it was the cheapest way forward.

"Okay, here, the airport fee. I don't need a receipt."

The fat man took the bills and made them disappear faster than anything he'd do that day.

"Very good. Everything is in order now."

* * *

AT TWENTY THOUSAND FEET, WITH NOTHING but blue sky and clear air visible through the porthole, the events of the past forty-eight hours seemed too fantastic to be true. But Vermeulen's aching body and blooming bruises weren't imaginary. His exhaustion trumped it all. The droning of the Antonov's engines lulled him into an uneasy doze. Whenever his head dropped too far down, some reflex in the reptilian part of his brain made him sit up straight again.

An hour into the flight, José came back and sat next to him. He held a thermos and poured Vermeulen a cup of black coffee. "Here you go. You look like you've been through the wringer. Why is everyone after you?"

Vermeulen took the coffee and sighed loudly after swallowing the hot liquid. "It's a long story. Knowing it would mean more trouble for you. You already know it involves your boss." He paused. "Why do you work for Houser?"

"I love to fly. This job lets me do that."

"There have got to be other places where you wouldn't have to break the law."

"Not nearly as many as you might think. Besides, I'm not breaking the law. I'm just piloting the plane. All flights are legal and approved. Okay, we fudge a flight plan occasionally. More often than not, it gets aid supplies to places that wouldn't get them otherwise."

"Is El Fasher your regular run?"

"For this plane, yes. We fly to El Fasher, Nyala, and El Geneina. They've got long enough runways. Our other Antonov is much smaller and can land at the secondary strips. I've been all over the place."

"Who do you supply? The Sudanese Armed Forces?"

"Them too, but we haul cargo for a lot of clients. I lost track of the whole alphabet soup of movements here. I know we've delivered to Southern Sudan."

"Doesn't that get you in trouble with the authorities?"

"Nah. It's not like they have the time to check on every flight. It's never been a problem. I assume Mr. Houser takes care of that."

"What about the cargo? You don't really know what's in the crates?"

"Well, you see the same kind of crates over and over, so you get an idea. I don't get paid to ask questions."

"What about this load? What's an AGM-114A?"

"I have no idea. All I know is it's special. This is not a routine flight. I just found out about it Saturday. Mr. Houser also told me to contact Global Relief and tell them we had unscheduled cargo space available."

* * *

THE COFFEE HAD REVIVED HIM. HE dug through his bag to find Ritu's diary. He'd read most of it on the flight to Port Sudan without finding any clues. He didn't hold out much hope to find anything in what remained.

The account of her disillusionment sounded familiar. Many people around the world, maybe most, considered the United Nations a good thing. It represented the antipode to the naked ambitions of states, especially the powerful ones. On TV screens around the world, the blue helmets stood for peace, de-escalation, and negotiations rather than attack. Unless you were an ardent nationalist, multilateralism just made more sense than unilateral attacks.

Up close, that image proved to be a lot more complicated. Vermeulen had experienced that in his years working for OIOS. Bismarck's comparison of a legislature to a sausage factory could easily be applied to the UN. While the outcome might be tasty, you wouldn't want to see the process.

On a personal level he had seen the same degree of naked ambition, incompetence, and self-centeredness he'd seen elsewhere. Just because someone worked for the UN didn't make them a better human being. At the institutional level, the bureaucratic inertia at the UN was no different from any government. He sometimes had to struggle with that even though his work for the Crown Prosecutor's office in Antwerp should have prepared him.

Ritu had begun full of idealistic fervor, eager to make a difference, and found that she had limited powers against the crushing forces of the status quo. It was a bitter pill to swallow. No wonder she sent her letter to the head of UNAMID. It was a logical step. Her disillusionment had turned to action. Someone wasn't doing their job and a woman died as a result. She was going to make sure it didn't happen again.

He reached the last entry:

I'm scared. I don't know what to do. Someone is following me. For the last two days, I've seen the same man several times.

At first, I didn't think much of it. There are many people working in Zam Zam. They are either working for or with the UN. So you see the same people a lot. I thought he might be working for one of the NGOs or the World Food Programme or another UN agency. How else could he get into Zam Zam?

Yesterday, I noticed he was looking at me from across several shacks. It wasn't the kind of look that makes you blush and look away. Not at all. It was a cold stare. Without any emotion. It chilled me to the bone. I stayed strong and stared back. He met my stare for a while before turning around.

He's tall, European, blond hair, a short goatee, wearing the usual khaki outfit. He's attractive-looking in a magazine sort of way. But the cold look in his eyes told me all I need to know about him.

Today, he was back. He followed us for the entire patrol. I didn't see him at every turn. We didn't have another staring contest, but I knew he was there.

Why? Did he come because of my letter? I hadn't seen him before that. Is he checking on my job performance, looking for something to discredit me?

I didn't tell Priya. I've bothered her enough with my complaints. I don't want her to think I'm paranoid, too.

It was dated March 8, two days before Roy was killed.

CHAPTER TWENTY-SIX

———————◆———————

IT WAS LATE AFTERNOON WHEN JOSÉ lined up the Antonov for the final approach to the El Fasher airport. In the minutes before, Dragan had given Vermeulen instructions for the arrival.

"Garreth Campbell is going to be there. He's Houser's point man in El Fasher. He mustn't see you. The moment the plane comes to a stop, grab your stuff and go to the back. Garreth usually waits by the door for José's report. I'll lower the rear ramp. The moment it's down, leave. Make sure you stay to the left of the plane. There'll be vehicles you can use for cover."

Tired and hungry, Vermeulen had no objections. Food and his bed were foremost on his mind. He did not want another confrontation with one of Houser's minions.

The Antonov touched down with a bump. The reverse thrusters kicked in, making any other sounds disappear. The plane slowed rapidly, bumping along on the concrete until it reached the turnaround at the end of the runway. From there it taxied past the small terminal to the cargo area. Before it came to a stop, Vermeulen took his bag and scrambled to the back of the plane.

As he waited for the ramp to open, the air inside the plane got hot again. He heard a few voices near the cockpit, but couldn't make out who was saying what. Ten minutes later, Dragan came back, opened a box affixed to the wall of the plane, and pushed a button. With a loud whine, the loading ramp sank to the ground.

A gust of hot wind laced with dust and burnt hydrocarbons swept into the fuselage. A grim reminder that the sea air of Port Sudan was gone for good. The ramp hit the ground with a metallic thud. Outside, a forklift waited. Vermeulen hurried down the ramp and took a right to make sure he stayed out of Campbell's sight, whoever he might be. He saw a flatbed truck standing not far away. A sticker on its door said Global Relief. He decided it was the best place for him to hide for now.

Halfway between the Antonov and the truck, he saw a white Toyota SUV pull up next to the truck. Its passenger door opened and Tessa got out. She waved. Vermeulen waved back and walked to the SUV. He kept from looking back, hoping that nobody on the other side of the plane noticed him walking across the tarmac.

"You look like shit," Tessa said.

They embraced each other.

"Thanks for getting me out of there," he said. "Who knows what would have happened?"

"We've been through an evening of cheap brandy, an ambush, and a cold night in a broken-down truck. I wanted to have at least one pleasant evening with you before they take you away."

She gave a gentle squeeze. He winced.

"So, what did happen to you?" she said.

"I got beat up pretty bad."

"I let you out of my sight for a weekend and all hell breaks loose. You've got to tell me everything. But let's get out of here first before anyone becomes suspicious. I owe Anya and don't want to get her into trouble."

"Let's get some food," he said. "I'm starving."

She hustled him into the rear seat and told Sami to step on it.

They drove around the plane. Standing there with José was a tall man in a khaki outfit with blond hair and a nicely trimmed goatee. If he hadn't known better, he'd have thought Dale Houser was supervising the unloading.

"Stop the car," Vermeulen said. Sami stepped on the brakes. "That man killed Ritu."

"Are you sure? I thought you said Houser did it," Tessa said.

"I was wrong. Amina told me that it was a blond man with a goatee, and I thought it was Houser, but he claims he was out of the country at the time. It didn't make sense until now. That man's name is Garreth Campbell, and he killed Ritu. Amina identified him and Ritu mentions him in her diary."

"What are you going to do? Arrest him? You have no authority to do that. Worst-case scenario, he'll have you arrested for stowing away on his damn plane. You'll make a ton of trouble for Anya and Global Relief."

He didn't really worry about getting arrested. That wasn't going to happen. Anya and Global Relief were a different story. Tessa was right.

Sami took off again. Vermeulen stared out the window at Campbell. Houser's point man in El Fasher. And an assassin.

Sami drove them to the al-Waha restaurant and left them there. Tessa coaxed him through the door and to the same table they'd sat at six days earlier. Samir was pleased to see them again. Tessa ordered roast mutton and tea for him.

"Let's start at the beginning," she said.

Vermeulen told her about the meeting with Mansour, the strange look from Fareed, being followed through Port Sudan, the International Club and Macklevore. Getting assaulted in his hotel room seemed more embarrassing now than when it happened. He skipped the details. Fortunately, the server brought their meal just then. He ate like the hungry man he was, methodical, masticating each bite efficiently, the next forkful ready when he swallowed. Tessa knew better than to interrupt him with questions.

When his plate was nearly empty, Tessa took out her phone and called Sami to pick them up.

"We're going back to the Crimson Lights Hotel. Sami and Wambui have scored some Tusker Lager. I thought you'd appreciate a cold beer, you being of Belgian heritage and all."

It was the best news he'd heard all week.

In the car, he remembered the crates from the blue container that had been loaded on the plane.

"Do you know what 'AGM-114A' stands for?"

"Sounds vaguely familiar. Where did you see it?"

"It was stamped on crates that came in a container and were loaded onto the plane. The odd thing is that they were supposed to be shipped to the Iraqi Air Force in Baghdad. Now they're in El Fasher. There's something not right."

She wrinkled her forehead. "Wait, I know. It's a model number for Hellfire missiles. You know, those things the U.S. fires from drones in Pakistan."

"Hellfire missiles?" Vermeulen knew about them. He'd seen the black-and-white videos of buildings or cars in shaky camera frames, punctuated by incomprehensible comments, followed by the sudden flash and the cloud of gas and dust of terrifyingly silent explosions.

"Did you say Iraqi Air Force?" Tessa said. "What are they doing here?"

"Obviously they have been diverted. The only forces here that could conceivably use them are the UN and the government. UNAMID isn't planning on arming its helicopters with missiles. They must be intended for the Sudanese Air Force."

"That's terrible news. That kind of escalation will doom the talks going on in Doha."

"Forget Doha. It's going to make life hell for a lot of people. How could Houser have gotten his hands on these? They don't just fall off some ship."

* * *

THEY CLIMBED THE STAIRCASE TO THE second floor of the Crimson Lights Hotel. Sami opened the door to his room. Wambui rose from a chair, beaming. Vermeulen clasped his hand and gave him what passed for an acceptable hug among men.

"Good to have you back, boss," Wambui said. "Heard there was a spell of trouble in Port Sudan. Here's a cold Tusker. I bet you've been wanting one for a long time."

"You'd better believe it. How did you get beer around here?"

"You can't deploy a battalion of Kenyan soldiers without their Tusker. The quartermaster's people know this and look the other way when the cases get loaded. Troop morale is more important."

Vermeulen took a deep swig and sighed with pleasure. It was the best beer he'd ever had.

The room looked plain. In Europe or the U.S., it would have qualified as a two-star room. In Sudan, it probably rated several stars higher. The large bed was covered by a wrinkled bedspread. There were two upholstered chairs, a small table, and a sofa.

Sami plopped into one of the chairs and Wambui took the other, leaving the sofa for Tessa and Vermeulen, who had to repeat the gist of his mission to Port Sudan to get Wambui and Sami up to speed. When Vermeulen told him about the crates of ammunition destined for the Kenyan contingent, Wambui was adamant that they got their supplies directly from home. Vermeulen pulled out his phone and showed him the photographs he had taken.

"Could Houser have landed a contract with your quartermaster?" he said.

"Never."

"How does the arms embargo work?" Tessa said.

"It prohibits the sale and delivery of weapons, ammunition, and related matériel to Darfur," Vermeulen said. "Any items sold to Sudan include a proviso in the end-user certification that these items cannot be transported to Darfur."

"Which, as we all know, Sudan ignores," Sami said.

"Yes. Therefore, most European countries no longer sell to Sudan. China and Belarus do, and they claim that they have been given assurances that their arms will not be used in Darfur." Vermeulen took another swig of beer.

"Right, we know how well those work. Are there no exceptions?" Tessa said.

"No," Vermeulen said. "The only exception the Security Council included was deliveries to UN-mandated troops in Darfur." As he spoke the sentence, he knew the answer. He slapped his forehead. "Of course. How dumb could I be? Houser uses forged end-user certificates that designate UNAMID troops as the consignee. The manufacturers are happy to make the sale. Everything looks legal."

"Who gets the ammo?" Tessa said.

"That's what we're going to have to find out. But it's not hard to imagine Houser selling his ammo to all sides."

Vermeulen was ready to get up again. Tessa pulled him back down.

"Not tonight, Valentin. You need rest. Doctor's orders."

She grabbed two more bottles of beer from the cooler. "Let's go to my room. You can show me Roy's diary."

The invitation to join her in her room came as a surprise. Not that he minded spending time alone with her, but he was also wary of her intentions. What did she want from him?

If Tessa noticed his hesitation, she ignored it as she coaxed him out to the corridor and into her room.

"Pull up a couple of chairs. I'll find an opener."

"I have one on my keychain," Vermeulen said as he pushed the chairs to either side of the table.

"A man after my own heart." She smiled. "At least when it comes to beer."

Her room was a replica of Sami's. Two chairs, a table, and a sofa. She pulled a chair so it stood next to the other.

They sat down.

Vermeulen smelled her familiar citrus scent and felt a little woozy. His worries disappeared.

"The diary?" she said.

"Oh, right."

He put the diary on the table. They started reading. More than halfway through, they reached the entry in which Roy recounted the death of the woman in the camp. Vermeulen wanted to flip the page. Tessa put her hand on his to stop him. He didn't move his hand. Neither did she.

"It must be a difficult job for policewomen," he said, pulling his hand back, suddenly self-conscious.

"Everything in a camp is difficult," Tessa said. "For everyone involved. Just talk to the aid workers. They face crises twenty-four/seven, and there's never enough of what they need. You're right, though. This is the most personal account I've ever seen."

She took a sip from her beer bottle.

"You want to finish reading? There isn't much more," he said.

"Sure."

They read the remaining entries. Roy's anger and then fear were palpable.

"I see why you wanted to go after that man by the plane," she said. "We need proof before we can do anything."

"How are we going to find that? He isn't going to admit it."

"You're the investigator. Do your job."

It was a challenge if ever there was one. She was right. He'd been following the trail of the APCs singlemindedly. As the case mushroomed in Port Sudan, his attention had shifted to survival. It was time to get back to investigating.

He sat back in his chair and pulled the pack of Gitanes from his pocket. He shook out a cigarette, then hesitated. "May I?"

"I'd rather you didn't. Can't stand the smell in my room."

"Fair enough," he said and drank from his beer instead. "If I'm going to do this, I need your help."

She turned to him, her face so close, he could smell the Tusker on her breath.

"Do you think you could work with me?" she said. "I think we make a pretty good team."

He looked into her eyes and knew she was right. His face moved closer to hers. He expected her to shrink back. She didn't. He wasn't sure of anything in that moment, except that he wanted to kiss her.

His usual doubts crowded into the foreground. She doesn't mean it that way, you idiot. She's just teasing. Get a grip.

Her head still hadn't moved back. Instead, it came forward. His lips touched hers, pushing his doubts away for good. They kissed gently. He pulled back and mumbled, "Yes, we're a pretty good team."

Her reply came quickly in the form of a more passionate kiss that lasted much longer. Standing up, he pulled her close and reveled in the sensation of her warmth against his body. He stood motionless, just letting their bodies meld. Pulling his head down, she kissed him again. His hands glided over her back, down to her buttocks and up the sides of her body. She let go of his head and started unbuttoning his shirt. He reciprocated. They laughed as their hands became entangled.

Tessa pushed him onto her bed and pulled his trousers off. She slipped out of hers, carefully put her glasses on the night table, and crawled in next to him. The feeling of skin against skin sent shivers down his spine. He caressed her stomach, feeling her skin ripple under the tips of his fingers as he followed the faint line of dark hair from her navel down to the elastic of her underwear. She planted butterfly kisses on his chest, each a little electric shock that puckered his skin. He released the clasp of her bra, dropped it on the ground, and pulled her on top of him. He could have stayed that way forever, their bodies blending, their skins becoming one. A different urge pushed into the foreground. They took off their remaining clothes and melted into each other.

CHAPTER TWENTY-SEVEN

———◆———

Dale Houser sat in his warehouse office. The ice in his scotch had melted. He gulped the last mouthful anyway. The burn in his throat took his attention away from everything that had gone wrong that day. The temptation to finish the bottle waited for that moment of weakness.

Houser pushed the bottle away. Getting drunk wouldn't help anything. So Vermeulen was gone. No big deal. He could deal with him later. At least the cargo was on its way. The retail value of the Hellfire missiles was three million dollars. That was for approved customers. The illegal value was more than double that. The best part was that he hadn't paid retail. The total bribes came to a couple hundred thousand. The rest was pure profit.

The only hang-up was the Sudanese suddenly balking at the price tag. Greedy bastards. Houser had anticipated that and kept every aspect of the transport secret. Only two people other than himself knew there were missiles in the container and where these missiles were at the moment—Tower and Campbell. He trusted them. Their bond was forged during the battles in the Falklands. It would withstand whatever anyone might throw at them.

Houser checked his watch. His Antonov should have landed in El Fasher by now.

As if urged into action by Houser's impatience, his phone rang. Garreth.

"Everything clear?" he said.

"Yes, the cargo arrived fine. It's in our warehouse."

"Has anyone seen the crates?"

"We unloaded the Global Relief stuff first and waited for them to clear out before we continued. The forklift driver is the only witness, and he knows who butters his bread. Besides, the labels on the crates are nondescript. For all he knows, they contain nothing special."

"Make sure there are extra guards at the warehouse. Let's take no chances."

"Wouldn't a change of the routine be suspicious?"

"You've got a point. But we can't take any risks."

"Okay, boss."

"I have some bad news," Houser said. "Vermeulen got away. He overpowered Ben, who acted like an idiot. He's disappeared."

"He probably just crawled into a hole in Port Sudan, waiting for the storm to blow over."

"No, I've met him. He isn't that kind of man. I'm certain he somehow made his way back to El Fasher."

"What makes you think that?"

"Where else could he be? That's where his investigation is. Here, he'd be hunted by us and Mansour's goons. In El Fasher, the UN will cover for him. I want you to find and eliminate him."

"Eliminate as in—"

"Yes."

"Okay. How much time to I have?"

"Very little. He has information that is detrimental to the company. Sooner rather than later, he's going to publicize it. That cannot happen. Under any circumstances."

"It's going to be difficult without proper preparation."

That was typical for Garreth, always wanting time for preparation as if he were on some training exercise.

"Then improvise," Houser said. "It's got to happen soon. Tomorrow at the latest, better yet tonight."

"You forget that I don't know where he is."

"Then find him, *now*. That's what I pay you for. Don't forget. It's your ass on the line if he spills the beans. You pulled the trigger."

Garreth didn't say anything.

"Is that clear? Make sure it's clean. No missing casings this time."

* * *

CAMPBELL STARED AT THE SILENT PHONE in his hand. This wasn't good. Not good at all. He liked to prepare for his jobs with care. For the Bangladeshi policewoman, he had spent a week tracking their patrols, arranging the mob, making sure the borehole was off-limits when the time came.

Houser's threat didn't surprise him. He'd used it before. *You pulled the trigger.* What nonsense. If it came to it, his testimony would nail Houser, too.

A conspiracy conviction was as bad as one for murder. Why didn't he ever appeal to his professionalism?

So, Mr. Vermeulen, where are you hiding? He pulled up his list of contacts he could rely on. They provided no useful information. Vermeulen hadn't been at his guesthouse, hadn't entered the UNAMID compound, and hadn't arrived on a commercial flight. Only three cargo flights had arrived that day, and one of those was the Assured Air Services flight.

It took almost half an hour to track down the numbers of the two other pilots. Neither one was pleased to be disturbed at this hour. Campbell managed to scare them by impersonating an official from the Sudanese Transport Ministry. The charade yielded no results. Neither pilot had transported an unscheduled passenger. El Fasher's airport was closed for the night. No one there to contact until the morning.

One more possibility crossed his mind. The TV journalist. Vermeulen had been hanging out with her. He could have gone to her hotel. A short phone call brought the desired result. A man fitting Vermeulen's description had indeed entered the hotel in the company of Ms. Tessa Bishonga. A small pang of jealousy rose in him. The journalist was quite a dish.

He drove to his apartment.

This wasn't a job for his M24 rifle. There'd be no opportunity to lie in wait a comfortable distance of six hundred feet away, focus on Vermeulen's forehead through the Leupold scope, and pull the trigger, knowing that he'd be dead 250 milliseconds later.

No, it'd be a close-quarters kill. Campbell selected his Ruger Mark III. Not as much punch as a Glock or Beretta, but it'd be quieter and less messy, more suited for the Crimson Lights Hotel or the WFP guesthouse.

After spending an hour cleaning the Ruger, he screwed on the suppressor and filled the magazine with ten .22 rimfire cartridges. Then he set out. With any luck, Vermeulen would not see the light of day.

Campbell reached the hotel at two thirty in the morning. There was a covered car park next to the main building. Several cars and pickups were already parked there. He nosed his truck into an empty slot and went to reconnoiter.

The hotel's entrance was locked. Not a surprise. This was El Fasher, after all. They rolled up the sidewalks after ten in the evening. There wouldn't be many late-night guests arriving. Those who did already had a key.

The hotel was a triangular two-story building, plain stucco over concrete blocks. A neon light attached to the façade of the upper story spelled the hotel's name appropriately in red. The main entrance bisected the long side of the triangle. There were two stairways to the second floor, one at each end of the long side. A second-story balcony spanned the length of the front. Oddly, none of the rooms had doors to the balcony, just windows. They were all dark. The only light visible was through a glass door that led to a common room.

A flat-screen TV hung on the wall. Several vinyl chairs and a sofa were arranged in viewing positions. Three tables with chairs stood scattered around. There was a Coke machine. Near the far corner stood a pool table. *Nice.* He hadn't known there was a pool table in El Fasher. Amazing what the influx of aid workers and UN staff had done for this sleepy town.

The entrance door was a simple metal door with a full-length glass inset. The lock didn't look complicated, but it couldn't be picked with a pocketknife. He briefly considered breaking the window, but decided against it. Too much commotion. There was a button for a bell. Presumably for the late-night partiers who'd lost or forgotten their keys. He couldn't imagine where in El Fasher one could party that late. Ringing it would be as bad as breaking the window. He made himself as comfortable as he could in the cab of his pickup. There was nothing to be done until the morning staff showed up.

CHAPTER TWENTY-EIGHT

———— ♦ ————

Tuesday, March 23, 2010

T HE RINGING OF HIS PHONE PULLED Vermeulen out of a deep sleep. It was way too early for anyone to call. His hand felt for the phone on his nightstand. It wasn't there. The ringing continued. Tessa turned over and rubbed her eyes. She sighed and grabbed the phone from her nightstand.

"Hans Reiker? I don't think you should answer him." She held the phone out of his reach. "Let's sleep a little longer."

He stretched his arm, trying the grab the phone.

"I really must talk to him. He's got important information."

She sat up, pushed the answer button, and said, "Mr. Vermeulen's office. How may I direct your call?" She listened, barely able to keep from bursting into laughter. "Just a moment, please."

She handed the phone to Vermeulen.

"Hello, Hans, what have you got for me?"

"Since when do you have a secretary? I thought you were in Darfur."

"I don't and I am. Someone playing around with my phone."

There was a moment of hesitation. "Ah, yes. Is this a good time to talk?"

"Perfect. Have you found something?"

"Yes. The head stamps of the cartridges you photographed indicate that these rounds were made in China and Israel. I consulted UN databases and our own records. The Israeli ammunition most likely was shipped to Chad in 2008 or 2009. Part of an arms sale that also included Tavor assault rifles, which are chambered for the 5.56mm NATO rounds you found."

Tessa was drawing little circles on his stomach with her index finger. It tickled.

"Can you hold on for a moment?" he said to Reiker and pushed the mute button.

"Please stop it, Tessa. This is really important. Reiker knows where the casing for the bullet that killed Ritu Roy came from."

Tessa gave him a mock pout and got up. "I can't believe I rank just below some spent casing. Well, your loss."

"You know you don't. Hans is doing me a great favor, and I don't want to put him out."

"I know. It's okay."

She wiggled her butt and disappeared into the bathroom.

"Okay, Hans, I'm back. Did Chadian rebels bring these to Darfur?"

"That's our assumption," Reiker said. "The Chinese ammunition are plain vanilla AK-47 rounds made by ammunition factory 31. Nothing surprising there. The most interesting find is the head stamp you sent without a picture. Are you sure those digits are correct?"

"Positive."

"It was made by the Royal Ordnance Factory at Radway Green in the UK. The stamp indicates that it was manufactured in 2009 and that the cartridge was match grade, which means it's made for sharpshooters. The date is well after the imposition of the UN and EU arms embargoes. That casing shouldn't be in Darfur."

"Why not?"

"All UK arms sales are filed with the UN Register of Conventional Arms. Radway Green ammunition is sold mostly to NATO armies. In 2009, that's where most of it went. With one notable exception. Assured Sovereignty—now there's a name for an arms dealer—ordered a large consignment for delivery to Kenya. That's all I know. You'll have to do the rest."

"Thanks, Hans. This was extremely helpful. I have something else for you that might make your work easier. I happened upon a warehouse of Assured Logistics—same owner—and found all kinds of ammunition bound for UN troops. Except, I think this is all fraudulent. I'll send you the pictures."

"Sounds good. Now get back to whatever you were doing when I called."

"I'm afraid it's too late for that."

* * *

CAMPBELL WOKE WITH A START WHEN someone knocked against his window. Orange clouds colored the sky. The sun hadn't quite made it above the horizon. The clock in the dash said that it was a quarter to six. He scooted up in his seat.

A man in a white shirt and gray trousers stood next to his pickup and motioned for him to lower his window.

"This is not a public parking space," he said when the window was down a crack.

"I'm sorry," Campbell said. "I arrived very late and wanted a room, but the hotel was locked."

"We have no rooms free."

"Are you sure? A friend of mine is staying here, and she told me there might be a room."

"I'm the manager. I know my bookings. The Crimson Lights Hotel is booked for the next two weeks."

"Could you check? My friend said she'd asked."

The manager shrugged and turned toward the hotel. Campbell stuck the Ruger into his waistband and covered the butt of the pistol with his vest. Then he got out and followed the manager.

The entrance was already open. He could've kicked himself for missing his opportunity. The manager walked behind the registration desk, opened the registration book, and ran his fingers down the list of entries.

"No, there is no opening. Your friend must have been wrong. Who is it?"

"Tessa Bishonga. She's a journalist."

The manager's demeanor changed rather abruptly.

"Oh, you're a friend of Ms. Bishonga. Welcome. Still, I'm afraid she was mistaken. There are no rooms available."

"Oh, well. Thanks for checking. What's her room number? Since I'm here, I might as well say hello."

"I'm afraid we don't give out room numbers."

"I understand. Could you ring her room and let her know I'm here?"

The manager had a pained look on his face. "I'm sorry, but it's very early in the morning. Ms. Bishonga has standing instructions not to wake her before seven thirty."

Campbell shook his head and stared outside. He wanted to grab the man by the throat, stick his pistol against his head, and march him to Tessa's goddamn room. That wouldn't do. Houser had ordered a clean hit. Which was as much in his interest as in Houser's.

"Do you have a piece of paper and an envelope? I want to leave her a note."

The manager handed him a piece of stationery and a pen. He moved a little down the counter and pretended to write a note. He folded the paper and stuck it in the envelope. He sealed it and scribbled Tessa's name on the front.

The manager took the envelope and stuck it into one of the cubbyholes behind him. Campbell could see the digits "209" above the hole.

"Could you recommend another place to stay?" he said.

The manager shrugged. "You could try the guesthouses operated by several of the UN agencies and aid organizations."

Campbell turned and left. He felt the eyes of the manager on his back and so had no choice but to go back to his truck. Just his luck that he should happen upon a conscientious employee. Any other place, he'd have been able to bullshit his way to the second floor.

The hotel sat on a large plot surrounded by a stone wall. Most of the plot was sandy, but just across from the car park, an enterprising soul had planted three rows of trees, perhaps hoping that these would eventually grow tall enough to provide shade. Planting trees was a bet against the future. So far, the bet had paid off. The trees were still alive but had a long way to go before they'd provide any shade. They did, however, provide cover for Campbell's pickup. Which meant he didn't have to drive all the way out of the compound. He wedged the truck between the last and the middle row.

He approached the hotel from the far side of the trees, well out of view of the main door behind which he assumed the manager lurked.

He took two steps at a time to the second floor and walked into the corridor. Industrial carpet muffled the sound of his steps. The rooms all faced the front. He counted eleven doors. That meant Room 209 was toward the other end, near the second staircase. That was perfect. Just a quick dash downstairs—no need to run past a lot of doors that might open unexpectedly.

The room was quiet. With his ear to the door, he thought he could hear some mumbling. They were probably awake.

He knocked, trying to mimic the soft but insistent knock of room service personnel worldwide. There was some rustling inside.

"Room service," he said, pulling the pistol from his trousers.

* * *

THE KNOCK ON THE DOOR INTERRUPTED the thoughts of a mutual shower Vermeulen and Tessa had been contemplating. They heard the room service announcing itself. She looked at him.

"Did you order room service?"

"No, but coffee would be good, wouldn't it?"

"I didn't order any room service," Tessa said loud enough to be heard through the door.

There was a moment's pause. Then the voice said again, "Room service." Tessa got up.

"I didn't order anything," she said, louder. "You've got the wrong room." Silence. Then another knock.

"Room service. Compliments of the management," the voice said.

"Have you ever gotten free coffee here?" Vermeulen said.

Tessa shook her head.

"No" she whispered. "I've stayed here five times already and the management never offered me anything complimentary. They have no reason. With all the UN and NGO presence, they're always booked. Are you sure nobody followed us here?"

Vermeulen nodded.

"Just a moment, please," she said. "I have to put some clothes on."

She did that, but then opened the window facing the balcony. She stepped out the window and disappeared.

Vermeulen got up.

Another knock came from the door.

"Room service, compliments of the management."

"Just a moment," he said and put on his shirt and trousers.

Tessa came back through the window.

"Psst," she hissed. "It's Campbell. He's got a gun. Quick, let's get out of here." She ran into the bathroom, flushed the toilet, and made all kinds of getting-ready noises.

"Hang on another second," she shouted at the door and pulled Vermeulen to the window. "Let's go to Sami's room."

Vermeulen was at a loss as to how Campbell could have known that he spent the night with Tessa. Or that he was back in El Fasher in the first place. It didn't slow him down. He grabbed his jacket and bag and followed Tessa. He pushed the window shut as far as it would go from the outside. Tessa knocked on the glass next-door. A long minute later, the curtains moved and Sami's sleepy face appeared.

"What's going on?" he said after opening his window.

"Somebody is trying to kill me," Vermeulen said. "He's outside Tessa's door with a gun in his hand, pretending to deliver room service."

Sami's face snapped from sleepy to full attention. They climbed in, and he closed the window and pulled the curtains.

"What do you want to do?"

"I don't know. Part of me wants to go out there and kick him in the nuts. Probably not the smartest move."

"You'd better believe it," Tessa said. "He's got a gun with a silencer—a real assassin."

They heard a bang and splintering of wood.

"He's just kicked the door in," Sami said. "What are we going to do?"

"He knew my room number," Tessa said. "He probably knows that you're next door. We can't stay here for long."

Vermeulen felt the Glock in his pocket.

"We're not entirely defenseless," he said, pulling the pistol from the jacket pocket.

"I don't think a firefight in a hotel is a good idea," Tessa said.

"That wasn't my plan. We can chase him away. Sami, call the front desk and complain about the noise."

Sami picked up the phone and explained with a cranky voice that a loud noise next door had woken him up. Would they please check on that and tell his neighbor to be quiet?

A few minutes later there were steps outside, a surprised shout at the broken door. More steps, more voices. Sami opened the door a crack and peered outside. Vermeulen peeked over his shoulder and saw hotel employees arguing with each other.

"I think we're safe for the moment," he said. "Whoever broke into the room left via the balcony."

He didn't see the white pickup standing between the trees.

CHAPTER TWENTY-NINE

———————◆———————

THE OFFICE OF THE MILITARY COMMANDER of UNAMID was just as busy as it had been during Vermeulen's first visit. This time the commander was in. The same three clerks from the Nigerian contingent sat staring at their monitors. One of them, a large female corporal, looked up whenever someone new came into the shed. If she recognized the newcomer, she nodded and went back to her typing. This gave the visitor permission to continue to the assistant's desk behind the partition. If she didn't, she raised her left eyebrow with an expression that made visitors reconsider whether their business was important enough to bother the assistant.

She didn't remember Vermeulen and so gave him the eyebrow treatment. With no time to mess with subordinates, he went through the door straight to the assistant's desk. He heard a chair fall back behind him and assumed the corporal hurried to stop him.

The assistant, a second lieutenant, also Nigerian, looked up. "And who might you be?"

The corporal appeared at the door. "I'm sorry, sir. He barged right through," she said with a tone of exasperation.

"I'm Valentin Vermeulen with OIOS, and I need to see the force commander immediately."

"Do you have an appointment?"

"No, this is an emergency."

"I'm afraid the general is busy."

"Then he'll have to get unbusy."

Vermeulen turned toward the commander's door.

The assistant jumped from his desk. "You can't just barge in there."

"Watch me."

He was a step away from the door when the assistant pulled on his shoulder. Vermeulen stopped and brushed the hand away.

"You touch me again, and I will make sure the Secretary-General will personally dismiss you and send you home. I imagine your military career would not survive that."

He said this quietly, without looking at the man. Then he knocked on the door and entered the commander's office.

Lieutenant General Adeyemo sat behind his desk. His uniform jacket hung on the chair back.

"Mr. Vermeulen," he said with a congenial smile. How he knew his name was a mystery to Vermeulen. "I'm sorry I missed you on your last visit. I'm glad to meet you, finally. I trust my deputy was able to address your concern."

"Thank you, General, he did."

"What can I do for you?"

"I have sensitive information about arms transfers in violation of Security Council Resolution 1591/2005."

The general wiped his face with his hands. "What kind of information?" he said.

"Five crates containing Hellfire air-to-ground missiles were shipped to El Fasher for the Sudanese Air Force."

The general shook his head as if his day had just gotten a lot worse. "How do you know this?"

"I was on the plane that brought them here."

The general raised his eyebrows, but he was smart enough not to ask the obvious question. "Where are they now?"

"I assume some warehouse near the airport. That's why speed is of the essence."

The general wiped his face again. All traces of congeniality had vanished. "What would you like me to do about it?"

"I'd like you to order a couple companies of UNAMID troops to move to the airport and confiscate the weapons. It's a flagrant violation of the arms embargo by the Sudanese government."

The general shook his head. "You have an exaggerated sense of my powers."

"I don't think so. All I'm asking is that you follow your mandate to prevent armed attacks and protect civilians."

"You didn't do your homework sufficiently, Mr. Vermeulen. While you are correct about preventing attacks and protecting civilians, my mandate does not include enforcement of the 2005 resolution or disarmament of any of the parties."

"This isn't the time for splitting hairs, General. It's vitally important that these missiles not reach the Sudanese Air Force. Once deployed, there won't be any peace to keep."

The general shook his head. "I understand that, Mr. Vermeulen. I've been here a year and a half, and I know full well how these missiles will destroy what little we have achieved. But my mandate is to assist in the implementation of the Darfur Peace Agreement and to protect civilians. I'm afraid that does not include confiscating Sudanese weapons, even if they've gotten here in violation of Resolution 1591."

"These weapons will kill civilians. How can you look the other way?"

The general's face changed from weary to angry. "Don't you tell me how to do my job. I'm commanding a cobbled-together mission with a cowardly mandate only the UN Security Council could conceive. I'm responsible for the lives of twenty-five thousand soldiers and police whose countries and families expect them to come back alive. I can risk their lives only within the strict limits of the mandate. If I go beyond that, I'll have fifteen governments and the Under-Secretary-General for Peacekeeping wanting my head."

The general paused and took a deep breath.

"Do I wish I had a more robust mandate? Of course I do. That, and a couple battalions of well-trained troops, and I'd make sure nobody so much as farted in Darfur without my permission. Those are not the realities I face. I hope you understand that."

Vermeulen nodded. Making the general angry didn't help anything. "I apologize for my earlier comment. Can't you contact New York and get special permission? I think a quick operation would be bloodless and the Sudanese would be embarrassed."

"You don't know the Sudanese. They say all the right words, but on the ground they constantly challenge us. In some parts of the North, we can't even go on patrol without getting permission from the local garrison commander. When we ignored that, our troops were attacked in the dark by unknown men in unmarked vehicles."

"So we just let them deploy the missiles?"

"I'll notify New York. Where did these missiles even come from?"

"According to the crates, they were destined for the Iraqi Air Force."

A wan smile crossed the General's face. "That doesn't surprise me at all," he said. "It doesn't take much money to make that happen. I'll notify New York and the U.S. liaison. I'm sure the Americans would like to know where their lost cargo ended up. That alone might keep the government here from deploying them. Who knows?"

Vermeulen didn't think the general's prognosis stood a snowball's chance in hell. The UN would get bogged down in stalemate, and the U.S. would be too embarrassed to admit that their Iraqi protégés were corrupt enough to sell a load of Hellfire missiles to the highest bidder.

He stood up. "I appreciate your time, General. I understand that your job here is very difficult. Let's hope your course of action has the desired results."

The general got up, too, and stretched out his hand. Vermeulen shook it.

"I know you disagree with me, and I can see you don't believe my course of action has any chance of success. But I urge you not to take matters into your own hands. You can't predict what will happen. So I ask you to leave these things to me."

Vermeulen nodded and headed to the door. When he reached it, he turned. "I can't promise that, General. I assure you that whatever happens, it won't jeopardize the UN mission."

* * *

So the 'Room service' trick hadn't worked. No big deal. It had been a spur-of-the-moment decision, and Campbell knew it was a little too obvious. The front desk might make the wakeup call; but room service, compliments of the management? That was really stretching it. Worth a try, but no big deal when it failed.

More importantly, Vermeulen hadn't seen him. All he knew was someone was after him, but not who. That was a key advantage, and Campbell was going to use it.

He leaned against a light pole near the force commander's office and pretended to read the latest issue of the magazine the publicity office of UNAMID put out once a month. Who's new to the force, who's leaving, silly training exercises, and of course, lots of coverage of a couple of projects that supposedly helped the locals.

The Ruger with its suppressor was stuck in his shoulder holster under his bush jacket. To the passersby, he was just another European consultant on break. The compound was busy; a constant stream of white military vehicles and pickups inched their way through the narrow lanes. The people milling about could have been extras for some video celebrating diversity, except most of them wore uniforms. His UNAMID cap and aviator sunglasses helped him blend in just fine.

The door of the force commander's shed opened, and Vermeulen stepped out. Campbell lifted the magazine a little higher. Through the slit between his visor and the magazine, he saw Vermeulen scan the area in front of the office. Vemeulen's head turned right past him. Campbell waited for that little hesitation, the telltale sign that his presence had been registered. It didn't happen. The man was as good as dead.

* * *

VERMEULEN HAD SEEN CAMPBELL THROUGH THE window of the commander's office. It wasn't much of a cover, standing there leaning against a light pole. Straight from some 1950s spy movie.

Back at the hotel, he and Tessa had debated how to deal with him. Tessa wanted to shoot him on sight.

"You've got a gun. He's trying to kill you. It's self-defense."

"I'm not going to give you the full legal definition of self-defense, but shooting him on the street doesn't qualify."

"He's after you. Just get him first."

"Unfortunately, the George W. Bush definition of self-defense doesn't cut it. Besides, I have different plans for him. I need him to testify against Houser."

"How are you going to do that?"

"I don't know yet. I'll make a plan with Priya Choudhury."

A squad of Tanzanian soldiers marched past the commander's shed. Vermeulen fell in step with them to put some distance between himself and Campbell. The squad marched toward the square where the memorial had taken place only a week earlier. When they reached the edge of the square, Vermeulen peeled off to the right and ducked into a large tent that served as the vehicle repair garage.

The shop was busy. A pickup sat up on a lift and was missing a rear axle. The engine of another truck hung from a hoist. A wrecked vehicle sat in the far corner, good for spare parts. Three more vehicles were going through what looked like oil changes. One mechanic was busy cleaning air filters with compressed air. The dusty roads had to wreak havoc on engines.

The mechanics had raised several of the tent's panels to let some breeze circulate. That gave Vermeulen a chance to keep an eye on the path. Campbell should come along any minute.

He took out his phone and dialed Choudhury's number.

"Where are you?" she said.

"South end of the square. At the repair shop."

"Did he see you?"

"You bet."

"Did he follow you?"

"I'm sure he will," he said. "He's in a hurry. He doesn't have time to set things up carefully. He's improvising. Once I see him, I'll double back from here and get behind him. You'll come across the square and we'll have him boxed in."

Vermeulen sounded more confident than he felt. He'd been a target only once in his life, when some hit man for a Brussels crime syndicate had gotten it into his head that killing the prosecutor would make the charge against his boss go away. With around-the-clock protection, Vermeulen never had to face the killer.

This time, so much could go wrong. He touched his jacket pocket. The heft of the Glock in it gave him some assurance.

He peered out of the repair tent. The Tanzanians were doing drills. They looked just as excited as he'd been during his army days, which is to say, not at all.

Campbell stood some thirty feet away at the edge of the square and looked straight ahead. He probably assumed that Vermeulen had continued across the square after the Tanzanian squad stopped. This was the moment to double back and get behind him.

Past the repair shop, a narrow lane ran parallel to the street he'd come on. A long storage tent provided good cover. Vermeulen hurried back until he reached a walkway that led back to the main street. Once there, he ducked behind one of the administrative sheds and peered toward the square.

Campbell was gone.

* * *

CAMPBELL STARED ACROSS THE SQUARE AND wanted to kick himself. Vermeulen had disappeared. Had he managed to cross the square before Campbell had gotten there? Not likely. The man wasn't a sprinter. The fact that he had even pulled this disappearing act worried him. Did Vermeulen know he was being followed? That didn't make sense. How could he have recognized him? They'd never met. Unless someone had warned him. That Bangladeshi woman cop? The journalist? That didn't really seem possible. He'd been stealthy. It was one of the things he was good at.

The UNAMID compound was laid out in a basic grid pattern. Main streets following the cardinal directions created blocks that were intersected by narrower lanes. The spaces in between were occupied by a dense array of aluminum sheds and tents to accommodate the needs of the sprawling operation.

Campbell was a sniper—the one skill the military had taught him. Everything else, he'd learned on his own, working with Houser. The first lesson in sniper training was making sure that your back was covered. A sniper is so focused on the target ahead that it's easy to forget a threat coming from behind. That lesson seemed particularly pertinent right now.

Vermeulen could've doubled back to get behind him. The man showed remarkable initiative for a desk jockey, so it was definitely possible. Campbell resisted the temptation to turn around. Don't let him know you know.

The Tanzanians were still doing their drills on the square. Other UNAMID personnel walked past him. Where was Vermeulen?

He saw the garage and the large storage tent to his right. Both provided excellent cover. Vermeulen must have decided to loop back. Well, two could play that game. He cut through the repair shop and darted past the storage tent.

Across the open space that lay between the storage tent and the aluminum sheds along the main street, he saw a figure run from one shed to the next. It had to be Vermeulen. He waited. Yes, there he was. Vermeulen crouched behind a different shed, about a hundred feet away. If only he had his rifle, it'd be an easy shot and the thing would be over. It would be loud, but he'd get away in the confusion. The Ruger with the suppressor was quiet, but it required proximity for a sure kill. At a hundred feet, chances for a sure hit were marginal.

There was no cover between him and Vermeulen. The only option was to continue to the end of the lane and cross over to the street.

A corporal from the Nigerian contingent stopped and eyed him with curiosity.

"Are you lost?" he said.

Campbell stared back with his *Get lost!* look. It was enough to send the soldier on his way.

The small distraction proved to be crucial. When he reached the main street again, Vermeulen was gone.

* * *

VERMEULEN DIDN'T HAVE THE BENEFIT OF sniper training. In his army days, the intelligence unit only fired shots during its mandatory firing range exercises. Nobody ever told him to watch his back. Nobody had to. It was something he'd learned in the bureaucratic trenches, first in the prosecutor's office and then at the UN. Over the years, it had become second nature.

So it wasn't a stretch for him to suspect Campbell of having followed him. That suspicion was confirmed when he looked back and saw a shadow flit between two tents along the walkway he'd used only minutes earlier.

His plan was falling apart. Campbell had been smart enough to see through his maneuvers. It was a bad situation—two men circling each other, waiting for the moment where they were close enough to pull the trigger. He had to coax Campbell into a spot where he could surprise him.

The square was still occupied by the drilling Tanzanians. A group of policemen walked past him toward the open space. He repeated his earlier strategy and fell in step with them. Two of the cops looked at him, probably wondering why this stranger was walking with them. He nodded and said, "Hello." They nodded back.

Since backtracking had failed the first time around, it made no sense to try it again. Instead, he chose the street that led east from the square. As soon as he made it past the first structure, he ran fast, then ducked behind the fifth shed. The space between the two structures was no more than three feet. He leaned against the wall and caught his breath. His right hand grasped the Glock in his pocket.

He strained to listen for steps on the path. The drone of two air conditioners made it difficult to hear. The people who worked in these makeshift offices stayed inside unless they had to run an errand. Unlike most of the soldiers, the civilian employees got to enjoy the cool inside.

His phone vibrated in his pocket. Probably Choudhury. He didn't answer.

There was another sound. A rustle like sand shifting underfoot. It didn't come from the path. It came from behind him.

The cold metal of a gun muzzle pressed against his neck.

CHAPTER THIRTY

———◆———

Priya Choudhury stood near the northwestern end of the square and stared at her phone. Vermeulen wasn't answering. It meant he was busy dodging Ritu's killer, which was part of the plan. It also meant she'd lost track of his location, which wasn't. The western and northern sides of the square were fully visible, but the Tanzanians blocked her view of the area where she assumed Vermeulen would be waiting.

They should've planned this better, accounted for the random events that might interfere. Case in point, those soldiers drilling in the middle of the square. But then, improvising meant using the random to one's advantage. She hurried across the open space, keeping the squad between herself and the southern part of the square. As she reached the soldiers, they finished the drill and began to march back to the main street at the southern end of the square. She followed them until she reached the first shed, where she stopped.

The clues she'd found at Zam Zam had told her that Campbell was a trained sniper. No ordinary guy with a gun could have fired three shots, all of them clean hits over a distance of six hundred yards. The guy had military training. He'd be careful and circumspect. He could well anticipate Vermeulen's movements.

She examined the rows of sheds and tents that lined the square and the streets. To get behind Campbell, Vermeulen's best bet would have been to turn right when he reached the square and use the repair tent as cover. She could see the lane running parallel. It was the most obvious choice. If Campbell expected that, he would have followed him. Which meant that he was now behind Vermeulen. And Vermeulen was nowhere to be seen.

Up to this point, her desire to avenge Ritu's death had been her driving force. She wanted to face the killer and make him pay for what he'd done. It hadn't been easy to agree to Vermeulen's demand that the man be arrested. She still thought it was too good a fate for him. Vermeulen had implored her to let go, and he'd been right. Now he was in trouble, and that changed things. He'd surprised her with his initiative. He wasn't at all like the other UN bureaucrats she'd met. Maybe he was smart enough to anticipate Campbell's moves. In that case, where would he have gone? Not across the square. That was obvious. The only other option was the street leading east. She hurried in that direction but stopped almost immediately. Better not use the street. It was too obvious. She crossed over the sand behind the repair shop and eased forward.

* * *

"YOU'RE NOT GOING TO GET AWAY with it," Vermeulen said.

"I don't see why not," Campbell said behind him. "A .22 Ruger with a suppressor is surprisingly quiet. I'll be out of here before anyone notices."

A hand patted Vermeulen's sides. It stopped and lifted the Glock from his pocket.

"We know who you are," Vermeulen said.

"You've never seen me. And you'll die that way."

"Wrong. You are Garreth Campbell," Vermeulen said. "You killed Ritu Roy with bullets that were traced back to Houser's company, the same Houser who just smuggled crates of Hellfire missiles to El Fasher. I've already reported that to the force commander here. Houser is going down, and you should ask yourself if you want to go down with him."

"Nonsense," Campbell said. Then, sounding less certain, "Turn around."

Vermeulen turned. Campbell's pistol looked strangely front-heavy, with the suppressor almost as long as the gun itself.

"I wouldn't be so sure," he said. "You killed Ritu Roy. I have a witness for that. That's an attack on the UN forces. Don't think they won't prosecute that. Even if they don't, the Bangladeshis will. I know Houser told you to kill her, but I'm sure he's not going to take the fall for that."

"Once you're dead, that storm will pass, too. Houser is too well connected. I'm not worried."

Vermeulen had run out of things to say. Where was Choudhury? They should have coordinated better. But then, no plan survives the first contact with the enemy.

He looked over Campbell's shoulder and smiled like he saw someone behind him.

"Nice try," Campbell said. "But it's the oldest trick in the book."

"It may be an old trick," Vermeulen said, raising his voice. "But one time out of a thousand it might not be a trick. Did you think I'd come here on my own? Against a trained sniper? Well, think again."

"Who'd help you? Your journalist friend?"

"No, Priya Choudhury." He almost shouted her name. "And she has absolutely no compunction about blowing you away the same way you blew away her best friend."

Campbell's eyes flickered. "Well, then, I'd better finish this quickly."

He pointed the pistol at Vermeulen's head.

* * *

CHOUDHURY GLANCED AROUND THE EDGE OF yet another shed. Nothing. On to the next one. Still nothing. This was taking too long. A quick dash to the fourth shed. Another glance. Where was Vermeulen? If she'd chosen the wrong street, he'd be in real trouble.

Another run to the next shed. She heard voices and stopped. The noise of the air conditioners drowned out most of the conversation, but the voices were ahead of her. She heard Vermeulen shouting her name. It sounded desperate. She hurried around the next corner and saw the back of a man who pointed his gun at Vermeulen.

Campbell!

Her first instinct was to shoot the man. The cold hatred rose again from the bottom of her stomach. She was facing the man who'd killed Ritu. Her agreement with Vermeulen seemed immaterial now, the niceties of arrest and trial a waste of time. This man was about to take his last breath.

Her police training kicked in. A 9mm bullet fired this close would blow right through Campbell and hit Vermeulen. Back home, her magazine would have held hollow-point cartridges, which didn't exit the target but caused massive internal injuries. Those bullets were not allowed here because the Hague Convention banned ammunition that expands inside the human body. Her entire unit had been issued regular full metal jacket NATO cartridges.

She inched close to the aluminum wall, hoping for a better angle. There wasn't one. The other option was to shoot the man's foot. That left him in possession of his gun, and he could still fire.

The radio on her belt touched the wall of the shed. Not hard, like a bang. No, it just barely brushed against it. To her ears, it sounded like she'd hit a gong.

* * *

VERMEULEN SAW CHOUDHURY COME AROUND THE corner. He saw her raise her gun and aim. Then she hesitated. He knew she was a cautious person, but this wasn't the moment for caution. Was she looking for a better angle?

Christ, just shoot him. The angle doesn't matter as long as you hit him. Then he remembered a rule they drilled into him at basic training. Pay attention to what's behind your target. He was behind the target. *Good woman*, he thought. She was right to be cautious. She leaned against the wall of the shed. Something on her belt touched the wall.

The sound changed everything. Campbell didn't hesitate. An unarmed man in front of him was less dangerous than an unknown enemy behind. He spun around.

Vermeulen figured that Choudhury had plenty of training to deal with armed assailants. His job was to get out of the way. He dropped to the ground and rolled as close to the wall as he could.

The silence that followed couldn't have been more than a blink of an eye. But it seemed like an eternity.

* * *

Choudhury's hesitation only lasted a moment. She saw Campbell spin around and recognized him immediately. Vermeulen's description had been vague. It could have fit any number of Europeans in El Fasher. She had seen this man hanging around the camp, talking to one of her colleagues at the mess hall. Just a lonely contractor looking for romance, she'd thought. Now she knew why he'd been there. He'd been keeping tabs on her.

A rush of hot anger flashed through her. It passed just as quickly. A cold calm followed. She'd succeeded. She was facing the man who killed her best friend. There would be no trial. There would be justice, her justice.

She saw Vermeulen dive down. Smart man, exactly what she'd hoped for.

Campbell's eyes signaled his intentions. She dropped to her knee just as Campbell fired. His bullet whistled above her head.

She pulled the trigger once, made a microscopic adjustment and pulled it again. A double-tap at the center of body mass, just as she'd been trained. Campbell dropped as if the ground below him had given way.

CHAPTER THIRTY-ONE

———◆———

D EALING WITH THE AFTERMATH OF THE shooting lasted into the early afternoon. The Kenyan Military Police were in charge of the investigation. A lieutenant questioned Vermeulen, who told him the bare minimum. He was investigating a conspiracy to defraud the UN. Campbell, part of the conspiracy, had followed and cornered him. He was about to kill Vermeulen when, by sheer luck, Constable Choudhury passed. In the resulting exchange of fire, Campbell was killed. The lieutenant asked him a few perfunctory questions and told Vermeulen he was free to go. Maybe Wambui had put in a good word for him.

Immediately after killing Campbell, he and Choudhury had argued over how to handle the situation. She was eager to show that Ritu hadn't been a victim of random mob violence, that Campbell had been her assassin. It was all about vindicating her dead friend.

Vermeulen saw it from a strictly legal perspective. Their evidence pointing to Campbell as the shooter was weak, just a spent casing, Amina's testimony, and an entry in Ritu's diary. The descriptions of the shooter fit any number of Europeans in El Fasher. Vermeulen himself had thought it was Houser.

Campbell was also a private citizen, not connected to any of the contingents of UNAMID. That put him into a legal no-man's-land. Strictly speaking, Ritu's death fell under either Bangladeshi or Sudanese jurisdiction, because she was a Bangladesh national and because the crime occurred in Sudanese territory. The Bangladeshi commander had already closed Ritu's file, and the Sudanese weren't going to investigate a shooting in the UNAMID headquarters.

The simple explanation they agreed on settled the matter best. Choudhury's actions were justified by the mandate, which permitted the use of force for the protection of UNAMID personnel. Case closed.

Vermeulen had no doubt that Choudhury would be the unofficial hero of her unit. No way would she keep to herself the fact that Campbell had killed Ritu, that she'd accomplished what she set out to do.

He, on the other hand, wasn't anywhere near being done. He called Tessa to tell her what happened.

"I thought you wanted to arrest him?" she said.

"It didn't work out that way. He cornered me, and Choudhury got there just in time."

"You crazy man. One of these days your half-assed plans will come back to bite you. What are you up to now?"

"I have to check in at my office. There's Jirel, the APC fraud, and the Hellfire missiles."

* * *

At fifteen minutes past two that Tuesday, Dale Houser finally lost his patience. He'd been pacing in his warehouse office, waiting for Campbell's call, for news that Vermeulen had been dealt with. He pulled his phone from his pocket and pushed the redial button for Campbell's number. The ring sounded increasingly forlorn. It continued for a few seconds until a different beep indicated that the call had rolled over to voicemail.

He left his third message. This was unusual. Campbell always got back to him after the first message. It was a point of pride for him not to leave his boss waiting. Maybe his battery had run out. But in that case the call would have gone to voicemail without ringing first. Had he left his phone somewhere? That wasn't like Campbell at all.

At three, he called again. The phone rang again for several seconds. Another message would do no good. He was about to hang up when Campbell answered. Except it wasn't Campbell. A voice with an East African accent said, "Who is this?"

"Where is Campbell?" Houser said.

"Who are you, and how do you know Mr. Campbell?"

"Since you are in possession of Mr. Campbell's phone, shouldn't you explain who you are first?"

There was a moment's hesitation. "This is Corporal Omondi, Kenya Military Police on detachment to UNAMID. Who are you?"

Houser stared at his phone. This wasn't good. It wasn't good at all. He was tempted to hang up right then. But he needed to know. Besides, Campbell worked for him, and he had every right to call his employee.

"This is Dale Houser, president of Assured Sovereignty. Mr. Campbell works for me, and I've been trying to reach him all day."

"I'm sorry, Mr. Houser, but Mr. Campbell is dead."

The message hit Houser like a vicious blow to the stomach. Its stark simplicity only amplified it. Campbell dead? He slumped into his chair. How could that be? The man was in perfect health. He didn't smoke, drank with moderation. How could he be dead?

"How …?"

"I'm afraid I can't comment on that. The investigation is still ongoing. The Mission spokesperson will issue a press release when the investigation is completed."

"He is … was my employee. I have a right to know how he died."

"The information will be released in due time, Mr. Houser. Until then, this is all I can tell you."

"Are you sure it's Campbell?" The stupidity of the question struck Houser the very moment he asked it. They had his goddamn phone. Of course it was Campbell. He ended the call.

"Garreth, you were a loyal friend," Houser said to the closed door of his office. "You had my back at Mount Longdon. You've had it many more times since then. What happened to you?"

He dialed the airport office of Assured Air Services.

"I need to go to El Fasher. Now!"

* * *

GIANOTTI JUMPED UP FROM HIS CHAIR when Vermeulen entered the office. He'd obviously been waiting.

"You won't believe what I found out."

"Well, let me sit down first," Vermeulen said. He put his bag on his desk and pulled out his chair. "Okay, let's hear it."

"I've made a major discovery," he said, adding enough of a dramatic pause to make Vermeulen feel antsy.

"Once a month, usually on a Monday, the commander of the Nepali police unit, Superintendent Jirel, puts on civilian clothes, drives up from Zam Zam, and visits the El Fasher branch of the Bank of Khartoum."

Vermeulen nodded.

"You might wonder why the man, so far from home, has to visit this bank so regularly." Gianotti was obviously enjoying this moment. "Well, he withdraws a certain sum of cash and puts it into his leather briefcase."

"From his account?" Vermeulen said.

"I didn't check. I figured it has to be his. You can't withdraw cash from someone else's account, can you?" Gianotti's smile disappeared. "Come on! I'm not done yet."

Vermeulen shrugged.

"He then walks two blocks to a branch of the National Bank of Sudan, where he wires the cash abroad."

"How did you find that out?"

Vermeulen instantly wished he hadn't asked. Gianotti broke into a glamorous story in which he, like James Bond, followed Jirel around town the day before and then wheedled the rest of the information from talkative tellers.

"Are you sure he didn't see you?" Vermeulen said.

Gianotti screwed up his face. "Of course I'm sure. I knew what I was doing."

"The teller didn't get suspicious?"

"Not at all. Valentin, I was born to do that kind of job. So much better than going through the books."

"I bet it was. What do you make of it?"

"The way I see it, someone sends him money and he wires it elsewhere."

"Well, that's bloody obvious, isn't it? Think for a moment. Who's sending the money and who's getting it?"

Gianotti sulked for a moment. "Okay," he said, rallying back. "But this is pure speculation. The UN pays the Nepali government for the APCs, right?"

Vermeulen nodded.

"The UN is paying for new equipment, but the actual vehicles are old and far less valuable. If the people handling these accounts in the Nepali government think these are new vehicles, they would expect the full payment. But if they know the APCs are used, they wouldn't expect that much money. Someone could skim the extra money off the top and send Jirel his share. How am I doing?"

Vermeulen was impressed. Gianotti had put two and two together.

"Why doesn't Jirel just keep his money in Nepal?" he asked.

"Maybe he doesn't think it's safe there? With his money abroad, the government will have a hard time getting to it if the scam is ever discovered."

"Right," Vermeulen said. "He moves it to a different bank to interrupt the money trail. Good job, Gianotti. I'll tell Bengtsson that he should assign more complex jobs to you."

Gianotti beamed and turned back to his computer. Vermeulen sat down at his desk and pondered the news. There were still many holes. Was Houser getting a share of the money? Or was Jirel operating on his own, as Houser claimed? What about Mansour?

He lit a Gitane. Gianotti harrumphed. Vermeulen remembered their deal from three days ago.

"Sorry, I forgot."

There was no shade outside the door, and he walked around the shed until he found a spot out of the sun.

Funny how the APC scam that had started his entire investigation now seemed like just another small-time fraud. Yes, they'd nail Jirel for it. It seemed curiously unsatisfying. Jirel was nothing but a bit player in this whole affair.

Houser, on the other hand, was as elusive as ever. Things couldn't have turned out better for him. Campbell was dead. Houser could walk away from everything. There was a chance that Jirel might have some incriminating evidence, but Vermeulen doubted that. It was in Jirel's best interest to keep quiet. Even if he agreed to talk, Houser would simply show the original end-user certificate, which listed the APCs as used, and put all the blame on Jirel.

Then there were the Hellfire missiles.

* * *

VERMEULEN WALKED STRAIGHT INTO THE FORCE commander's office. The front office staff had obviously been instructed to let him in without delay. The conversation with Lieutenant General Adeyemo turned out as badly as Vermeulen had expected. The Department of Peacekeeping Operations didn't want to rock the boat and forwarded the information about the violation of the embargo to the Security Council in the hope that it would convene an emergency session. Until then, General Adeyemo was not to undertake any unilateral action under any circumstances.

"I'm afraid that's all I can tell you, Mr. Vermeulen," Adeyemo said. "I know it's not what you wanted to hear, and believe me, I didn't want to hear it, either. Nothing would have given me more satisfaction than commanding one of our squads to seize the missiles. My hands are tied. I hope you understand."

"Thank you, General. I appreciate your taking it this far. Do you think the Security Council will act?"

Adeyemo shook his head.

"No. I don't expect it."

Vermeulen nodded.

"Just as I thought. Thanks again."

He shook Adeyemo's hand and left the shed. Outside, his phone rang again. It was Bengtsson from Nairobi. That could only mean worse news.

"What the hell are you doing there? I got a call from the Under-Secretary-General, who got a call from the U.S. Military Staff Committee at their UN mission saying that any information related to missing missiles is classified and may not be mentioned, reported, or otherwise made public. I didn't even know what they were talking about."

Vermeulen let out a deep sigh. "During my investigation of the APCs, I came across information that the same company that sold the vehicles—and most likely was involved in the fraud—had also gotten its hands on a number of Hellfire missiles that it sold to the Sudanese government in clear violation of the arms embargo. The missiles are sitting at the airport here. I asked the force commander to confiscate them. He contacted New York instead."

"The Under-Secretary-General also received a call from the British mission to the UN complaining that an OIOS investigator was harassing a British businessman in Port Sudan. She told me to tell that investigator to back off. So, from now on, leave Mr. Houser, whoever he is, alone."

"Houser is the one who sold the missiles to Sudan. His company acquired them somehow and shipped them here."

"How do you know that?"

"I was on the plane. I saw the crates."

"You were *where*?"

"I was on the plane. It's a long story. You're probably better off not knowing it."

It was Bengtsson's turn to let out a deep sigh. "I'm sorry," he said. It was the first time that Vermeulen had heard him apologize. "I know you're doing your job. It bugs the hell out of me, but I have to call you off."

There was a moment of silence. Bengtsson continued, "Those two-faced Americans are driving me up the wall. Always screaming about UN reform and cutting waste. Did you know that the U.S. mission to the UN has its own waste and fraud hotline? Not the OIOS hotline. No, their own fucking hotline, as if we can't be trusted. The moment you point the finger back at them, they tell you to back off. If their companies skim millions off the top, it's called legitimate business. If some poor sod in Kenya pockets a few hundred dollars, it's called fraud. And the Brits are even worse."

Vermeulen could hear Bengtsson's breathing. The rant was unexpected. Bengtsson had never said anything remotely controversial. Vermeulen's respect for him rose several notches.

"I hear you, Mr. Bengtsson. I feel the same way. But these are the realities. We can't change them. I'll wrap up the APC case and we'll get the audit results to you. Gianotti has been very helpful. I think he'll be a good man for the OIOS."

"Glad to hear it. Just to be clear. You are ordered to forget anything you know about those damn missiles, and you are ordered to stay away from Mr. Houser."

CHAPTER THIRTY-TWO

———◆———

THE CALL LEFT VERMEULEN DAZED. HE'D expected the reaction of the UNAMID commander, but Bengtsson's order came as totally unexpected. He wanted to scream. Tell everyone around him that they were playing bit parts in a huge farce. That they weren't keeping the peace. That they were covering for greedy profiteers. That those who weren't profiting from the conflict didn't give a rat's ass about it. That it was all a sad joke costing a lot of money without making any difference in the lives of those most in need of help.

He knew better. He'd done this job long enough. No, ranting wouldn't do. He needed a new plan. Bengtsson's order was clear. Stay away from Houser and don't speak to anyone about the smuggled Hellfire missiles. Straightforward, no room for misinterpretation. And completely inane.

Visiting Port Sudan again was not in his plans. So staying away from Houser was easy. But if Houser didn't stay away, Vermeulen would deal with the man. No question.

As far as not mentioning the missing missiles, he knew only one thing: those missiles could never reach their intended recipient. Once they were deployed, the civil war would resume with a degree of ferocity not seen before. With the UN out of the picture and the Americans pretending the missiles had never disappeared, there was really only one option to prevent their use. They had to be destroyed. Tessa knew as much as he did, and the order didn't apply to her.

Back in his office, Vermeulen found a note from Gianotti telling him that he was out wrapping things up with the Jirel investigation. For being a pencil pusher, Gianotti sure had been bitten by the investigative bug. Good for him.

He might still discover that following the rules religiously won't help you solve your cases.

He called Tessa.

"How did it go?" she said.

"Predictably."

"The UN won't do anything?"

"Worse. The UN won't do anything and I'm not allowed to talk about it."

"What? Who said that?"

"My boss in Nairobi."

"Are you going to listen to your boss?"

"Sure. But that doesn't mean *you* have to."

"What do you mean?"

"Did you ever get Masaad's satellite phone number?"

"Yes."

"Good. We need to talk to him."

"About what?"

"A small excursion to El Fasher."

She was quiet for a beat.

"D'you think he's up to it?" she said.

"I'm sure. He's got all the incentive. I'll be over soon."

"Okay."

A beep indicated an incoming call.

"I have another call. Are you at your hotel?" he said.

"No."

"Let's meet at my room."

He pressed the Flash button.

"Yes?"

"Valentin, it's me, Tony. I need your help."

"What happened?"

"I got a call. Someone wanted to meet to give me more documents about Jirel's transactions."

"Who?"

"I don't know. He didn't give a name."

"Where are you now?"

"The taxi dropped me in the parking lot at the northern edge of Lake Fasher."

"And?"

"I don't know. Something feels—"

Vermeulen stared at his phone. The connection had been broken.

* * *

WAMBUI PICKED HIM UP FIVE MINUTES later. He could have taken a taxi, but two sets of eyes were better than one. Wambui raced through the compound, earning them angry shouts and raised fists. Once they were outside, El Fasher's late-afternoon traffic swallowed them and they slowed to a crawl.

"Where did he say he was?" Wambui said.

"In the parking lot at the northern edge of Lake Fasher. He sounded scared."

"Why did he even go there?"

"I don't know. I thought he was done with his investigations. He had the money laundering scheme figured out. It was enough to make the case against Jirel."

He suspected that Gianotti hadn't been as stealthy in watching Jirel as he'd claimed. Which meant that Jirel knew he'd been trailed and had every reason to get rid of Gianotti. That worried Vermeulen.

The traffic eased up as they hit the main road. From the mosque, Vermeulen could see a sliver of the lake ahead and to the right. The low sun twinkled on its surface. Wambui pulled into the parking lot two minutes later.

"I don't see Gianotti," Wambui said.

"He may have hidden somewhere. We'll have to check."

A white SUV with the UNAMID decal sat in the far corner against the concrete barrier that separated the parking lot from the lake. Wambui stopped next to it.

"Is that Gianotti's?" Wambui said.

"No, he took a cab. He's gotta be around here. Let's split up. I go left and you go right. Take the causeway across. We'll meet at the southern end."

"Not a good idea, Valentin. This must be Jirel's car. He'll be armed. You don't want to face him unarmed."

Vermeulen pulled the Glock from his pocket. "I'm not unarmed."

He followed the promenade around the eastern side of the lake. The shadows of the trees on the opposite side were getting longer, covering the western end. He reached the fence that separated the municipal soccer stadium from the lake. Shouts came from the field. A dozen or so players were doing warm-up exercises, but they weren't wearing any team jerseys. Maybe a pickup game was about to start.

The fence gave way to a high wall. Only bits of plaster were still sticking to the cement blocks. The rest had fallen to the ground below. The heat of the day was still radiating from the wall.

"Gianotti. Are you there?" No answer.

A shot rang out when he'd covered almost half the distance to the southern end. It was followed almost immediately by a second shot. A double-tap. Which meant the shooter had police or military training. It had to be Jirel.

He hadn't seen any muzzle flash, and the sound echoed in a way that made it hard to locate its origin. It hadn't come from behind him. Vermeulen ran forward.

"Gianotti! Where are you?"

The soccer stadium gave way to a patch of overgrown vegetation that had long ago defeated any attempt at control. A low wall was the only barrier that kept it in check. He reached the southern end of the lake. The water looked mucky, and a film of green slime covered the end close to shore.

Vermeulen ran past another parking lot. There were three cars, one of them another white pickup with the UNAMID logo. He heard voices ahead. They came from another overgrown area, larger and denser than the one he'd just passed. There was no wall, and the bushes reached all the way to the water.

If Jirel had shot Gianotti, there was a fifty-fifty chance he'd come this way. Maybe forty-sixty, since following the causeway was the shorter route back to the northern end. The second pickup worried Vermeulen. If Jirel had an accomplice along, they'd head for the second pickup parked in the lot just behind him. That meant they'd be coming his way any second.

He pulled the Glock from his pocket, pulled the slide back, and let it snap forward again. There were some bushes, but they didn't provide good cover unless he lay on the ground. The first of the trees was about thirty feet away. He dashed toward it.

The crack of another shot sounded. The bullet hit his left arm with a searing pain, as if he'd been struck with a red-hot branding iron. He kept running and slid to a stop behind the tree. Blood trickled from his arm. His jacket and shirt were ripped near the shoulder. He pulled them apart. The bullet had grazed him, leaving a gash in his arm.

A second shot rang out, and this time he saw the muzzle flash in the gloom of the vegetation. He aimed and fired at it. The bullet crashed through the bushes without any effect.

"It's over, Jirel," Vermeulen shouted. "You can't shoot yourself out of this. Just give yourself up. You know we will turn you over to your own government. For all I know, they'll set you free."

Silence.

"Do you hear me, Jirel? Don't make a simple case of fraud worse by doing something stupid."

"It's too late for that," a voice shouted.

The bastards had killed Gianotti.

"Why did you kill him?"

"He was following me. Then he told me he had all he needed for prosecution. I couldn't let him do that."

"Give yourself up. It's the best choice. Don't make things worse."

"I think not. Things will improve dramatically—"

Vermeulen heard a branch crack behind him. He flung around and stared into the barrel of a pistol aimed at his heart. Gupta. Jirel's second in command. The two of them had worked together.

"Drop the gun," Gupta said. "Put your hands behind your head."

Vermeulen let the Glock tumble from his hand. Blood was running from his arm. The wound pulsed painfully with each heartbeat. It made raising his arm impossible. Gupta didn't seem to care.

He could've kicked himself. Jirel had strung him along so that Gupta could sneak behind him. He should've seen that ruse. Not that he'd had much choice. Wambui was still out there. No reason they should expect him.

"What are you going to do? Shoot me? That's even dumber than fleecing the UN. My colleagues know I came here. They'll be looking for me any moment."

"All the more reason to shut you up for good," Jirel said. He had emerged from the thicket and seemed rather pleased with himself.

"We should finish this quickly," Gupta said. "Even in El Fasher, random shots fired in the middle of the town attract attention. We don't need the local police to show up."

"Don't worry," Jirel said. "Once they see the blue berets, they'll back off. They don't want to mess with the UN. Okay, Mr. Vermeulen, step toward the lake."

The edge of the water was no more than twelve feet away. Jirel intended to shoot him and let him drop into the lake, where he'd disappear underwater until his insides were bloated enough to bring him back to the surface.

He took slow steps backward. The green slime looked poisonous in the evening light.

"Okay. Step into the water. Move it. I want you in up to your knees."

Vermeulen stepped into the tepid scum. Water ran into his shoes. That alone was enough to make him angry. Those shoes had been expensive. Now the leather would be ruined. The green slime stuck to his trousers. They'd be ruined too.

The next step brought him to cooler water. The lake was deeper than he'd assumed. The bottom slanted downward at a steep angle. That's when he knew his way out. It involved ruining his entire wardrobe.

He turned his back to Jirel and faced the middle of the lake.

"What? Too scared to face the gun that will kill you? I would've expected a little more bravery. But then, you work for the UN. Not really a surprise."

"Why should I be scared?"

Vermeulen took a deep breath and dove into the water. Once under, he used his legs and the good arm to dive deep and to the right. The water was much colder than he'd expected. Which was good, because it numbed the pain in his arm. He heard dull percussions and a hissing sound. Bullets hitting the water. He wasn't where they thought he'd be.

Three more strokes and he was running out of air. His lungs burned. He forced himself forward. At the last possible moment, he surfaced slowly.

Green slime covered his head. He gasped for air, inhaling foul-tasting scum in the process. He was at least thirty feet from the bank and a good distance to the right of Jirel and Gupta. The two men were dark shadows on the bank. In the growing gloom, he doubted they could see him. The algae provided perfect camouflage.

What it didn't do was give him a way to get out of the water and arrest the killers. He wasn't willing to let them get away, or for that matter, to spend any more time covered with green slime. He was getting cold. To arrest the Nepalis, he needed to find his Glock again. Not likely. Wambui was the only other option. Where was he, anyway?

The answer to that question came in the form of two shots, followed by screams. Vermeulen saw the two shapes at the bank fall down. A third shape rose from the ground behind them and shouted, "Hands behind your heads." Wambui had things under control. The beam of a flashlight danced over the two Nepalis. They were no longer holding their pistols.

Vermeulen struggled out of the water as fast as he could. By the time he made it to shore, Wambui had already cuffed Jirel and Gupta with zip ties. In the beam of the flashlight, Vermeulen saw that each was bleeding from a leg wound.

"It was the easiest way to immobilize them," Wambui said, almost apologetically.

"Did you find Gianotti?" Vermeulen said.

Wambui hesitated. "Yes, he's dead. I found him in the thicket. One of them shot him through the heart."

The dull anger that had been lodged in Vermeulen's gut for the past hour burst into white-hot rage. Gianotti was just a dumb kid who'd stumbled into his first real case and wanted to impress Vermeulen with his initiative. Whatever money Jirel and Gupta had skimmed wasn't worth his life. He stepped in front of Jirel.

"You happy now, scumbag?" he said and kicked the man. "You ended an innocent life. For what? A few dollars. You greedy bastard. I'm going to make sure you rot in jail for the rest of your life. Count on that."

He was about to kick Jirel again when Wambui pulled him back.

"Leave him, Valentin. He's not worth it."

CHAPTER THIRTY-THREE

———◆———

SORTING OUT THE MESS AT LAKE Fasher took a while. Wambui had called the Kenyan MPs, who took control of the scene, collected what evidence they could find, and arrested Jirel and Gupta. One of their medics cleaned Vermeulen's wound and bandaged it. It was eight o'clock when he got back to his room at the WFP guesthouse. His anger had given way to exhaustion.

As he reached for the door handle, the door opened and Tessa came out, ready to embrace him. She saw his condition and shrank back.

"Eww. What did you do? Bob for crocs?" she said.

"Long story. I've got to take a shower."

"I'd say. What is that on your arm?"

"Just a scratch."

"It looks like more than that. Get yourself cleaned up and I'll deal with it then."

He grabbed his Dopp kit and hurried to the ablution shed. The warm water and plenty of soap and shampoo got rid of the dirt and green scum. The scrubbing didn't get rid of the emptiness he felt. Yes, Gianotti had been a pain at times, but was that a reason to be rude to him? He was just a new kid, hoping to learn the ropes. Vermeulen was glad they'd found better terms that morning. Gianotti's death didn't serve any purpose. He caught himself. *No death served any purpose.* The misery in Darfur had no justification. Warped people making devious plans they hoped would bring them power or money or love. All it did was create more misery.

He stopped scrubbing because his skin was raw. After putting on his last change of clothes, he went back to his room.

Tessa re-dressed the arm wound after cleaning it thoroughly with antiseptic from his first-aid kit. He told her what happened at Lake Fasher. Tessa had never met Gianotti, had only heard what Vermeulen said about him, which wasn't very complimentary. But she understood his sadness.

"What's going to happen to Jirel and Gupta?" she said.

"They fall under their own country's jurisdiction. They're in lockup right now until the Nepali government decides what to do with them. I have an inkling that they'll be in trouble. Jirel went on and on about his valiant career fighting against the Maoist rebellion in Nepal. The Maoists are now part of the government. I bet they won't let him off easy."

"What are we going to do next?"

Her question brought him out of his maudlin state.

"Have you talked with Masaad yet?" he said.

"No, I wanted to wait for you."

"Good. First we need to know where the missiles are. There aren't that many storage places around the airport. I bet Wambui can find out."

He dialed his number.

"Winston? Valentin here. Could you find out where Assured Air Services stores its cargo? Yes? Great. I'll wait for your call."

He sat down on his bed and let himself fall backward. The wound on his arm burned; his eyes itched from the mucky water of Lake Fasher. The weariness of a long day dodging assassins and finding his dead colleague washed through him like a dark flood.

Tessa crawled to him and kissed him gently. "Sorry you had to live through this day, Valentin. It must've been awful."

She squatted behind his head and began massaging his shoulders. He groaned and let himself sink into her fingers. The shrill ring of his phone interrupted the moment. He pushed himself upright and answered. It was Wambui.

"You found it? Good."

He opened his notebook, scribbled a few lines, and ended the call.

"Their warehouse is near the entrance to the airport. It's the largest structure there. It has a fence around it, and a few armed guards. Not enough to stop the UJM. Let's make the call."

Tessa dialed the number. Vermeulen sat next to her, listening in. The clicks and hisses went on for quite a while. Then he heard a voice.

"I'd like to speak to Commander Masaad," Tessa said. "This is Tessa Bishonga. I interviewed him a few days back near Jabal Deidu. I have a few follow-up questions."

More clicks and hisses. Then a pop that made Tessa pull the phone from her ear.

Masaad's voice was surprisingly clear. "Ms. Bishonga. How nice to hear from you. I trust you made it back safely to El Fasher. You shouldn't have escaped during the ambush. It was a very dangerous thing to do."

"We had no choice. Sticking with you didn't look any safer. In any case, we got back without any trouble."

"What can I do for you?"

"I have information that's very valuable to you. I want to pass it on."

"Please do."

"But I have a condition."

Vermeulen sat up straight and stared at her. A condition? What was she doing? He opened his mouth, but she put her finger on his lips.

"What condition?"

"I would like your permission to broadcast our interview."

"No. That's why I asked for the tape. It can't ever be broadcast."

"I have to admit that Sami gave you a blank tape. He kept the one with the interview."

There was silence at the other end. Then a cough.

"Why do you even bother trying to get my permission?"

"I think you can play an important role in the peace process, and this interview would be the first step."

"Please don't flatter me. I prohibit you from broadcasting it. If you decide to do it anyway, you are no longer welcome in Darfur. My men will find you."

"You haven't even heard the information I'm willing to trade for it."

"I can't imagine your having anything valuable enough to make me change my mind."

"How about the whereabouts of eight crates of Hellfire missiles that have just been smuggled to Darfur?"

There was another silence at the other end.

"How do you know this?"

"My friend Valentin Vermeulen traveled in the same plane as the missiles."

"Where are they now?"

"Do I have your permission to broadcast the interview?"

More silence.

"Listen, Commander," Tessa said. "I'm going to give you a chance to destroy an important offensive asset of the Sudanese Air Force. It will be a serious blow to them. They will be weakened. That's your opportunity to emerge as a peacemaker. The interview will be the first step."

Tessa put her hand over the mouthpiece.

"He's talking to someone, probably his deputy."

"Why didn't you tell me about this plan of yours?" Vermeulen said.

"Because you wouldn't have approved. It's bad practice to give something for nothing. The information about the missiles is vital for him. We might as well get something positive in return."

She put her hand up to silence Vermeulen.

"Yes, Commander?"

"I don't like the way you're railroading me into becoming a peacemaker. Because there can be no peace with al-Bashir. I grant you permission to broadcast the interview. Maybe you are right, maybe you aren't. In either case, it's a small price to pay for the defeat we will inflict upon our enemy. Where are the missiles?"

"They are stored in the warehouse of Assured Air Services near the airport. The warehouse lies near the entrance to the airport. It's the largest structure there. I believe you have very little time."

She ended the call at eight forty-five.

* * *

ABOUT THE SAME TIME, A LEARJET 36 landed at the El Fasher airport. It taxied past the passenger terminal and stopped at the cargo area. Dale Houser unbuckled his seatbelt and walked to the door, where he waited impatiently until the plane came to a stop. The copilot emerged from the cockpit, opened the door, and lowered the stairs.

"There you go, Mr. Houser."

Houser nodded.

Nobody was waiting for him. He caught himself looking for Campbell, then remembered that he'd never see him again. He pushed those thoughts back and concentrated on the here and now, like settling the price of the merchandise.

Having a client welch on a deal or demand new concessions wasn't new to him. When you sell weapons, it comes with the territory. In the early years of his career, a Liberian warlord had held a pistol to his head, demanding to get his AK-47s for next to nothing. Houser hadn't blinked. He had told the man to inspect the crates. They contained rotten potatoes. Then he told him he'd get his weapons if he forked over the money. Once he had his money and was safe, he called the man and told him the guns were under the stinking vegetables.

It wouldn't be any different with the Sudanese. They'd balk, Houser would explain patiently the kind of destruction they would visit on their opponents, and then they'd transfer the money. It always worked that way.

After ten minutes, a black SUV drove up. Campbell would never have been late. He would have opened the door for him. But these days were gone.

He got into the rear of the car and told the driver—someone in his employ whom he'd never seen—to take him to his warehouse.

The sight of the armed guards reassured him. Campbell had chosen the right number. At first glance, there wasn't any indication of stepped-up security, a telltale sign that something valuable was stored inside. As they rolled to a stop at the entrance, Houser noticed more guards in the shadows. Nobody was going to break in.

He went to the door. A short man dressed in a white shirt and gray trousers opened it from the outside. Houser vaguely remembered him as the crew supervisor hired by Campbell. The man had short black hair, a narrow brown face with a large nose, and thin lips. Houser couldn't remember his name.

"Welcome, Mr. Houser. An honor to meet you in person."

"Thanks ...."

"It's Hakim, Mr. Houser."

"Yes, of course, Hakim. Show me the latest cargo."

They walked into the storage area. Hakim threw a switch. Bright lights flooded the space. The eight special crates stood near the front. Houser inspected each crate.

"Everything is in order, Mr. Houser. Mr. Campbell, Allah bless him, set up extra security. Nobody has shown any interest in our facility."

Houser nodded. "That's good to know. Make sure it stays that way."

He told the driver to get lost and drove himself to the Crimson Lights Hotel. Assured Sovereignty owned a flat in El Fasher, but that flat had been used by Campbell and Houser was in no mood to deal with his ghost. He needed to focus on the next two days. They'd be crucial in getting the deal finished. Then there would be time to mourn his comrade's death.

* * *

AT A QUARTER TO ELEVEN, FIVE pickups left a desert encampment about three hours south of El Fasher. The pickups had been painted white with cheap latex paint in the preceding hours. It was a sloppy job, but in the darkness they could pass for a UN convoy. Once the sun came up, they'd be driving alone in different directions. A lone pickup with a bunch of passengers in the back, driving along some dirt track, didn't attract attention, no matter what its color was.

Dark figures huddled under blankets on the beds of the first four pickups. The last truck carried several barrels of fertilizer and diesel fuel under a tarp. They wound their way west through a wadi. Once on the tarmac, they sped up, settling into a comfortable cruising speed. The night was clear. A quarter moon shed a faint silver glow over the quiet desert scape. Barring any incidents or car trouble, they planned to arrive in El Fasher by three the next morning.

Commander Masaad sat in the passenger seat of the first pickup. He was relaxed. The plan was improvised, given how little time they had, but the outcome would be spectacular.

CHAPTER THIRTY-FOUR

———◆———

Wednesday, March 24, 2010

THE UJM TEAM ENCOUNTERED ITS FIRST snag two hours into the drive, when the right rear tire of the last pickup blew out. Its driver had a hard enough time keeping the truck from skidding into the ditch by the side of the road. He was quite proud to have brought the truck to a stop without overturning it and losing the heavy cargo. It was the oldest truck the UJM had, and its tires were almost bald. Changing the tire took a lot longer than Masaad liked. The load required the use of two jacks. The broken surface of the road didn't help, either. Fortunately, one of the other pickups carried a decent spare tire. The repair set the team back by a half-hour.

Back on the road, Masaad recalculated the time. According to his GPS position, he was an hour and a half from El Fasher. They'd still arrive in time. He read somewhere that the best time for a night assault was four in the morning because that's when the sleep cycle is at its deepest and those on guard duty were most likely to have dozed off. He didn't know if the explanation was sound, but he'd followed that strategy and his ambushes were generally successful.

The phone call from Tessa Bishonga had come as a surprise, as had the news that she still had the videotape of the interview. The anger he'd felt after hanging up had been stronger than any emotion he'd felt in recent months. It was directed at himself. How could he have underestimated her? Had he been lulled into complacency by her engaging style? How stupid! The woman was a journalist. She knew how to manipulate men. That's how she made a living.

As quickly as he'd flown into a rage, he'd calmed down again. The information she'd passed on was worth more than the interview. He didn't buy her talk about being a peacemaker. There could be no peace in Darfur as long as al-Bashir ruled Sudan. But a major setback of the sort he and his men were about to inflict could weaken the coalition that kept the dictator in power. It could also change the balance of power among the rebel movements. It would push him into the limelight, because he'd destroyed the most dangerous new weapon in the government's arsenal and because he'd shown the world that the embargo was little more than a fig leaf.

Masaad smiled. Tomorrow morning, there'd be a whole new set of opportunities. He was ready to seize them.

* * *

HOUSER SAT UP IN HIS ROOM at the Crimson Lights Hotel. There'd been some haggling about getting a room, but he put enough cash down. Every hotel had at least one spare room. It wasn't what he was used to, but it served his needs.

The night dragged on. Sleep was impossible. Campbell's death didn't leave him alone. The loss of an old comrade was bad enough. The lack of any information about his death made everything worse. He'd called several contacts after arriving in El Fasher. Nobody had more information. One mentioned reports of a firefight in the UNAMID headquarters. Another reported shots fired at Lake Fasher in the early evening. That was too late to be relevant.

The shots at the headquarters had to be the ones that killed Campbell. What happened there? Campbell was too smart to be tricked by Vermeulen. Or was he? Houser's estimation of Vermeulen had increased since the man managed to disappear from the warehouse in Port Sudan. He had proved to be much more resourceful than your ordinary bureaucrat. He was a real threat. That's why Houser had ordered Campbell to eliminate him in the first place. Somehow, the tables had been turned. How?

Houser remembered Ben Tower telling him that Vermeulen had taken his Glock. He jumped up. His mourning of Campbell's death had kept him from drawing the most obvious conclusion. Vermeulen had been armed. He had killed his man. That's why the UN was all tight-lipped about it.

He hammered the table with his fist. The cheap thing cracked but remained standing. He punched it again. The crack grew, but it still stood there, resisting his force, taunting him like Vermeulen. He delivered a vicious blow, breaking it in half. His breathing grew ragged as he stomped on the closest table leg. It splintered but didn't break. The next leg required two kicks before breaking. Sweat pearled on his forehead. He kept kicking and punching the remains of the table until they were reduced to a pile of splinters.

Exhausted, he fell back on his bed.

Tomorrow, Vermeulen would pay.

* * *

SLEEP ALSO REFUSED TO COME TO Vermeulen. The day had been exhausting enough, but Gianotti's death kept him awake. Tessa breathed calmly next to him. He envied her.

There was no escaping the conclusion that he was responsible for Gianotti's death. He should've kept him checking invoices in the office rather than allowing him to shadow Jirel. Gianotti had no experience outside an office. His enthusiasm to conduct a "real" investigation got the better of him. Vermeulen should have anticipated that. Tomorrow, he'd have to call Bengtsson with the news. He dreaded that call more than any other. The guilt kept gnawing at his innards, refusing to let sleep come.

* * *

THE FIVE PICKUPS REACHED THE OUTSKIRTS of El Fasher at three twenty in the morning. They separated and took different routes to the airport. Fifteen minutes later, all except the last truck had parked a few blocks from the Assured Air Services warehouse. Twenty UJM fighters filtered singly and in pairs to the designated meeting spot, an overgrown area just east of the fence surrounding the warehouse. Masaad sent three fighters to reconnoiter the layout and defenses of the structure. The others hunkered down. They were the best-trained soldiers of the UJM. Masaad could tell they were excited, even if they did their best to remain calm.

Fifteen minutes later, the scouts came back and reported to Masaad. He nodded.

"Listen," he said, keeping his voice to a whisper. "There are seven guards outside. We don't know if there are more inside. That means we need to eliminate those outside without any noise. Hands and knives only, no shots."

The men nodded and slipped into the dark.

Masaad liked the ratio—two of his men for each guard, plus backup. He leaned against the fifth pickup with the heavy cargo. Its driver had remained in the cab.

At four, his deputy reported back. All the guards had been neutralized. No shots had been fired. Masaad smiled. He got into the pickup. His man drove it through the open gate to the loading door of the warehouse. He kept the pickup idling. The other fighters massed around him.

Masaad reviewed the strategy. The lead man, Masaad's deputy, would open the door. The next man would throw in two flashbang grenades. After the explosions, the rest would storm in. Masaad told them to set the rifles to semiautomatic mode. Automatic fire in a confined space was a recipe for disaster.

"Remember, there are crates with ammunition in there. Aim before you shoot."

The fighters nodded. Adrenaline pulsed through their arteries. They were ready. Masaad gave the signal. The deputy opened the door. The man behind him tossed two black cylinders into the warehouse. The deputy pulled the door shut. Two earsplitting explosions reverberated through the night. Masaad could only imagine how loud they must have been inside the building. The deputy yanked open the door again and the fighters streamed inside.

Masaad got back into the pickup, ready to drive it into the building the moment the loading gate opened.

* * *

The sound of two explosions tore Houser from the fitful sleep that had finally come. His parachute training kicked in without hesitation. An attack. He was dressed in less than a minute. Two minutes later he stood outside. The sound of gunfire came from the northeast, exactly where his warehouse was located. He jumped into his SUV and tore out of the parking area.

The tires spun on the sandy track that led from the hotel to the main road and the airport entrance. He lowered the windows and heard more gunfire. Who'd be attacking his warehouse? The Sudanese forces? That made no sense. They were his customers. They knew he'd supplied them with weapons they couldn't have obtained otherwise. Would they be stupid enough to destroy that relationship?

The Hellfire missiles. That had to be it. The army didn't want to pay his price. So they decided to get them for free. A flash of anger blew through him. Those bastards would not get away with it. If they stole the missiles, he'd make sure they'd never receive a single shipment of anything. Even if he had to personally blow them up. He'd deliver guns and ammo to the rebels for free. He'd get them helicopter gunships. He'd ....

The track joined the road near the entrance to the airport. His warehouse loomed just beyond. The gunfire had stopped.

* * *

The explosions also woke Vermeulen. He sat up in his bed. Tessa kept breathing slowly. He shook her shoulder.

"Did you hear that?"

She groaned.

"Did you hear the explosions?" he said.

"What?"

"There were two explosions just now."

"I didn't hear anything."

"Now there's gunfire."

Tessa sat up. "Yeah, I hear that. What's going on?"

"I assume it's Masaad."

"This soon?"

"You told him that he had little time."

Tessa yawned and stretched like a cat. "What do you want to do?"

"I want to see this. You too?"

"Sure."

They got dressed and hurried to their car.

* * *

THE FIGHTING TOOK MUCH LONGER THAN Masaad expected. He sat in the idling pickup and listened to the volleys inside the warehouse. What was happening inside? Twice he grabbed his rifle and almost jumped from the truck to join the fray. He stayed in the pickup. *Stick with the plan.* His men were good enough to deal with their opponents. He assumed that security at the warehouse had been stepped up, given the unusual cargo that had arrived the afternoon before. Nobody would let a bunch of Hellfire missiles sit in a warehouse unprotected.

One of the UJM fighters stumbled out the door. He was bleeding from his leg. Another followed. He eased the first fighter to the ground and applied a rough tourniquet around the man's thigh, using his belt. Then he went back inside.

The gunfire ended. The idling engine was the only sound in the night. Masaad wasn't concerned that the noise of the battle would attract attention. They'd be gone before any police or soldiers were mobilized.

The large loading door creaked open and dim light spilled out into the dark night. Masaad's man drove the pickup into the warehouse. One of the others directed them to five crates that had been stored away from the other boxes. The driver backed up right against the middle case, turned off the engine, and set the brake.

The fighters were already assembled near the fence. Masaad lowered the large door and turned off the light. A minute later they all melted into the darkness. The wounded man was supported by one of his comrades. They lagged behind enough to see a set of headlights appear at the gate.

* * *

IN THE BEAM OF HIS HEADLIGHTS, Houser saw two figures disappear into the bushes near the fence. Those had better not be his guards. He was realistic enough to consider that possibility. Why should they stay and be shot at to protect someone else's property?

He slid the gate open and drove to the entrance. No sound came from the warehouse. That seemed odd. No matter who won the skirmish, they would be celebrating. His pistol in hand, he eased open the door. It was dark inside. He slipped into the warehouse.

There was no sound. Nothing. That didn't make sense. Were they waiting for him?

He moved a few steps farther, expecting the light to come on, expecting soldiers with guns.

The light stayed off. The men with guns didn't turn up.

It made absolutely no sense. His guards might run away if attacked, but they wouldn't just walk off the job.

He inched closer to the light switch. He held his breath, turned the light on, and immediately ducked. The brightness blinded him momentarily. There was no gunshot.

When his eyes adjusted to the light, he saw the bodies of his guards. They hadn't run away. They'd stayed and fought. And lost.

Except for the bodies of the men and the bloodstains, nothing had changed. The crates were still there. All of them, as far as he could tell. He'd suspected the Sudanese of attempting to steal the Hellfire missiles. But they were still there, just like everything else.

Except there was a pickup parked against the missiles. Did he surprise someone? Someone who came to steal the missiles but ran when he turned up? No, that couldn't be it. A pickup could, at best, carry one crate. Besides, the pickup's bed was already fully loaded. The cargo was covered with a dirty tarp.

Houser shook his head. This was just crazy. He walked to the pickup and lifted the tarp. There were four barrels on the bed. The stink of diesel fuel was unmistakable.

It took only a second for his brain to compute that information. The next second, he was racing to the exit. It was a truck bomb. It could go off at any moment. He'd seen the force of fertilizer bombs. The pressure wave alone was enough to rip someone's lungs apart.

Who'd rigged the bomb? Who'd destroy the missiles? Not the Sudanese. There was no time to sort that out. He had to get away from the building.

He reached his car, jumped in, and started the engine. Through the open window he heard the sound of a jet engine above. He turned the car toward the gate. A streak of light cut through the night from the west. It zoomed toward his warehouse. A second streak followed close behind. The noise grew unbearably loud. It was the last he heard.

A massive explosion grabbed the SUV and lifted it into the air. A second explosion tossed the car fifty feet farther. It rolled three times before coming to rest on its roof.

* * *

VERMEULEN AND TESSA HAD JUST REACHED the road leading to the airport when Vermeulen saw two streaks race across the night sky. Tessa had seen them, too. She slammed on the brake. Vermeulen heard the sound of jet engines. *That can't be good*, he thought.

A second later, two huge explosions followed and robbed him of his hearing. The shockwaves pressed against his body, squeezing the air from his lungs. He gasped and swallowed to ease the pain in his ears.

He saw a red-orange fireball rise ahead of them, followed by black smoke. Tessa shook him. He turned and saw her mouth move. He couldn't hear anything at all.

"What?" he shouted.

All that came out was a croak.

* * *

MASAAD HAD JUST STOPPED NEAR THE northern edge of town. The other pickups had dispersed into their prearranged directions. He pulled out a burner phone and began dialing the number that would set off the bomb; then, hearing the sound of jets, he looked up. Something raced across the sky and headed in the direction of the airport. The explosions that followed shook his truck. The massive fireball made the night disappear.

He stared at the phone. He hadn't dialed the last digit.

It took him only a moment to work it out. The streaks in the sky had been cruise missiles. He'd heard their unmistakeable sound back in 1998 when the U.S. attacked the pharmaceutical factory in Khartoum. So the Americans weren't going to let their Hellfire missiles fall into the wrong hands after all. He'd wondered about that. He shifted into first gear and drove off. There had to be a way he could turn this situation to his advantage.

CHAPTER THIRTY-FIVE

---◆---

Wednesday, March 31, 2010

THE FLAT-SCREEN TV ON THE CREDENZA showed an Al Jazeera anchorwoman against a map of Sudan that dissolved into an aerial shot of Darfur.

"That's it!" Vermeulen said, dialing up the volume on the remote. He sat on the sofa in his daughter's apartment in Düsseldorf. Gaby, next to him, had taken the morning off to watch with him.

"And now a special report from Darfur," the woman said. "Reporter Tessa Bishonga has managed to do what no one else has accomplished. She interviewed the leader of the United Justice Movement, Fahad Masaad. The UJM has long been regarded as a holdout against the settlement of the conflict. Commander Masaad was a no-show at the Doha Peace Forum and a vocal opponent of the proposed comprehensive settlement of the long-running conflict. Is that still true? According to Tessa Bishonga, we may have to change our opinion."

The program cut to a short visual intro to Darfur, a view of Jebel Marra, the grand mosque of El Fasher, images of burnt hamlets, an aerial view of a refugee camp that might have been Zam Zam. Another cut and the image of Masaad appeared.

"You were right there?" Gaby asked. "Right in that tent?"

"Shh, yes, let's listen."

The interview played mostly as Vermeulen remembered. It had been edited to include shots of Tessa listening intently. Vermeulen knew that these had been taken beforehand by Sami. When the interview was over, Tessa appeared over a live feed and answered questions from the anchorwoman. In her answers, she stressed that rather than being an obstructionist, Commander Masaad was detail-oriented and wanted to ensure that the small, practical aspects of the Doha negotiations were not overlooked in the haste to achieve an agreement.

"He's as interested in peace as the other parties, probably even more. But he made it clear that the implementation of the agreement must follow the letter and the spirit of the final communiqué of Doha. And, most importantly, it must directly involve the affected populations."

The image switched back to the anchorwoman, who narrated the intro for the next report. He looked at her.

"So what do you think?"

"Were you really attacked right at the end of that interview?"

"Yes. It was quite harrowing. But we got away."

Gaby frowned. "Yeah, you still got hurt." She pointed at the arm immobilized by a sling. "And your hearing is still not okay. Dad, I don't want you to do this job anymore. You're a lawyer, not some Rambo guy. If I'd known you were facing that kind of danger—"

"Well you didn't, so it's okay. And that's not normal. Most of my assignments are really boring."

The wound on his arm had gotten infected by Lake Fasher's water, resulting in three weeks of medical leave. He could've gone to his apartment in New York City, but he decided to recover in Düsseldorf. Gaby found him a small sublet for the time, and he'd been walking the Rhine promenade daily. The weather was still iffy, but sunny days outnumbered the blustery ones. The day before, Tessa had called him, telling him that her interview would be airing on Al Jazeera.

"What do you think of Tessa? I wouldn't want to date a woman without my daughter's approval."

"She's very smart. I mean, that was a great interview. And she's good-looking." Gaby smirked. "Probably too good-looking for an old man like you."

He reached over and pinched her arm. "Who says I'm old?"

"Well, you've got your arm in a sling and you walk the promenade. That's what old people do." She laughed out loud. "Just kidding, Dad. You are a fine specimen of the middle-aged male. I do wish I could meet her. You never know about a person until you speak with them."

You've got that right, Vermeulen thought.

* * *

THAT AFTERNOON, VERMEULEN WAS LEANING AGAINST the railing and watching a barge maneuver the bend in the Rhine. It was from Holland and almost came too close to the bank to manage the turn. He saw laundry strung up near the aft cabin, fluttering in the sunny breeze. A small dog ran the length of the ship and barked at him. He wondered if all barge skippers had a dog on board. What might life be like, living on a ship, making the trip from Rotterdam to Basel and back? Probably like any other job. Still, the idea of floating past cities, villages, and castles sounded pleasant.

The antibiotics were working. His arm was slowly getting back to its normal shape. Along with the swelling, the pain also diminished. In a week, he'd start physical therapy. After that, there'd be another call from New York and another assignment.

The OIOS had dealt with the aftermath of the affair in a surprisingly flexible manner. Undoubtedly, Bengtsson had taken the lead, outlining Vermeulen and Gianotti's initiative in identifying Jirel and Gupta as the perpetrators of the fraud. Both received commendations from the Under-Secretary-General, Gianotti posthumously.

As Vermeulen expected, the matter of the missing Hellfire missiles was covered up. The U.S. government neither confirmed nor denied the cruise missile attack. Houser's body had been found in his SUV with a broken neck. The ammunition still at his warehouse in Port Sudan was confiscated by the Sudanese authorities, as was his aircraft. José would have to find another employer.

There was a tap on his shoulder. He turned. There, before him, stood Tessa.

"W-what are you doing here?" he said.

"I'm happy to see you, too."

She gave him a hug that morphed into a lengthy kiss.

"You can't get rid of me that easily," she said after they came up for air.

"Who said I wanted to get rid of you?"

"Well, you never called. What's a girl to think?"

"I'm sorry. How come you are in Düsseldorf?"

"I wanted to check up on your recovery."

"I just saw you on TV."

"The live feed came from the TV studios just up the street. Let's go and meet your daughter."

"Up the promenade in one of those buildings."

She grabbed his good arm and they turned south.

"Do you think Masaad will take advantage of the opportunity?" he said.

"That, like so much in Darfur, remains to be seen."

Photo by Joanna Niemann

MICHAEL NIEMANN GREW UP IN A small town in Germany, ten kilometers from the Dutch border. Crossing that border often at a young age sparked in him a curiosity about the larger world. He studied political science at the Rheinische Friedrich-Wilhelms Universität in Bonn and international studies at the University of Denver. During his academic career he focused his work on southern Africa and frequently spent time in the region. After taking a fiction writing course from his friend, the late Fred Pfeil, he embarked on a different way to write about the world.

For more information, go to:
www.michael-niemann.com
www.facebook.com/MichaelNiemannAuthor/

A Valentin Vermeulen Thriller, Book 2

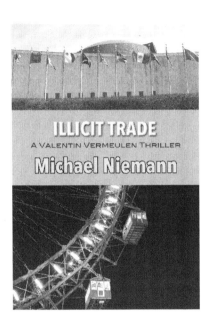

Two Kenyans who entered the U.S. with forged UN documents are killed. UN auditor Vermeulen suspects crimes worse than fraud. After riling "The Broker" in Newark, he follows the clues to Vienna. Hustler Earle Jackson soon regrets trying to con the Broker. Using the dead Kenyon's passport, he flees to Nairobi. Both men are now the targets of a vast and vicious criminal network.